NCIS:™
LOS ANGELES
BOLTHOLE

Also available from Titan Books

NCIS: Los Angeles™: Extremis
by Jerome Preisler

NCIS:™
LOS ANGELES
BOLTHOLE

Jeff Mariotte

Based on the CBS television series
created by Shane Brennan

TITAN BOOKS

This book is for my Marcy Spring,
with all my love.

NCIS Los Angeles: Bolthole
Print edition ISBN: 9781783296330
E-book edition ISBN: 9781783296361

Published by Titan Books
A division of Titan Publishing Group Ltd
144 Southwark Street, London SE1 0UP

First edition: November 2016
1 3 5 7 9 10 8 6 4 2

A CIP catalogue record for this title is available from the British Library.

Printed and bound in the United States.

PROLOGUE

Ramadi, Iraq,
February 2007

Easy Street was anything but.

Al-Qaeda in Iraq forces were operating freely out of Ramadi's Ma'Laab district, and Operation Murfreesboro was about to be launched to bring the district under control and take out the bad guys. The first step was going to be installing concrete barriers along what the U.S. forces had taken to calling "Easy Street," to wall in the neighborhood. Once egress and ingress were controlled, terrorist operations would stop. Or that was the plan.

Trouble was, al-Qaeda snipers were working the rooftops of Ma'Laab, making even recon missions dangerous, much less the actual erection of the barriers. And enemy IEDs kept turning up on the American patrol routes.

Which was where the Navy SEALS came in.

A tiny handful of SEALS, the thinking went, could make the neighborhood safe enough for the Army to operate. The Navy encouraged such thinking, and the fact that the Army resented that just reinforced the Navy's position. Officially, the branches cooperated. Unofficially—well, people were human, after all, and pride was one of the seven deadly sins to which members of the armed forces were sometimes most susceptible. Along with the other six. The annual Army–Navy Game was a mere shadow of the genuine rivalry between the two services.

That explained why Lieutenant Kelly Martin and Leading Petty Officer Bobby Sanchez found themselves inside the Ma'Laab neighborhood one dark winter night. Through an informant, they had a lead on the identity of one of the AQ snipers who'd been threatening both American troops and the Iraqi Army troops working alongside them. Three Iraqis had been killed and one American soldier badly wounded—he might still pull through, but the prognosis was poor—and the word on the street was that this particular sniper was claiming credit for all those shots.

Rather than being sent as part of a large force to find and take out the sniper, the two SEALs went in alone, confident in their ability to navigate the narrow, midnight roads undetected, kill the sniper, and get out again.

As it turned out, the sniper wasn't alone. Three men were sitting with him in his living room. Martin and Sanchez later learned that two were his brothers and the third a distant cousin. At the moment, all that mattered was that the four men were sitting around a table loaded with an array of weapons, and when the SEALs rammed in the front door, each man lunged for the guns.

Sixteen pops sounded—suppressed, but still audible to the pair of SEALs and probably to people in neighboring apartments—and the four men were dead; sprawled this way and that. Blood trickled down walls and oozed from corpses, though the initial spurts—powered by hearts that were still beating—had stopped. The smells of gun smoke and blood and sweat and death mingled in the small room. The two SEALs performed a quick, efficient search of the place, turning up IEDs and cellphones rigged to detonate them, more guns and plenty of ammunition, and a laptop hidden inside an underwear drawer. They took the laptop and set a charge that would, five minutes after they left, blow up the IEDs; with their explosive force added to the small charge, the entire building would probably come down. Maybe the whole block, depending on how well constructed the buildings were and what other explosives might be contained within them.

If that happened, innocents would probably die. Martin knew that. But he also knew that if they didn't blow up the IEDs, then someone else would come along and find them and use them against the Americans and their Iraqi allies. Probably soon, since he doubted that the sound of the door being bashed in had gone unnoticed.

And then Americans would die, as would Iraqi soldiers trying to fight to build a country that was not in the iron grip of a tyrannical despot. Martin wasn't interested in the politics of it, he was interested in saving the lives of American service members—even if they were Army—and accomplishing the mission so they could all get home as soon as possible, ideally in one piece.

War was hell and people died. Even innocents. He couldn't devote too much energy to thinking about that, because if he did the sorrow would paralyze him. He did what he had to do to protect himself and his own, and he hoped that his actions would open the door to some kind of self-rule that would one day benefit the vast majority of Iraqis.

Five minutes later, Martin and Sanchez were almost a mile away, somewhere in the warren of streets near the edge of the Ma'Laab. They heard the blast, saw the sky lighten as fire reached toward it. Martin, not a religious man, spared a quick thought for any noncombatants caught in its fury, and a corresponding but darker one for terrorists who hid among the very people they claimed to be fighting for, precisely to make finding and killing them more difficult for people of conscience.

When Martin heard gunfire, for a fraction of a second he thought it was some delayed echo from the explosion bouncing off the walls around him. But it went on, growing more intense, and it became clear that it was coming from ahead of them, not behind. He and Sanchez locked eyes—Sanchez's were, in that moment, the eyes of a zealot, utterly lacking in doubt or uncertainty of any kind—and Sanchez said, "Come on!"

He started jogging forward without waiting for a response. Martin followed. There was a firefight going on, beyond the confines of the Ma'Laab, and that meant there were Americans involved because the Iraqi Army and police didn't go up against al-Qaeda without Americans by their sides.

The SEALs burst across Easy Street, where soon concrete barriers would be in place, and raced toward the sound of the fight. They found it only a few blocks from Easy Street, at a low, freestanding building that could have been a warehouse or a small factory, but which Martin knew was a museum affiliated with Ramadi's University of Anbar. The university wasn't particularly old, but among its faculty were scholars and intellectuals reaching into Iraq's past, and some of them had amassed a limited but important collection of artifacts stretching back to Sumerian days.

By the time Martin and Sanchez reached the scene, the gunfire had died out. They found four Americans—private security contractors, not military, though it was often hard to distinguish the difference—surrounded by seven dead Iraqis. Two of the bodies were clad in khaki uniforms of some kind.

One of the security contractors raised his weapon toward Martin and Sanchez, then lowered it when he saw they were Americans. The man was tall, gangly, with a youthful face that was drenched in sweat despite the cool night. His eyes were a luminous green that practically sparked with some inner fire. Martin didn't think he would ever forget those eyes. They made him uncomfortable. They were the eyes of a man who had just killed several people and wished there were more.

"What happened here?" Martin asked.

The contractor ticked his head toward a truck painted the color of sand. "We were driving in from OP Virginia," the man said. "Delivered some supplies out there earlier. We came around the corner and were ambushed."

"You all okay?"

"We are, yeah," the contractor said. "They're not."

"I can see that. How'd they do it?"

"Just waited for us to come around the corner, then they started shooting from the shadows."

Martin eyed the truck. It was neatly parked about twenty yards back from the corpses, near the museum's entrance. He couldn't see any damage to it—the windshield looked whole, the tires solid, and there were no evident bullet holes.

"I'm sure you guys have more important things to

do," the contractor said. "Everything's copacetic here. We'll check out the truck and get back on the road."

"You sure?" Martin asked. "We can provide—"

The guy cut him off with a dismissive wave of his hand. "Don't worry about it. We're cool."

Martin caught Sanchez's eye. Sanchez shrugged. "Whatever."

"Okay," Martin said.

"Thanks for checking in," the contractor said. "Appreciate it."

As Sanchez had so succinctly put it, Martin thought, *Whatever*. Something felt hinky about the whole thing. He didn't like it.

But he had his job to do, and he had done it. Getting involved in the affairs of contractors was outside his purview.

In his opinion, they were nothing but mercenaries. Many were ex-military, jumping ship to private companies that promised to pay vastly higher salaries than the Department of Defense could. Martin had turned down offers that seemed exorbitant to him.

The difference was that real warriors didn't do it for the money, they did it for their country. The loyalties of mercenaries were not to any flag, but to the company that held the dollars out in front of them.

Civilian leaders had decided to outsource many of the tasks that had previously been performed by service members to private companies, and it wasn't Martin's place to second-guess the whims of the Pentagon brass.

But he didn't have to like it. And he didn't have to like contractors who opened fire on foreign nationals, knowing that if there were any complaints about their actions, their employers would simply spirit them stateside.

Ducking responsibility for one's actions didn't correspond to courage, in his view. Just the opposite.

Martin was still steaming when he hit his bunk, the encounter with the contractors having put a sour gloss over the whole night's work, despite the successful kill of the sniper who'd been targeting Americans. He hoped the captured laptop would provide actionable intelligence on other AQ members operating inside the Ma'Laab. When he finally fell asleep, it was with thoughts of what might be learned running through his head.

1

June 9

"Someday, G," Sam said, "you're gonna want to settle down with the right lady. She'll be smart and sweet and funny and pretty, and you'll want to put that ring on her finger. And in a little while—a year, two, maybe five at the outside—she's going to want you to unpack your bag and stop sleeping on the sofa." He glanced over at Callen's dismissive expression. "You know I'm right."

"You know what they say about bridges," Callen replied.

"Don't burn 'em while you're still standing on 'em?"

"Don't cross them until you come to them. If I meet that mythical woman, and if she's everything you say she is and we decide to get married, then I'll worry about unpacking. Until then, there's no reason to jump the gun."

Sam eased the black Challenger around a wide bend in the road. Like most Los Angeles streets, this one had been pretty straight, until it wasn't. "Now you're mixing your metaphors."

"Mixing my… what do *metaphors* have to do with anything?"

"Jumping a gun has nothing to do with crossing a bridge, that's all I'm saying."

"The bridge was your thing. I was never even on the bridge. But if I was, and you were on it, too?"

"Yeah?"

"I'd throw you off, just to watch you fall."

They were joking with each other because that was how they interacted best, but also because they were almost at the worst kind of crime scene, and neither one wanted to spend time dwelling on it until forced to.

And that was about to happen. Sam braked to a stop in front of a modest California bungalow. Two LAPD cars were already there, a cruiser in the driveway and an unmarked unit standing in the patchy yard. A palm tree stood at the edge of the corner lot, throwing uneven shade toward the house. It wouldn't be enough to ward off the heat; already topping eighty-five, at 9:00 A.M., the day was going to be another scorcher in a summer full of them.

Sam glanced at his partner. "Ready?"

"As I'll ever be."

"Let's do it."

They climbed out of the vehicle and crossed the lawn, which was mostly weeds. A porch fronted the house, its stucco a faded pink, like salmon left too long in the sun. A young uniformed officer stood at the top of the three stairs, blocking entry. He held a clipboard in his hands. "Sorry, sirs," he said. "Authorized personnel only."

Sam and Callen flashed badges. "NCIS," Callen said. "Office of Special Projects. We're what they mean when they say 'authorized personnel.' Look it up in the dictionary and you'll see our pictures."

"Yessir," the young cop said, flushing to almost

the color of the house. "I mean no, sir, that won't be necessary. They're expecting you."

"You want us to sign in?" Sam asked. He hadn't slowed his pace; the officer had already stepped aside to avoid being mowed down.

"Not necessary, sir. I'll just mark you down as OSP. Also?"

Callen paused in the doorway. "Yeah?"

"I'm sorry."

Sam understood that what the man was sorry about had nothing to do with his behavior, which had been by the book. He meant it on a more personal level, and Sam appreciated the gesture. It didn't really help, but then, nothing would, in this situation.

Sam, after all, had been a Navy SEAL. And so—if the report that had brought them here was accurate—had Bobby Sanchez, whose corpse they were about to view.

Civilians sometimes thought warriors were accustomed to death, that it didn't faze them. The truth was, they had to encounter it more often than anybody else, so they couldn't let it slow them down, hamper their reflexes or dull their instincts. But every death hurt—especially that of a brother-in-arms.

They found Sanchez in the living room. Two detectives—Sam knew one of them, a hard charger named Sabrina Melloy—and a uniformed cop who looked ten years and twenty pounds past retirement were with him.

"The Marines have landed," Melloy said. "Oh, wait, you're Navy. You're the guys who chauffeur the Marines."

"It's a little more complicated than that," Callen said. "Actually, a lot more complicated."

"Ignore Detective Melloy," Sam said. "She used to date a Marine. She's never been the same."

"Happens to the best of them," Callen offered. "Sad."

"If you three are finished," the other detective broke in, "I can tell you what we—"

"Save it," Sam said. "Let us draw our own conclusions."

The second detective was a man, older than Melloy, with thinning red hair, a drooping mustache, and sad eyes. The blue suit he wore was faded at the knees. He looked at Sam for a long moment, then shrugged. "Have at it. A field investigation unit will be here in a little while. This is the fourth homicide of the day, so they're a little backed up. And it's not even nine-thirty. Going to be a bad one."

"Looks that way."

The male detective tilted his head toward the door. "Let's get out of their way, folks." To Sam and Callen, he added, "We'll be right outside. I'll let you know when the crime scene folks show up."

"Thanks," Callen said.

The LAPD officers left the house, and with them went the last distraction from the reason Sam and Callen had come. Sam stepped back to the corner and tried to view the scene through fresh eyes.

The house probably dated from the first couple of decades of the twentieth century. It was built in a simplified Craftsman style, employing lots of dark wood, with wainscoting about two-thirds of the way up the walls and exposed ceiling timbers. The living room was separated from the dining room by a pocket door, but the dining room had been converted to a bedroom at some point. The kitchen was on the other side of the living room, visible from here only because its floor was tiled instead of hardwood. The furnishings were nothing fancy, and they'd been tossed around as if a tornado had targeted this specific room. There was a couch and a couple of chairs that could have come from Target or K-Mart or any other discount department store, a wooden coffee table and end tables, pictures on the wall that had probably been purchased in their frames, with little emotional connection to the house's current occupant.

Said occupant—Lieutenant Robert Sanchez—was on the floor between the couch and the coffee table, which had been tipped over on its side. Blood had pooled and congealed all around him, dark against the floorboards and visible mostly because light from outside glinted off it. But even if he hadn't seen it, Sam had smelled it the moment he'd passed through the front door. Blood and more—the unmistakable scent of death.

Bobby Sanchez had died, and he'd gone the hard way.

All the fingers on both hands had been broken, and both thumbs had been cut off. His jaw was shattered and his left eye had been gouged from its socket. He was naked, and his skin was covered with cuts, mostly shallow but some deep, from the soles of his feet to the top of his shaved head. His flesh was so bruised it was impossible to tell where one contusion left off and another began. His wrists and ankles were bound with nylon rope.

"SEALs are trained to withstand torture, right?" Callen asked.

"Yeah."

"Maybe that training didn't do Sanchez any favors. You think he gave up whatever somebody wanted to know?"

"Everybody has a breaking point," Sam said. "Can't say what his was, but what he went through would have been way too much for most people."

"You didn't know him, right?"

Callen already knew the answer to that. Sam wouldn't be here if he'd known Sanchez. Or he might have been, but the case would have gone to another team. No matter how hard agents tried to leave personal feelings at the door, they were only human, and a close emotional connection to a case tended to act as blinders. Sam, in particular, had been told that he sometimes got too involved. He supposed that was true, though he had no intention of changing. That involvement was what drove him. He wanted to right the wrongs, to seek justice on behalf of people who couldn't do it for themselves.

People like Bobby Sanchez.

"Right," he acknowledged.

"Looks like he was worked over for a long time. Neighborhood like this, you'd think somebody would've heard something."

Sam had been thinking the same thing. "Let's talk to those detectives."

He was glad not to be looking at Sanchez's body anymore, although he knew the image would stay with him forever. They found the detectives in the yard, talking to the two unis.

"Excuse me, Detective Melloy? And…" Callen let the sentence trail off. Sam figured he didn't know the older detective's name, either.

"Jackson," the man said. "Mickey Jackson. Mick."

"I'm Callen, he's Hanna."

"I know. What can we do for you?"

"Have you started canvassing the neighbors? See if anybody saw or heard anything?"

"We're still waiting on the manpower for that, but we

will," Jackson said. "My guess? The house next door is vacant. This is a corner lot, with a good-sized yard, so the place around the corner isn't too close. Sanchez lived alone, and I get the feeling this isn't a neighborhood where people poke their noses in other folks' business."

"How do you figure?"

"I'm a detective. I detected that no one has come around since we got here, looking to see what's going on, and from that I deduced that people here mind their own beeswax."

"He's good at that deducing stuff," Melloy added.

"How was Sanchez found, then?"

"One of yours," Melloy replied. "A Navy counselor named Jim Hawthorne had an early appointment with him today. When he got here, no one answered the door. He walked around back and the kitchen door was ajar, so he went inside."

"Where is he now?" Sam asked.

"Being questioned at the station, although he'd probably rather be on some other counselor's couch. He was really shaken up."

"We'll need to talk to him," Callen said. "This is our investigation, now."

"Of course it is," Jackson said. "I know how this works. Feds come in, step all over the locals—"

Sam cut him off. "It ain't like that."

"No?"

"He's one of ours. You'd feel the same way if he was LAPD, and we'd understand."

"I've seen how understanding you guys are. One time the Bureau—"

Melloy touched his arm. "Sam and Callen aren't the Bureau. You haven't worked with them, but I have. They're okay."

Jackson shrugged. "You say so."

"We'll keep you involved," Callen said. "Your guys can process the scene, just be sure we get the full data set—not just the conclusion. You'll be in the loop. Like Agent Hanna said, Sanchez was a SEAL. That makes him family. We're not trying to step on anybody's toes, but we run the investigation."

Jackson breathed a sigh of resignation. "Okay, whatever. We'll work the scene, canvass. Let you know what we come up with."

"And we'll do the same for you," Sam replied.

"Appreciate it."

"We're all on the same side here," Melloy offered. "Let's try to act like it."

"I will if they will," Jackson said.

"Detective Jackson," Callen said, "you've got my word."

2

Jim Hawthorne was a civilian counselor who divided his time between the Naval Medical Center in San Diego, the Robert E. Bush Naval Hospital in Twentynine Palms, and VA facilities in Long Beach and L.A. As if that didn't keep him busy enough, he also made home visits in certain cases. Bobby Sanchez had apparently been one of those cases, and Callen wanted to find out why. Detective Melloy had made a phone call, at his request, and the LAPD had delivered Hawthorne to the Boatshed by the time Callen and Sam arrived.

"I already told the police everything," Hawthorne said. "About ten times, in fact."

"They just want to make sure you got your story straight," Sam said. "We operate a little differently here. We don't need to hear it ten times. We just need to hear it once. As long as it's true. If it's not, that's when we start having problems."

"Look, I don't want any trouble with you. We work for the same people, right? You're NCIS, I'm a Department of the Navy civilian."

"He's right, Special Agent Hanna," Callen said. "Go easy on him and he'll tell us what he knows."

"That's right!" Hawthorne looked at Callen like he had tossed him a lifeline when he was about to drown. He was thin, with a shock of curly auburn hair and a neatly trimmed beard. He wore wire-rim glasses with oval frames, reminding Callen of that Beatle who'd been shot. John Lennon, that was his name. Hawthorne was fifty-two, according to the personnel file Nell had sent over to Callen's phone, so old enough to remember the Beatles as something more than historical figures. The counselor wore a blue Oxford shirt, button-down, faded Levi's, and brown Mephisto shoes. Sensible, not cheap but not outrageously pricey. Callen figured he'd been a hippie, but at the tail end of the scene, when most of the original hippies had already cut their hair and found jobs.

"Peace, brothers," Callen said. "There's no need for conflict. Jim—is it okay if I call you Jim?—just tell us what happened this morning at the Sanchez house."

Hawthorne blew out a breath, as if he'd been holding it for days. He ran long fingers across his damp forehead. The day was hot, and sometimes the team liked to keep the Boatshed on the steamy side when they were going to be interrogating suspects. Callen didn't know yet whether Hawthorne was a suspect, but they'd opted for warmish, just in case.

"I had an appointment with Bobby. I was supposed to be there at seven-thirty."

"That's early," Sam said.

"Bobby hasn't been sleeping much. Nights are hard for him, so he likes to make his appointments early in the morning."

"What are you seeing him for?" Callen asked.

Hawthorne frowned. "That's confidential. I'm sure you understand."

"What we understand," Sam said, "is that a Navy SEAL was tortured and murdered. I think any issues of doctor–patient confidentiality are less important now than finding out who did that, and why."

"Yes, well…" Hawthorne steepled his fingers on the table. "You can probably guess a lot of it. Sanchez saw action in Iraq and Afghanistan, among other places. And the kind of action SEALs tend to see is different from what most sailors encounter."

"Yeah, I know," Sam said. "Been there, got the nightmares. So you were helping him with PTSD?"

Hawthorne squirmed uncomfortably in his seat. Even though the patient was beyond caring, he looked uncomfortable about giving away too many details. Callen had to appreciate that, even though it made his job more difficult.

"Yes, that's right," the counselor finally said.

"Anything else?"

"Trust me, PTSD is a handful. It's one of those things that can't be diagnosed through lab tests or anything like that. It's more a set of symptoms. When a patient presents with the right ones—cognition and mood symptoms, avoidance, reactivity and arousal, and re-experiencing symptoms, for at least a month, he or she is considered to be suffering from PTSD."

"And Sanchez had those?" Callen asked.

"Big time. Like I said, he hardly slept. He didn't like to talk about the things he'd done and seen, and sometimes he claimed he didn't remember a lot of the details. He was constantly on edge, startled almost out of his wits by sudden, loud noises. Borderline paranoid, I'd say. He was the kind of guy who liked to sit with his back to the wall, and checked out the windows a lot."

"Maybe it wasn't paranoia," Sam suggested. "Maybe someone really was after him. You know, considering what happened to him."

"Believe me, I've thought about that. Since this morning, especially. I always thought it was just the trauma, and if he knew about any genuine threats, he never confided in me about them."

"What happened to him wasn't random. Someone doesn't just go into any old house and do that to the guy inside," Callen said. "That was personal. Sanchez was targeted."

"I... didn't really get a good look," Hawthorne said. "As soon as I saw him, I ran out and called nine-one-one."

"You didn't stick around?"

"I went back to my car and sat in it with the motor running until the police arrived. I didn't know if whoever had done that was still around, you know? If anyone came out of that house, or came toward my car, I'd have floored it out of there."

"Tell us exactly what you saw," Sam said. "From when you got out of your car the first time."

"Like I said, it was early. The neighborhood was quiet. There were a few cars on the roads, people going to work. A block or so from Bobby's house there was a bus stop, and some people were there, you know, with lunch pails, briefcases. Just a regular weekday. I stopped in front of his house, got out, went to the front door. His doorbell's broken—or that's what he says, but I think he disconnected it. He really didn't like having visitors. Anyway, I knocked, like I usually do. Most of the time, he's ready for me and opens the door before I even have a chance to knock, but when I do knock, he's always there right away. Like he's been watching me since I pulled up. I expect he usually was.

"Anyway, this time I knocked, and nobody answered. That was really unusual. I waited a minute, and knocked again. Nothing. I actually checked the calendar on my phone, to make sure I had the right day. I did, so I went around to the back, because Bobby had a back door that opened out of the kitchen. I thought maybe he was back there, out in the yard or in the kitchen. When I got back there, the door was open. I poked my head in, called him a couple of times. He didn't answer, and I started to get really worried."

"Worried why?" Sam asked. "Did you think he had enemies who meant him harm?"

"Not that so much," Hawthorne replied. He stroked his bearded chin, like a professor in a cartoon. "But with PTSD, suicide is always a concern. I half-expected to find him dead by his own hand."

"Obviously you didn't."

"No. Like I said, when I got into the living room and saw him—all the cuts, all the blood—I knew he was dead. I took off out of there and called for help."

"Did he ever name any enemies who might want to hurt him?" Callen asked.

"No, nothing like that. He always felt like he was in some kind of danger, but I think it was a vague, nonspecific danger. More a reflection of the fact that on combat missions, the possibility of violent death was always there, and that level of alertness wasn't easy to shut down."

Callen passed a card across the table to Hawthorne. "Thanks for your help," he said. "If you remember anything else, let us know. Anything at all, no matter how insignificant it might seem. You never know what might turn out to be important."

Hawthorne's expression was so grateful Callen was almost embarrassed by it. Strike the *almost*; he was embarrassed. Hawthorne looked like a guy whose life sentence had just been commuted. He hadn't suspected the counselor had anything to do with Sanchez's death, and having met the man, he was certain of it. Sanchez put up a fight—the condition of his living room testified to that. He could have taken Jim Hawthorne blindfolded, with both arms and legs tied behind his back. No, whoever had done that to Bobby Sanchez was a considerably more dangerous person—or persons—and he, or they, had to be found.

Callen got the feeling that Sanchez's death was the beginning of something, not the end. And anything that started that bad was only going to get worse.

3

June 14

"Spider-Man or Batman?"

"Deeks, that's not even a question. Spider-Man or Batman what? Which one would I date? Neither. They're both fictional, and that's just the beginning of my objections."

"I wouldn't expect you to date either of them. That's kind of my exclusive province."

Kensi didn't answer.

"Isn't it?"

She sighed. "Yes, Deeks. Unless I decide to go on the prowl for someone who doesn't bother me with nonsensical questions while I'm trying to work."

"Nonsensical? You're the one who asked me which Ninja Turtle I am."

"Oh. My. God. Is this about that? You're still upset about that? That was—"

"That was at an intimate moment," he reminded her. "And it's difficult to maintain the appropriate mood when you're trying to figure out whether your partner would be more romantically interested in Leonardo, Michelangelo, Donatello, or… I'm blank."

"Raphael."

"Raphael! That's the one. I was just going to say that."

"Sure, you were."

"Mr. Deeks, Ms. Blye."

Henrietta Lange's voice cut through the moment's tension and the stillness of the bullpen. Both agents looked up at her, barely taller than the balustrade at which she stood.

"Would you join me upstairs, please?"

"We would be happy to, Hetty," Kensi replied. "Thrilled, even, if it'll get Deeks to stop pestering me with absurd questions that don't really have answers."

"That sounds like a fascinating philosophical challenge," Hetty said. "What was the question, Mr. Deeks?"

He and Kensi were both starting up the wooden stairs, she two steps ahead of him. He didn't mind the view. "The question was, Spider-Man or Batman?"

"By which he means—"

Hetty cut her off. "The meaning is obvious, Ms. Blye. 'Which would prevail in combat?' The answer is equally obvious. Batman."

"Exactly," Deeks agreed.

"Why Batman?" Kensi asked.

"Spider-Man has the proportionate strength of a spider, thanks to being bitten by a radioactive one, while Batman is simply a human, albeit one who has trained extensively in the martial arts and is in peak physical condition. In the end, however, Spider-Man is young, immature, and somewhat idealistic. Batman, on the other hand, is a narcissistic sociopath of the highest order. In a fight, he simply would not quit, while I can't say the same for Spider-Man."

"And there you have it, my dear," Deeks said.

"From the voice of experience."

"You do realize, Hetty, that they're both fictional characters. How they would do in a fight would be up to whoever was writing it."

They had reached the top of the staircase, and Hetty was already on her way into the Operations Center. Now she stopped and slowly turned toward them. "Of course I realize that, Kensi. I'm not an idiot, after all."

"No!" Kensi blurted out. "I didn't mean to imply… I was just…"

"I know, dear. It's all right. I'm simply having some fun. At your expense, for which I apologize."

She turned again and disappeared into the darkened room. Deeks and Kensi followed. As they entered, Eric Beale was walking out clutching several file folders. "She said Batman, didn't she?" he asked.

"What other answer is there?"

"Nell and I had the same argument once, and Hetty made a perfectly valid case for Spider-Man. I honestly believe she chooses whichever answer she thinks will end the conversation sooner."

Kensi faced Deeks, and he braced for her "So there!" face. But Hetty spoke again before she could pull it together. "Mr. Deeks, what I'm going to ask you to watch will be particularly difficult for you, I believe. I suggest you prepare yourself."

Kensi's expression went flat, then sympathetic. Deeks wasn't sure how to take Hetty's warning. How was he supposed to prepare himself without knowing what it was he was preparing for? "I, uhh, I'm prepared. I guess. As prepared as I'm going to be."

"Very well. Watch, please."

As soon as the words escaped her lips, video started playing on several of the room's screens, including the largest. Deeks looked there. The video was from a bank surveillance camera, inside the bank. "It has been edited," Hetty said, "to focus on the important parts. This happened this morning at the Certified National Bank branch in Malibu."

The camera was stationary, mounted high above the counter, on the customer side. The video was a little grainy. At first, it looked like a normal morning. Three tellers were working, each with a customer at the window. Two more customers waited in the queue. Two of the tellers were women. The gender mix of the customers was similar, with three women and two men. One of the men was barefoot, wearing board shorts and a Hawaiian shirt.

Another woman strolled into the bank and took her place in line. Almost immediately behind her came three men in long, dark coats and stocking caps. As they entered, each man reached up and rolled down his cap, turning it into a full-face mask. From beneath their coats, they pulled long guns. AR-15s or something based on that platform, Deeks guessed, though it was hard to be sure with the poor video quality.

From there, events proceeded as expected. The men made the tellers back away from their windows and ordered the customers and other staff to toss aside their cellphones and lie on the floor. One of the men went over the counter and started emptying drawers, while another took the bank manager with him to the vault.

It was over in less than two and a half minutes, and the three were on their way out the door, each one carrying what looked like a heavy bag of money.

"One point one million," Hetty said, as if reading Deeks's mind. She was good at that, and not just with Deeks. "We'll cut to the outside now."

As she spoke, the scene switched to one filmed by an exterior camera. The men burst from the bank and dashed to a waiting brown station wagon. The doors were open, as was the rear. They threw their bags of money in the back, piled into the seats, and the vehicle was in motion before the doors were closed.

But they weren't out of the woods yet. A pair of patrol officers had reached the scene, and were standing beside their cruiser, shielding themselves behind the doors. One held a handgun, the other a shotgun. They aimed at the oncoming car, and the one with the handgun got off a couple of shots, then ducked from the hail of fire coming his way. The cop with the shotgun was, Deeks guessed, waiting for the wagon to get close enough to make the weapon useful. But before that happened, a couple of rounds fired from the passenger-side window hit him. Deeks could almost feel the impacts as the officer flinched, turned, and fell to the street.

"That's enough," Hetty said. The screens went dark.

"Is he…?"

"He's still in surgery. Mr. Deeks, you know him, I believe."

"I thought he might be… is that Tony?"

"Officer Anthony Scarlatti, yes."

"Oh. Oh, man."

Deeks felt Kensi's hand on his arm, then snaking across his back.

"Friend of yours?"

"Kind of. His dad, Tony senior, was one of my training officers. Kind of a mentor when I first got onto the cops. Tony junior was just a kid, then, but before long he was a rookie on the force. Tony senior was killed by a drunk driver who plowed into him while he was walking back to his car after giving a motorist a verbal warning, and I sort of took Tony junior—just Tony, now—under my wing."

Kensi squeezed tighter. "I'm sorry, Deeks," she said.

"What's the prognosis?" Deeks asked.

"His condition is critical. The doctors are doing what they can. They're cautiously optimistic."

"Good. What about those... bastards, who shot him? Are they...?"

"We were able to enhance the image enough to get a license plate number. The vehicle is registered to someone named Mitchell Bostic, of El Paso, Texas."

"He came all the way from Texas to rob a bank? I mean, it wasn't a bad haul, but—"

"How does the OSP fit in?" Kensi interrupted. "Is Bostic Navy?"

"Our only interest—other than the natural concern we have when any law enforcement officer is targeted— is Officer Scarlatti's connection with Mr. Deeks. The investigation is in the hands of the Los Angeles Police Department and the FBI. At this point, they know little to nothing about Mr. Bostic, and have not identified his compatriots. I wanted Mr. Deeks to hear it from me before it hit the news. When I get back to my office and give the word, the name and photograph of Mr. Bostic will be broadcast across the entire Los Angeles basin. One does not shoot a police officer in this city and expect to get away with it."

"You okay, Deeks?" Kensi asked.

Was he? He wasn't sure. He had been close to Tony once, but that had been years ago. Still, he didn't want to have to see Angela, Tony senior's widow, at a funeral for another of her Tonys.

"I'll be all right," he said at last. "But thanks. And

thank you, Hetty. You'll keep me posted?"

"In thirty minutes, you won't be able to escape the news, Mr. Deeks. No matter how much you might want to."

"That's good. Let's flush this guy out."

"I assure you, that is what those running the case intend to do."

"If I can do anything to help—"

Hetty cut him off. "You'll be the first to know. Well, the second, actually."

"Who'll be first?"

Her eyes widened, as if in shock. "Why, *me*, of course. Always."

4

To no one's surprise—her own, least of all—Hetty was right.

Television, including the networks and the cable news channels, ran with the bank robbery story, showing the largely unhelpful video footage and incessantly repeating Mitchell Bostic's name for most of the day. If history was any guide, there was every likelihood that they'd run with it for days, unless some other horrific crime or national disaster supplanted it. The correspondents and professional hairpieces knew virtually nothing, of course, but that didn't stop them from interviewing "experts" who also knew nothing, and repeating the same paucity of details in ever more breathless tones, as if vital new information had just come across the wires.

Deeks was upset because there was no new information. He had hoped that the release of Bostic's name and pictures of his car would have spurred a flood of tips. Said tips wouldn't have come directly to him, of course, but either through his contacts at the LAPD or via Hetty, he'd have heard about any promising ones. Instead of information—or even better, intelligence—all he'd heard during the day could have been the relentless chirruping of crickets in the evening.

Not that it was his case—or anybody else's, for that matter. Hetty had made clear that NCIS was officially hands-off. Still, Deeks was an interested observer, and a legitimate consumer of the media. It wasn't his fault that the media he was consuming on this particular day happened to be focused on local news.

He was ready to call it a day. He'd heard about a new food truck in Bell Gardens, which was supposed to have an incredible baked ziti. Kensi was ready to go, car keys in her hand, when his phone buzzed. He offered Kensi a shrug. "Deeks," he said.

"Marty?"

He didn't recognize the voice. "Yeah?"

"It's Chris Gilpin."

Deeks had to scan his memory banks for that one, but then it came to him. Gilpin was a detective Deeks knew from the LAPD. They'd never exactly been friends. Deeks suspected that Gilpin was on the take—he lived a little too large for what he earned, and that was always a cause for concern. But no dirt had ever surfaced, that Deeks had heard about, so maybe he'd been wrong. Maybe Gilpin had made some good investments, or had family money or a profitable side job.

"Chris," he said. "Been a long time. What's shakin'?"

"You were tight with Tony junior, right?"

"With both Tonys, yeah. Terrible news."

"Damn right it is. Anyway, I got someone you should meet. She came in today, after the story ran on TV for about the millionth time."

"She?"

"I think you should hear it from her. Trust me, you'll want to."

"About Tony?"

"Just meet with her, Marty."

"When?"

"What are you doing now?"

Deeks thought about that baked ziti. He'd almost given up on finding lasagna as good as his mom's, but there were other dishes in that neighborhood, and a good baked ziti was one of them. His mother made a heck of a smalahove, too, but Kensi had explicitly rejected the idea of any dishes made from sheep's heads, so that was off the menu permanently.

He caught Kensi's eye, read her disapproval there. "Nothing, I guess," he said, glancing away. "Where do you want to meet?" *Say Bell Gardens*, he mentally implored.

"Don't you have someplace there? Some boat house or something?"

"The Boatshed. Sure, that would work."

"I'll bring her over. Thirty minutes?"

"Cool. See you then."

He ended the call and turned back to Kensi. "Please don't kill me. Because I know you could."

"I could," Kensi agreed. "But I don't want to. Yet. I'm pretty hungry, though, and you know what happens when I get hungry."

"You get hangry."

"Yes. You don't want that, do you?"

"No, of course not. Where can we eat that's close enough to be at the Boatshed in half an hour?"

"There might be a candy bar in one of my desk drawers we could split."

"Seriously, Kens—"

"I am serious. The only places close by that I'd want to

eat at would take considerably longer than a half hour."

"I think there's some food in the cupboard at the Boatshed."

"If there is, it's probably been there long past its prime."

"It's about Tony Scarlatti, babe."

"I figured. It's okay, Deeks. The food truck was your thing, not mine. We can eat a little late. As long as we eat sometime."

"You mean it?"

"I do now. I won't guarantee that I will later. Who are you meeting?"

"A cop named Chris Gilpin. And a mystery woman."

Kensi arched an eyebrow. "Ooh, a mystery woman? Who is she?"

"If I knew that, she wouldn't be a mystery."

"Point taken."

"You're really not mad?"

"I'm really not mad, Deeks. Just—"

"Just what?"

"Just when you do buy me dinner later, it better be a good one."

Gilpin had grayed some since the last time Deeks had seen him. His jowls had thickened, as had his gut. His piercing blue eyes seemed to have shrunk behind folds of flesh. True to form, he was wearing a suit that had probably cost a month's salary. He had bought the silk shirt twenty or thirty pounds earlier, though; when he sat, it gapped open between the buttons.

Julianne Mercer, the slender young woman with him, looked nervous. She had big brown eyes that wouldn't hold still, and long, straight dark hair that she twirled with her fingers. She was wearing a long, men's-cut Tee shirt with a word on it that Deeks assumed was the name of a band he'd never heard of, and jeans so tight they might have just been painted on. She couldn't meet his gaze, and it took seemingly intense effort to release her hair long enough to shake his hand.

After the introductions were made—Kensi had accompanied Deeks to the Boatshed, on the off chance that having another woman in the room would make the "mystery woman" more comfortable—they all sat around the long table. Deeks tried not to stare at Mercer, but he was curious. "If Kensi doesn't get some dinner pretty soon, she's going to start eating my fingers," he said. "What is it you wanted to tell us?"

Julianne Mercer stared at the tabletop, feverishly winding her hair around her fingers. "Go on," Gilpin said. "Agent Deeks is one of the good guys. He can help."

"Maybe. I'll try, if I can," Deeks said. "Kind of depends on what this is all about."

"It's about Mitch Bostic," she said. Her voice was thin and quiet, as if she were far away and speaking through a tube.

"I kind of figured that from Chris's call," Deeks said. "What about him?"

"He doesn't exist."

5

"Maybe you could be... a little more specific?" Deeks said.

"He's not real," Mercer said. "He's a fiction. Made up."

Deeks knew he shouldn't have been so surprised. He and the others on the OSP team often inhabited phony identities. When they had time, they built legends—unbreakable fake histories, complete with lifelong identity trails, yearbook photos, former "friends"—everything necessary to make an assumed life stand up to the closest scrutiny. But her flat way of saying it threw him.

"Can you explain?"

"I don't know how else to say it. There is no Mitchell Bostic."

Kensi spoke up. "Let me try. I think we get by now what you're saying. Mitchell Bostic is an assumed identity. How about if you tell us how you know that?"

"Yeah," Deeks said. "That's what I was getting at."

Mercer took a deep breath, held it in for several long moments, then let it out slowly. "I know, because I'm his girlfriend."

"But you said he—" Deeks began.

Mercer interrupted. "That's not his real name. Mitch Bostic is really Kelly Martin."

"And you're Kelly Martin's girlfriend," Kensi said.

"That's right."

"And Kelly Martin is here in L.A.? Robbing banks?"

"He would never do that," Mercer said. "He's not a criminal. He's a Navy SEAL. Or he was, anyway; he just retired a couple of months ago."

The light bulb blinking on in Deeks's brain was just this side of literal. "And that's why you brought her to us," he said to Gilpin. "Because Mitch Bostic is really a former SEAL named Kelly Martin."

"Now you see why I thought you should hear it from her." He sounded relieved, as if he had transferred a heavy weight off his shoulders and onto those of NCIS.

"So where does Bostic come in?" Deeks asked.

"I haven't known a lot of Special Ops types," Mercer prefaced. "So I don't know if it's true or not. But Kelly told me that a lot of them have boltholes set up."

"Boltholes?" Deeks asked.

"A new name. A new identity. Maybe a house and a car and a good stash of money. Someplace far from where they live, so it won't be easy to connect them and they're not likely to run into people they know. Kelly's was in El Paso, Texas. He said from there it would be easy to blend in, or if necessary to cross the border and melt into the population in Juarez."

"But why would he need that? Why would any soldier need a bolthole?"

"I get that," Kensi said. "Special Operations forces handle a lot of sensitive missions. Sometimes they're as much spies as soldiers. They're on the front lines, and they make plenty of enemies. He probably figured that the day might come that somebody tried to get revenge on him, and he might need to disappear for a while."

"That's it exactly," Mercer said. She flashed the first grin Deeks had seen on her, a quick one, there and gone in an instant but it brightened the whole room. "He said there were plenty of bad guys who had it in for him—and you couldn't always trust the good guys."

"That's for sure," Deeks said. In his experience, the good guys were almost as likely to be bad as the bad guys. Or maybe it only seemed that way because he invariably started out trusting the good guys, whereas if he knew someone was bad from the start, they couldn't disappoint him.

Which brought up another question. "Who knew about his bolthole? Obviously you did."

"Only two people in the world knew about the Bostic identity. Me, and his swim buddy, a SEAL named Bobby Sanchez."

If words could knock a guy out of his chair, those would almost have done it. "Hold on. Bobby Sanchez, the—"

"The one who was killed a few days ago," Mercer finished for him. "That's right."

"Wow."

What had not been an NCIS case a few minutes earlier was suddenly part of a much bigger case—and undeniably NCIS business.

"If his bolthole was in El Paso, why is he in Los Angeles?" Kensi asked. "Don't people know him here?"

"I don't know," Mercer said. "I was out of the country, in Belize, for a shoot." She flashed another quick grin. "I'm a model—not, like, a supermodel or anything, but I do catalogs and websites and stuff. We were in a jungle area, and cellphones were useless. I talked to Kelly once on the one satellite phone we had. He was staying at my place while I was gone. But then the next time I tried to call him, a couple of days ago, I couldn't reach him. I got back into town last night, and it looked like he hadn't been there for days. Then I saw all the stuff on TV about Bostic today."

"So you've seen the video?" Deeks asked.

"Yes. Non-stop."

"Is the car his?"

"I've never seen the Bostic car, or his place in El Paso. But it's the right make and model, anyway."

Gilpin spoke up for the first time since introducing Julianne Mercer. "It makes sense," he said. "We spent all day trying to figure out who Bostic was. He has a good ID set up, with bank accounts, credit cards, driver's license, passport, all that stuff. But there are weird blanks in it, if you dig deep enough."

"Like what?"

"He has a birth certificate. Born in Lancaster, Pennsylvania, thirty-one years ago. But he never attended elementary school there. Can't find any other educational records, either, except a diploma from the University of Texas at El Paso at his home there."

"So his family moved around," Kensi suggested.

"That's what we thought. They owned their house, though. The title wasn't transferred until fourteen years later, when they sold it. According to local phone directories, they always lived there."

"Homeschooled?"

"That's a possibility. That's Pennsylvania Dutch country, so there are lots of small Amish schools, but the Bostics weren't that."

"Keep digging," Kensi said. "Chances are you'll find a death certificate, or a newspaper report that Mitch Bostic died before starting first grade."

"That's what it sounds like. Easy enough for Kelly

Martin to latch onto his identity, in that case."

"He never told me the details of how he did it," Mercer said. "He just wanted me and Bobby to know, because if he ever had to use it, it meant the shit had hit the fan and he wanted us to know what was up."

"I wouldn't want to be standing in front of that fan right now," Deeks said. "Bobby Sanchez is dead and the Bostic ID has been activated, so it's bound to be pretty messy there."

"Yeah," Mercer said. "Anyway, I want you to find him and make sure he's okay. He wouldn't be robbing banks and shooting cops—he just wouldn't. So something must have happened to him. I'm worried sick."

Deeks pulled out his phone. "I have to let G and Sam know about this," he said. "They're the agents working the Sanchez case. You'll probably have to tell your story again. That okay?"

"As many times as necessary, if it'll help find Kelly."

Deeks pressed Sam Hanna's icon, and the call was answered on the second ring. "What's up, Deeks?"

"So you know that case you've been working all week without getting anywhere?" Deeks asked. "I've been on it for five minutes, and I know more than you do."

"How so?"

"It's complicated. Come over to the Boatshed and—"

"Deeks, I'm on my way home. My family—"

"Trust me, this is big. You want to get it from the source."

He heard a heavy sigh, then Sam said, "Okay. I'll call G and we'll meet you there in twenty."

6

Eric Beale had enhanced the security video from the bank to the extent that he could, and Callen studied Julianne Mercer's face as she watched it for the third time. They had shown it to her in slow-mo once, then paused on each of the bank robbers individually and zoomed in on them. Now they were watching it at regular speed, and had told her to focus on gait, posture, body language. Callen had seen it more than enough times; he was focused on her, watching for any hint of recognition.

Nothing.

At the end, she shook her head. "None of those guys are Kelly."

"You're certain?" Sam said.

"Absolutely. I know Kelly. I know his build, the way he walks, the way he… moves."

There was a wistful note in her pause, and Callen wondered if "makes love" had been on the tip of her tongue. Or maybe a slightly more graphic word, instead.

He didn't doubt her certainty, but it was foreign to him, just the same. He could probably watch video of Sam or Deeks or Kensi, even with their faces masked, and know whether it was them or not. But that was because they worked together, day in and day out. They'd been under fire together. The circumstances of their profession made them close.

Beyond them, however—and probably Jethro Gibbs, and of course Hetty—he wasn't sure there was anyone else in his life who he could be as sure of. Could he pick a masked Joelle Taylor out of a lineup of women with similar physiques? Maybe, maybe not. He had to figure the same was true in reverse—outside of the people he worked with, was there anyone who could recognize him if his face were hidden and they couldn't hear his voice?

He didn't think so. Sometimes, he wondered what that would be like. To be so close to someone. To know them so intimately, and to be known the same way. Thinking about it was scary, sometimes, because with that kind of knowledge came a vulnerability he had never allowed himself. That person would know his flaws, his weaknesses, his moments of doubt.

Sam said it didn't matter, because when you loved someone enough to let them inside like that, you also trusted that they wouldn't use what they knew against you.

Callen wasn't sure he was capable of that much trust. For others, it was baked in, probably, from early childhood. When you trusted your parents and siblings, maybe it was easier to keep on trusting into adulthood. Callen hadn't known his long enough for that, and one way or another, they'd always left him. Years in foster care hadn't done anything to encourage it, either; on the contrary, when you never knew if you were going to remain part of a "family," you learned to hold your emotions close, to not open up to others.

You trusted only yourself—and even that could be open to question.

"No," Mercer said, then reiterated. "Kelly's not there. I'd know if he was."

"You don't recognize any of the others?" Sam asked.

"No. I wouldn't, necessarily—there aren't many people I know like I do Kelly."

The four agents sat silently for a few moments, considering. They had let Gilpin leave; they'd make sure Mercer got home. Finally, Kensi broke the quiet.

"So he was here in L.A. when you left for Belize, but sometime in there he went to El Paso."

"Right."

"What day did you talk to him last?"

"It was... let's see. It was Sunday. Sometimes it's hard to keep track when you're on a shoot. Nothing matters but the photographer's schedule."

"And Sanchez's body was found on Monday."

"That's right," Callen said. "When that hit the news is probably when Kelly Martin decided it was time to become Mitch Bostic."

"Do you have any idea why, Julianne?" Kensi asked. "Is there anything or anyone you can think of that might have meant Sanchez harm, or Kelly? Any mutual enemies they might have had?"

"He doesn't talk a lot about the ops he works on," Mercer said. "Lots of them are classified. Most of them are dangerous. He tells me I don't want to know, and he's right."

"How did you meet him?"

Mercer closed her eyes briefly, as if picturing the moment. When she opened them again, they looked huge and luminous. She really was beautiful, Callen thought, even though she wasn't wearing any makeup and had seemed to attend to her hair only by wrapping it around her fingers. He wasn't surprised that she was a model.

"I did a gig at a Wounded Warriors fundraiser. They wanted some pretty girls dishing up food, handing out glasses, and so on. It was a benefit, so no money for me, but I didn't have any work that day, and it was a good cause. Anyway, Kelly was there. He was *sooo* handsome: tall, with broad shoulders and incredible arms. He had a kind of scruffy beard and his hair was a mess, but his smile made the whole room seem happy. I guess he liked what he saw, too, because he came over to talk to me. After the event, we kept talking. We had dinner the next day, and lunch the day after that. Finally, on our third date, he kissed me. We've been pretty much inseparable ever since."

"That's sweet," Kensi said. Callen knew that it bothered her sometimes to be the only female in the bullpen, but he was glad they had her. She could get away with things the others couldn't, and say things like "That's sweet" without sounding like a complete idiot.

"Sanchez has served in Iraq and Afghanistan, but also Yemen, Somalia, Djibouti, a couple of European countries, and other places I can't mention because the missions are that classified," Sam said. "Same for Kelly?"

"All those, I think, yes. Also the Philippines and South Korea. That I know of. Like I said, some missions he hasn't told me the first thing about."

"They've known each other a long time? Him and Sanchez?"

"They've been swim buddies since they both tried out for the SEALs together. Kelly says he doesn't know if he would have made it in if not for Bobby. Bobby says he's full of it."

"Sanchez's record is exemplary," Sam said. "Usually guys like that don't hang around with slackers. Not that slackers make the SEALs in the first place."

"Kelly's definitely no slacker."

Callen noticed tears brimming in her eyes. "You've got to find him," she said. As she spoke, a single tear slipped free and tracked down her cheek. "I've been so worried."

"We will," Kensi said.

"We don't want to keep you here all night, Julianne," Deeks added. "Are you okay to go home?"

"I guess so," she replied. "I'll need a ride, I guess."

"I'll drop you off," Kensi said. "You're in Westwood, right?"

"Yes. I really appreciate it, Agent Blye."

"Please, call me Kensi." She didn't add, "Agent Blye was my father," but Callen knew she sometimes thought it. Instead, she said, "Does anyone have more questions for Miss Mercer?"

"About a million," Deeks said. "But nothing crucial at the moment. Because I know some people are getting hang—uhh, hungry."

Kensi shot him a look that Callen was certain had to do with some conversation that had occurred before he and Sam had shown up. She didn't reply, though, just looked around the table. When no one spoke up, she rose from her chair. "I guess we'll be going, then."

Mercer stood more slowly, pressing her palms flat against the tabletop to push herself to her feet. She looked weary. Defeated. But beautiful just the same.

"Thank you," she said. "Thank you all, for anything you can do."

"We'll find him, ma'am," Sam said. "We're good at our jobs."

"I'm sure you are. I think Kelly would like you all."

"I'm looking forward to meeting him," Sam said. "Soon, I hope."

Julianne Mercer lived in a high-end apartment building on Westwood Boulevard. Kensi noted a camera watching them as she pulled up the drive, and inside the lobby, a uniformed guard sat behind a high counter that no doubt concealed multiple monitors. He greeted Mercer by name, and the elevator door slid open before they even reached it. When Mercer and Kensi stepped inside, the 11 button was already illuminated.

"Nice place," Kensi said as the door closed and the elevator started gliding up.

"I make a good living," Mercer said. "I feel safe here."

"I'm sure." There was a camera inside the elevator, too. Kensi would have Eric and Nell pull all the footage from this place so they could see what state Kelly Martin had been in—and whether he'd been alone—when he left for the last time.

"Are you and Mr. Deeks a couple?" Mercer asked.

"We don't... talk about our personal lives," Kensi said. "I'm sure you understand."

"Yes, of course. Sorry. I just kind of got that vibe."

When they reached the eleventh floor, Mercer got out and made a right. Kensi eyed the position of the hallway camera. At the door of apartment 1127, Mercer inserted a key and turned it, but Kensi stopped her before she opened the door. "Let me go in first," she said.

"Okay..."

Kensi drew her SIG Sauer, concealing it from the hall camera with her body, and went inside. She flipped a switch and lights illuminated an entryway that led to an expansive living room. On the far end, a glass wall revealed a balcony and a glorious city view. A good living was right.

She cleared the apartment, room by room. When she was finished, she brought Mercer in from the hallway. "Just being cautious," she said. "Do you have any security cameras inside the apartment?"

"God no," Mercer said emphatically. "Sometimes it seems like I spend most of my life with cameras pointed at me. That's the last thing I want when I'm in my own place."

"I understand. But until we find Kelly and figure out what's going on, I don't know if you're in any danger. This building seems pretty secure, but it might not be a bad idea to get a system of your own inside."

"I'll think about it."

"Good," Kensi said.

Mercer indicated the SIG, now holstered at Kensi's hip. "Are you good with that?"

"Very."

"Kelly's tried taking me to a shooting range a couple of times, but I can't get the hang of it. I don't really like guns."

Kensi shrugged. "It's a tool I work with. Like an electrician's screwdriver, or a carpenter's hammer. I appreciate that it's well-made and does what I need it to."

"Well, I hope you don't need it any time soon. And I hope you guys really can find Kelly."

"I won't lie to you, Julianne. He's a professional, like we are. If he doesn't want to be found, he can make our job very difficult. And if he hasn't been in touch with you, he might not want to be found. That's why I said you might be in danger—if he's keeping away from you because he's trying to draw the danger away."

"I understand, I guess."

"If he does contact you, get in touch with us right away. Even if he tells you not to. It's very important. You can decide not to tell us where he is, if you think that's best, but at least let us know you heard from him."

"Okay."

"And if you think of anything else that might help us locate him, please let us know that, too."

"I will. Definitely."

"Thanks," Kensi said. She started for the door, then stopped. "One more thing."

"Yes?"

"If you feel like you're in any danger—at all—call nine-one-one. Then call us. Immediately."

When she finally left, Kensi thought poor Julianne Mercer looked kind of terrified.

Perfect, she thought. *That's how she should feel.*

Because whatever her boyfriend's mixed up in, it's not good.

7

June 15

The long day turned into an all-nighter for the team. Eric and Nell traded off doing research and taking catnaps while the others studied the service records of Kelly Martin and—because they hadn't been involved in the case previously—Kensi and Deeks pored over those of Bobby Sanchez. Both SEALs had done plenty of wet-work and taken out their share of bad guys, any of whom might have had family and friends anxious for revenge.

Reading through the files, Sam Hanna's overwhelming feeling was one of familiarity. In many respects, he could have been reading his own history. It was tinged with a little bit of nostalgia, too, though overall, he was glad he'd made the career shift. Working for NCIS kept him stateside more often, and he got to see Michelle and the kids most nights and many weekends. Some SEALs managed married life, but many didn't, and of those who did, far too many left widows behind to raise shattered families.

He discovered his path had crossed with those of Sanchez and Martin once or twice, although he hadn't known them at the time. They'd operated out of Coronado, in Southern California, while he'd been out of Virginia. But they'd all been in Fallujah together, among other places. Looking at their photographs, he tried to remember the men, but his own memories of that bloody combat were scattered and indistinct now. These men, though he had never met them, were his brothers-in-arms. Every SEAL was bonded by the torturous experience of testing and more than two years of training, and more so by the willingness to die that others might live. He owed Bobby Sanchez justice, and he owed Kelly Martin every effort to find him and ensure his safety.

At three-fifty in the morning he was fighting off fatigue. The letters on the pages were alternately running together or scrambling into nonsense. But he woke up when Eric and Nell came down the stairs together, both wearing smiles that could only be described as triumphant. They descended in perfect lockstep, like a couple being wed on a staircase—which, Sam thought, was exceedingly unlikely to ever happen to those two.

Unless, of course, they married each other.

"Kaleidoscope got a hit," Nell said.

"On the car. Mitch Bostic's car," Eric clarified.

"A 2009 Ford Taurus station wagon," Nell added. "Texas plates."

"Where is it?"

"It's in a Ralph's parking lot on—" Eric said.

"Hollywood and Western," Nell finished. "Sorry," she said to Eric.

"Thai Town?" Sam asked.

"That's right," Eric said. "We backtracked through the video to see who dumped it there. It was only one guy, and he was masked, just like in the bank robbery footage. He left the car and walked off-camera, so we can't see who picked him up. I'll isolate the best shot of him and send it to your phones, but I doubt it'll be much help."

"Send the LAPD over to secure the vehicle," Sam said. "We're on our way."

"We are?" Callen asked. He'd been working on his own research, and he looked like Sam felt—like he'd rather be asleep.

"I want a look at it."

Callen scooted his chair back, rose, and stretched. "Sure," he said. "A little night air'll be good for us. Get the circulation moving. Wake us up."

"I'll alert the LAPD," Nell said. She started back up the stairs. Eric stood there a moment longer, as if he couldn't decide which way to go, then shrugged and followed her.

The online post was simple: "Mitch Bostic we have something of yours Sea Vue Motel."

The punctuation and spelling left much to be desired, but the meaning was unmistakable. Kelly Martin had numerous online alerts in place for the "Mitch Bostic" name—alerts that had been silent for years, then suddenly filling his email inbox since the bank robbery and "Bostic's" car had hit the news.

What the post didn't mention was a room number or any other contact information. He tried emailing the poster—the website was one mostly used for offering low-paying jobs, items for sale, and easy hookups, so there was an anonymous email system set up—but got no response.

It was, of course, a trap. That would have been

obvious to a fifth-grader, and Martin was a trained Navy SEAL. He could smell it a mile away.

What he couldn't sniff out was any way around it. The invitation was so obvious he couldn't bring himself to ignore it.

Anyway, he had survived traps before, and worse. This one was so blatant, he was more than a little curious about who wanted him to walk into it, and why. With luck, he would be able to learn something about what had happened to Bobby, and how his bolthole had been compromised, and maybe even get some payback for both. Even if he learned nothing, the payback could still happen.

He was in his own city, and even though his primary identity—the name he'd carried since birth, and the ever-aging face that went with it—was also compromised, he had resources here. He got his hands on a car—okay, *stole* was the word, and if he started lying to himself, he might as well hang it up—and some hardware and found out where the Sea Vue Motel was, and he walked into the trap.

The motel was quiet. It was late enough that most of the drug dealers and prostitutes who frequented the place were asleep or passed out or otherwise MIA. The office was dark, the door locked. Any tourists rolling into town at this hour would be unlikely to find themselves at the Sea Vue, and even if they did, the fact that they couldn't get into the office to rent a room would be a favor they'd probably never fully understand. If they were lucky.

But there was one guy smoking a cigarette in the shade of the second-floor walkway. Martin had parked at the edge of the property, and he watched the guy for a few minutes before leaving the beat-up Ford Bronco he had liberated from the long-term parking lot at LAX. The man was scrawny, dirty, and every time he leaned back against the wall, it looked like he might fall asleep there. Using, for sure, Martin judged. He wore a black long-sleeved Tee shirt and jeans that had blown out at the knees from age and use, not because some designer had convinced people to pay extra for the effect.

Martin pulled his FN SCAR from the bag he'd been carrying and slid from the driver's seat. He preferred the SCAR-H for this kind of work—the H was for heavy, the rest of it for Special Operations Forces Combat Assault Rifle, and he liked the larger load over the L (for light), but he was on the move all the time, on foot a lot, and even those few ounces made a difference. The close quarters variant was fine for this kind of work, and the weight difference meant he could carry a few more twenty-round magazines.

For the smoker, he figured the weapon's undoubtedly sinister appearance would do the trick. The guy barely seemed to notice him as he approached. He was sucking every last molecule of nicotine out of his smoke. One final flare, then he tossed the remaining fragment out into the parking lot, where it bounced and scattered sparks before dying. He was digging in his pocket, presumably for a key card, when Martin approached.

"Hey," he said.

The guy almost jumped, as if he'd had no idea that a vehicle had pulled into the lot and its occupant had sat inside it for five long minutes before climbing out with an assault rifle in his hands. Maybe he had been so deep inside his own drug-fueled thoughts, he'd missed the whole thing. He turned now, though, with a look that resembled panic on his face. The paranoia of the junkie, Martin thought. Everything was cool, until it wasn't.

"What's up?" the guy mumbled.

"I'm looking for some men. Probably four of them, staying in one room, or maybe two, next to each other. You seen them?"

The guy thought for a minute. Martin was afraid he'd fallen asleep. Then he started nodding, almost frantically. "Yeah, yeah, yeah. Yeah, I seen 'em."

"Where are they?"

The guy jerked his thumb toward his left. "In, in, uhh, one-seventeen. No, one-nineteen. Or twenty-one, maybe."

"Which is it?" Martin made sure the junkie saw the gun. "It's kind of important to get this right."

"Nineteen, I think. One-nineteen."

"All four of them?"

"Yeah, four. Four guys. I thought it was something freaky, you know? Four guys in one room like that."

"Right," Martin said. "Freaky."

"You know what I mean?"

"Yeah," Martin said. "You might want to disappear."

"Don't have to tell me twice, Jack. You never saw me."

"Never saw you."

The guy faded into the shadows under the stairs, and Martin went to study the scene. Room 119 was in the middle of the row on the ground floor. There was nothing especially notable about it, which made it just like the other rooms. Painted doors, numbers on plastic plates, dark windows with curtains drawn. The window air conditioner of 119 was on, dripping water onto the sidewalk. The slick, mildewed spot showed that it was nothing unusual. The night was hot, and the units for other rooms were blowing, too.

Between those and the incessant trill of crickets, Martin almost didn't hear the pad of the junkie's sneaker on the pavement behind him.

But he did. He threw himself down and to the side. The first round tore into the stucco. Martin rolled and came up firing. The junkie—no junkie at all, Martin knew now—had ducked behind a car, and Martin didn't have time to force him out. Another car had pulled into the lot, and a man who looked like a legitimate tourist stared at him for a moment before trying to throw the vehicle in reverse. Instead, he killed the engine.

There wasn't going to be any conversation. He'd been right about the trap, but even knowing it was there, he'd stepped in it. Now there was a guy with a gun somewhere behind him, and an innocent civilian in the line of fire. And the distant wail of approaching sirens. More upright citizens in this neighborhood than he'd expected.

He took cover behind a car, at what he hoped was a safe distance from the civilian who'd driven into the middle of trouble, and waited for the door to 119 to open.

He didn't have to wait long.

8

The parking lot was nearly deserted. Tall lampposts threw circles of light on the ground, and the wagon sat just outside one of those. A scrap of newspaper had blown up against one of the tires. An LAPD cruiser was parked nearby, and two bored officers stood outside it.

"Anyone paying attention to the vehicle?" Callen asked them.

"Not really," one said. "I doubt anyone gave it a second look until we showed up."

"Probably right," Sam said. "Not much to look at."

It wasn't. It was a sun-bleached brown color, the paint so oxidized that it looked like it had been driven through salt ponds. Given its intended purpose, as functional transportation for Kelly Martin's Bostic identity, it made perfect sense. He would have wanted a vehicle that would not call attention to itself, and he'd have wanted something that a Navy SEAL would never be caught dead driving. This car met both of those criteria.

"You guys touch it?" he asked the officers.

"No, sir."

"Good. We'll need a complete workup. Fingerprints, DNA, hair and fiber. Everything. And stat."

"There's a tow truck on the way. We'll take it in and check it out."

"Get a team out here, too. This parking lot's a crime scene, now."

The cop who had answered before looked resentful. "Got it," he said.

"I don't mean to come off like a jerk," Sam said. "I appreciate what you guys have done, and are going to do. But this car was involved in the shooting of a cop, and I want to make sure everything's done by the book. We find who's been using this car, I want to be able to get a conviction."

"Is this connected to that bank job?" the other officer asked.

"Yes. So no shortcuts, okay? Make sure we get what we need."

"You got it, sir."

Sam wanted to take a look inside the wagon himself, but he didn't want to risk smearing any existing prints, or leaving any clues that would point the wrong way. Locard's exchange principle held true for good guys as well as bad—every contact made with another person, place, or thing resulted in the transfer of physical materials. Touching the vehicle would leave traces of Sam Hanna on it—and in the process, might remove some trace of whoever had last been inside it.

So he would leave that up to the professionals, who could invest more time in it than he could.

"Let's take a drive, G. See if we can spot any other cameras in the area that might have caught them driving away," he said.

"Works for me," Callen agreed.

They were heading back to the Challenger when Sam's phone buzzed. He glanced at the screen. "Text from Eric. He's routing a live feed to our phones."

"Feed of what?" Callen asked.

"Let's find out."

At once, both phones were filled with a dark image, primarily illuminated by bright, intermittent flashes. Sam recognized them as muzzle bursts. Both men watched on Sam's phone as Callen made a call.

A moment later, he said, "This is streaming on Periscope, from the Sea Vue Motel in Culver City. A tactical team's on the way but they're not on scene yet."

The video was poor quality, and shaky. Hanna guessed that someone was shooting it on a mobile phone, from hiding, legitimately worried about being hit by a stray round. "What's it got to do with us?" he asked.

Before Callen could respond—if he even knew the answer—the screen brightened as a barrage of gunfire came from an open door and a window that had once had glass in it. In the foreground, the apparent target of all that lead threw himself to the ground behind a parked car. The people inside the room burst through the doorway and, still laying down covering fire, scrambled into a dark SUV. It looked like three men, and though the light was bad and the image tiny on his screen, Sam watched closely, trying to identify the model or see a license plate. But the camera angle was wrong. The men were still shooting out the vehicle's open windows as the SUV raced past.

Then Sam heard a pained grunt, and the image flipped around several times before coming to rest. Only now, it was facing toward the sky.

"He's hit," he said. "Whoever was shooting that video."

Callen listened to his phone. "Tac team's only a minute out, if that. There's a bus on the way, too."

"I hope it gets there in time," Sam said. Then he added, "Wait, look."

A shadow fell across the camera, then a hand reached down and picked it up. For a few seconds, a man's face was visible. Then he dropped the phone again. The last thing that could be seen before the feed went black was the sole of a boot rushing toward it.

"Did you see that?" Sam asked.

"Yeah," Callen said. "I think that was Kelly Martin."

Its name notwithstanding, the ocean couldn't be seen from the Sea Vue Motel. Not much could, Callen observed, except spent shell casings, broken glass, and blood. By the time he and Sam made it to Culver City, the shooting was long since over. The LAPD tactical team had arrived too late—the men were gone, the guy who looked like Kelly Martin was gone, and the citizen who had captured it on cellphone video was dead. The phone was found beside his corpse, turned off and wiped of fingerprints.

"His name was Morris Eubanks," the desk clerk who'd checked him in said. He was a wiry, rat-faced guy with three days' growth on his cheeks and chin, and tattoo sleeves decorating both skinny arms. "He didn't look like one of our regular type of clientele, so I asked him what he was doing here. He had an Oregon driver's license—Portland, I think. Said he was in town doing some sales calls, and just needed a place to put his head down for a few hours."

"What's the usual clientele?" Callen asked.

"You know, hookers and junkies, mostly. And their

customers, I guess. We don't pretend to be anything we're not."

And apparently bank robbers, Callen thought.

"You pretend to have an ocean view," Sam observed.

"That's just a name. It don't mean anything. Anybody who can see the sign can see that it's crap."

"Refreshingly honest," Callen said.

"I got no reason to lie to you."

"What about the four guys in room one-nineteen?" Sam said. "What was their story?"

"I don't know. I wasn't on when they came in. I didn't even know there was four guys in there. There's only one name down on it."

"Let's see," Callen said.

The clerk dug around behind the counter for a minute, then brought up a sheet of paper on which the guest's name had been typed and a signature scrawled.

It came as no surprise that the name was Mitchell Bostic.

"That's all you got?" Sam asked. "Don't you scan ID? Imprint a credit card?"

"We mostly deal in cash," the clerk said. "I told you who we cater to. If we did take a card, it'd probably be a stolen one."

"Do you look at driver's licenses?"

"If somebody wants to show me one, that's cool. I'll look at it. Like that dude from Portland, the dead guy. I looked at his. Had his picture on it, and the name matched what he gave me when he checked in."

Callen showed the clerk a photograph of Kelly Martin he had on his phone. "Was this guy a guest here?"

The clerk looked at it for a few seconds, then shrugged. "I ain't seen him. But that doesn't mean he wasn't. Just I didn't check him in or nothin'."

Callen started to ask another question, but the motel phone rang, cutting him off. "Sea Vue," the clerk said. He listened for a minute or so, then said, "Yeah, okay."

As he hung up the receiver, he looked at the agents with an expression of weary resignation. "That was the owner," he said. "He wants to know who's going to pay for the damage. You guys?"

"Above our pay grade," Sam said.

"Way above," Callen added.

9

"That's definitely Kelly," Julianne Mercer said. "Where is he?"

"This came from the scene of a firefight at a cheap motel in Culver City," Kensi said. "A salesman from Oregon was unfortunate enough to be on the scene, and was streaming it on his phone, until he took a bullet in the head. Kelly picked up his phone while it was still streaming. By the time the police arrived, he was gone."

Mercer's mouth fell open and rows of lines formed on her forehead. "A firefight? But he's okay?"

"As far as we know, he wasn't hit."

Kensi and Deeks had tracked Mercer down through her agent. She was doing an early-morning shoot for a department store commercial—"Mostly walking in the background," she said, "in my own clothes. But with one good closeup." They were shooting in a park in Santa Monica, with the Pacific Ocean as a natural backdrop. A few production trailers were parked nearby, just out of the shot.

"Was he part of the fight?"

"He appeared to be a significant part of it," Deeks said. "Maybe the most significant part."

"Who was he fighting?"

"It's a little hard to tell, but every indication is that it was the bank robbers who were using his car. They had checked into the motel using the Mitchell Bostic name."

"He hasn't been in touch with you?" Kensi asked.

"No. I've called and called, but I think he's probably tossed his phone."

"That would make sense if you wanted to disappear," Deeks said.

"Do you have any idea how he would have found the crew that hit the bank?" Kensi asked.

"No clue," Mercer said. "I don't know about these things. I guess, you know, he's a SEAL. They know all kinds of tricks, right?"

"They do indeed," Kensi said, thinking of some of the things she'd learned from Sam. "But I don't know if they include magical locating abilities. The room was rented for cash, no credit card or ID used. Do you think it's possible that he really is connected to them in some way? Maybe the fight was a falling out between thieves?"

"No. I told you before, he's not like that. There's no way he'd be hooked up with crooks."

Kensi nodded. "I know you said that. I'm just saying, sometimes people can surprise you. How long have you known him?"

"About four years, I guess."

"But you travel a lot. And he was deployed a few times in that time, right?"

"Yes. But—I don't know if you believe in soulmates."

"She totally does," Deeks said, wearing a smug smile.

"Don't listen to Deeks. Go on."

"Well, I do. And Kelly's mine. We're as close as two

people have ever been. I would know if he was capable of something like that."

Kensi wasn't sure they were as close as Mercer thought, given that Martin was back in Los Angeles and hadn't reached out to let her know. He might have been trying to protect her, worried that if he got in touch, it would somehow blow back on her. But the more likely scenario, if somebody had it in for him, was that they'd be watching her, expecting him to contact her. If he thought that, then keeping away might have been more out of concern for his own safety than for hers.

A production assistant wearing a dark blue Tee shirt, faded jeans, high top Converse sneakers, and a Paramount Pictures ball cap walked to the group with an anxious look on her face. "Sorry, Ms. Mercer," she said nervously. "Sorry. They're waiting for you on set. I'm sorry."

"Look, are we done here?" Mercer asked. "I have to go."

"Yes," Kensi said. "I think we're done. Just… get in touch if you think of anything."

"I will."

She started off with the PA, who glanced over her shoulder before she'd taken four steps. "Sorry!" she called back.

"If she wants to direct, she's gonna have to get a lot more forceful," Deeks said.

"Maybe she wants to work for a studio head," Kensi replied. "In which case, all she has to brush up on is her groveling."

"Ouch. What did a studio head ever do to you, Kensi Marie?"

"Have you seen some of the movies they've greenlit?

I think some of them are deliberately trying to whittle down America's collective IQ."

"That sounds positively criminal," Deeks said with a grin. "A little out of our jurisdiction, though."

"That's probably for the best, Deeks," Kensi said. "I'd hate to be brought up on charges for shooting one of them, but every time I come out of the theater after watching some stupid movie, a little part of me itches to pull the trigger."

"Maybe try therapy, instead." Laughing, Deeks ducked away from Kensi's wide punch.

"What do you have for us?" Hetty asked.

"Make it good," Owen Granger added. "We can't have a SEAL running around Los Angeles getting into firefights."

Eric looked up from his monitor. "I was able to—does something smell strange in here? Like… livestock?"

"That would be me," Granger said. "I'm taking care of a friend's horses for a couple of weeks, while she's out of town. I stopped in this morning and haven't had a chance to shower yet. Her place is way up in the hills, off Coldwater Canyon."

"We have a shower down in—" Nell began.

The assistant director cut her off with a sharp "I know."

"Never mind."

"Anyway, I grabbed a decent face shot from that cellphone video," Eric said. "The lighting was terrible, and the focus only so-so, but I cleaned it up and enhanced it. They've always been masked, before, but now that I have this face, I've been trying to find an ID, and maybe get a look at who his friends are."

"That's a start," Hetty said. "But we need—"

"Got him!" Nell broke in.

"Got who?" Granger asked.

"Kelly Martin," Nell replied. "I've been running facial recognition software, looking for him, and finally got a hit."

"Where is he?"

"He walked past a bank branch on Alvarado and the ATM camera caught him. Eight minutes ago."

"We don't need to know where he was eight minutes ago, dear," Hetty said. "We need to know where he is now."

"Scanning," Nell said.

"Eric, get the field agents headed toward downtown," Granger said. "We should have something for them momentarily."

"On it," Eric said.

"Ooh! Got him again!" Nell said. "He just crossed Olympic, then turned right. Headed southeast on Olympic, toward Westlake."

"Keep on him," Hetty instructed.

"I am."

"You got that, Eric?" Granger asked.

"Relaying it now," Eric said. "They're en route. Sam and Callen are closer. Kensi and Deeks just left Julianne Mercer in Santa Monica, but they're almost to the freeway."

"Tell them to turn around," Hetty said.

"Excuse me?"

"Was I not speaking English? Tell them to turn around."

"Hetty says turn around." He paused, listening, then said, "They're turning. They'd like to know why."

"Because they should pick up Ms. Mercer and take

her along. Kelly Martin is a trained SEAL, and he's already been in one firefight today. He'll be on high alert, with strong situational awareness. If he sees Mr. Callen and Mr. Hanna approaching him, he'll either bolt or start shooting. Neither would be constructive. But if he sees his girlfriend, he might not even notice that she's with Agents Blye and Deeks. And if he does, he might not care. Without her there, we have a less than fifty percent chance that he'll be taken easily. Since they've only just left her, getting her won't be too time-consuming, and well worth the slight delay."

"Did you get all that?" Eric asked into the phone. After a moment, he turned back to the others. "They're almost there. They'll pick her up and be on their way."

"Good," Hetty said. "And, Eric?"

"Yes?"

"I didn't mind explaining my reasoning just now. But you do understand that if I had simply said, 'Because I said so,' it would have been an equally valid response, don't you?"

"Yes," Eric replied. "I do."

"Excellent. Keep the teams aware of Mr. Martin's coordinates. But hold Sam and Mr. Callen back and let Kensi and Deeks approach first, with Ms. Mercer." When she finished speaking, she glanced up at Owen. "My office?"

"By all means," he said, and followed her from the room.

This time, Kensi parked on the grass.

A lighting tech had to dive out of her way, and he knocked over a stand of lights in the process. Someone holding a large reflector panel dropped it, and a breeze caught it and whisked it away. The director started screaming before they were out of the car, and Julianne Mercer stared at them, as if in a state of shock.

"Get in the car!" Deeks shouted.

"What? Why?"

"We found him, Julianne!" Deeks said. "But we want you there when we make contact. He won't trust us, but he will you."

"But I'm working!"

"If they're not out of our shot in precisely three seconds, you won't be," the director threatened.

"Julianne, it's important," Kensi stressed. "We want to take him safely, but we need you."

"One," the director said. "Two…"

"All right," Mercer said. She sought out the apologetic production assistant. "Where's my bag?"

The PA was already on her way, holding a messenger bag that Mercer could almost have carried Hetty in. "Right here."

"…three," the director finished. "You're—"

"Never mind, I quit!" Mercer said. "And by the way, you don't know jack about camera angles."

"Come *on*," Kensi urged. "We need to go!"

Mercer tossed her huge bag into the backseat and climbed in with it. "It's not that I object to losing this particular gig," she explained. "But if someone gets a rep for this kind of behavior, word gets around and other casting directors put you at the bottom of the pile."

"We wouldn't have interrupted if it wasn't important," Deeks said.

"I know. Trust me, I want to find Kelly as much as you guys do. More, probably."

While Kensi drove, Deeks got on the phone with Nell. "Plenty of cameras in that area," he said after a moment, "so she's keeping close tabs on him."

"What's he doing there?"

"Just walking, as far as we know," Deeks said. "My guess is he's still looking for the bank crew, but I don't know why he thinks they'd be around there."

"Since you still don't know how he found them at that motel, I guess that's not surprising."

"But we do," Nell said.

"Do what?"

"Know how he found them at the motel. There's just been so much going on, I haven't had a chance to tell you."

"How?" Deeks asked.

"They told him."

"Sorry?"

"Posts were made on a few different websites last night, all with some variation of 'Mitch B, see you at the Sea Vue.'"

Deeks chuckled. "Advertising for a gunfight," he said. "That's a new one."

"Maybe they didn't think he'd come in shooting. Maybe he has something they want to trade for."

"We'll know more in a little while," Deeks said. "Either Kensi will have us there in a few minutes, or you can scrape our corpses off the Santa Monica Freeway."

"I'm a good driver!" Kensi snapped.

"If by good you mean fast and occasionally reckless."

"I haven't killed you yet."

"There's a first time for everything."

"Oh my God," Mercer said from the back. "You guys *are* a couple. Nobody bickers like that unless they're in love."

"You caught us," Deeks said. "She can't get enough of me."

"Right, that's how it is," Kensi argued. "You should have seen him trailing me around, like a duckling imprinted on a human. I had to go out with him just to stop him from embarrassing himself."

"Kensi's nothing if not self-sacrificing," Deeks said. "North one-ten."

Kensi pushed the accelerator to the floor and shot across two lanes of traffic, narrowly squeaking past the front fender of an eighteen-wheeler. "Now you tell me."

"I thought you knew how to get there."

"I'd have to know where 'there' is, wouldn't I?"

"Exit at James Wood, then take Cottage to Olympic. Martin's just about to cross under the freeway. There's an urgent care center on Olympic, so we can park there and intercept him."

"You guys are sickening," Mercer said. "In an adorable way. But sickening, just the same."

Kensi whipped her Escalade north on the 110, then screamed down the ramp onto James Wood. Deeks was used to her driving—as used to it as someone could get who didn't have suicidal tendencies—and, although he wouldn't admit it to her, he appreciated her control behind the wheel. She concentrated on the task at hand, and when that task was getting somewhere in a hurry and in one piece, her skills were hard to beat.

Still, he braced himself when she flew around curves, because not to do so would either throw him into her lap or slam him into the door, seatbelt notwithstanding. The turn into the narrow alley called Cottage Place was especially sharp. They hurtled down uneven asphalt, between fences and walls that Deeks expected to scrape, and at the end of the alley, she made another wrenching right onto Olympic. Behind them, horns blared and tires squealed. The

SUV lunged forward, charging through the tail end of a yellow light at Francisco Street and another at Georgia before bumping up over the curb and into a parking lot.

They bailed out, Mercer hesitating only long enough to grab a smaller purse from inside her big bag.

"You walk ahead of us," Kensi said. "We'll be about ten paces behind. Sam, Callen, are you guys onsite?"

Callen's voice sounded through Deeks's earwig device. "We see you," he said. "I'm in the parking lot behind the palm-reading place, and Sam's across the street, by the movie theater, in case Martin runs that way."

Deeks eyed the theater and saw Sam, standing at the corner, seemingly checking out the movie posters outside the box office. "Got him," he said.

"Here comes Martin," Callen said. "Heading your way."

Deeks and Kensi hung back and let Mercer get out ahead. A block away, a muscular guy walked toward them with an easy, rolling gait. He wore jeans and a tight black Tee shirt and had a duffel slung over his shoulder. Deeks was watching for the moment of recognition, when he spotted Mercer, but it hadn't come yet. Maybe he was playing it cool, in case he was being watched.

Then Eric's voice came over the earwig, anxiety tightening his tone. "Guys, don't let Julianne Mercer get near Martin! Repeat—she's a hostile. Don't let her get close."

Deeks was still processing what he'd heard when he saw Mercer reach into her purse, then drop it and raise the gun she held in her hands.

10

"Gun!" Deeks shouted.

"Drop it, Julianne!" Kensi cried. "Don't be stupid! You're surrounded!"

If Mercer heard them, she didn't show it. She calmly leveled the weapon at Kelly Martin. Behind Martin, Callen drew his own weapon, knowing that if she missed her intended target, she might well hit him.

Martin's SEAL training and honed reflexes kicked in. Traffic was still rushing down Olympic. When he saw Mercer's gun, he tossed his bag to his left and hurled himself to the right and down, dropping off the curb just as her first round hit the sidewalk, inches away.

Callen had tenths of a second to assess the situation and make a decision.

Martin was on his feet again, darting into the traffic on the busy road. Mercer was tracking him, adjusting her aim for another shot. If she missed—even if she hit and the round passed through him—she was likely to hit a vehicle, maybe cause a pileup. So far Callen had no reason to think Martin was anything other than what she had said he was—a Navy SEAL whose phony identity had been compromised—and although he still didn't know if the man was connected to the bank crew, he knew for sure that Mercer had lied about her intentions. She had played them all, with the intention of killing Martin.

He could see her finger tightening on the trigger as she blew out her breath, waiting for a clear shot as Martin wove in and out of traffic. She was going to take the shot.

Callen took his first.

Popular entertainment filled people's heads with a lot of nonsense about shooting to wound someone. In movies and TV shows, someone in his position might shoot the gun out of Mercer's hand, or kneecap her to spoil her aim. A more "serious" depiction might include something about shooting her "center mass," since that was the easiest target.

But a shot center mass might leave her the opportunity to squeeze off several more rounds, straight into traffic. And Callen was confident enough in his own abilities to not have to rely on what was easy.

His round struck her just above the right eye and ejected a spray of red mist out the other side of her skull, and she collapsed in a heap.

He raced to her side, kicking away her weapon even though she appeared very dead indeed. As he did, he scanned the street for Martin, who had almost reached the sidewalk on the far side.

Which was where Sam Hanna slammed into him. They both went down.

Drivers were reacting now—slowing and stopping. Callen heard the sound of a fender-bender. Even in Los Angeles, a mid-morning shootout was too much to ignore. Half the people observing it probably thought they were a movie crew, but that was okay.

At any rate, the road jammed up, giving him safe

passage across it. Kensi and Deeks were rushing toward Mercer, so Callen darted between the cars and trucks. He reached his partner just as Martin struggled to his feet. Callen hooked one of Martin's legs and pulled it out from under him, and Martin went down again.

"NCIS!" Callen shouted as Sam clambered onto the other SEAL's back, grabbing at one of his flailing arms. "You're safe, Martin! Stop struggling!"

Sam wrenched the arm behind Martin's back, then clawed at the other one. "This would be a lot easier if you'd just calm down," he said.

"Show me a badge!" Martin demanded. Callen crouched a few feet in front of him, making sure the man could see not only his badge but the SIG Sauer in his right hand.

"Here you go. We've been looking for you. You're lucky we found you first."

Martin relaxed then, allowing Sam to zip-tie his wrists behind his back. That done, Sam took a small automatic from the man's ankle holster and a bigger one from a holster tucked into the small of his back. "Any more weapons?" he asked.

"Just in my duffel," Martin said.

"Secure that bag, Deeks," Callen said.

Deeks's voice came back over Callen's earwig. "That's no way to talk about the recently deceased. Nice shot, Callen."

"The *duffel* bag," Callen snapped. Sometimes Deeks still got on his nerves.

It had been a nice shot, and he took some professional pride in that. But his pride was tempered by regret.

Not regret that he'd done it—regret that it had been necessary in the first place. He didn't know anything about Mercer, but she had seemed nice enough. Kensi had been to her home, and she and Deeks had seen her working, so even at a more-than-cursory look, she appeared to be who she said she was. The way she had drawn down on Martin, though, indicated professionalism in a field other than modeling.

Callen had killed before, and he expected that he would have to again. Sometimes it was unavoidable, in his line of duty, and that line of duty was important. The life of a criminal or a terrorist was a small tradeoff if it meant protecting the nation and people he had sworn to defend.

Still, Mercer had been a human being. She'd had friends, family. She'd worked as a model. She had value above and beyond whatever her less savory qualities might have been. Callen believed that any human contained the possibility of redemption, but ending one's life also took away that option.

And he didn't have any illusions about how easy it might have been for him to follow that other course. His upbringing had not been one that automatically led toward a career in law enforcement, after all. If it hadn't been for the invisible hand of Hetty, he might have fallen in with the wrong element, become as expert at violence as he was now, but working toward opposite ends. *There but for the grace of God* wasn't just a saying, to him. As a child, he had been both unlucky and profoundly fortunate, and he was glad the fortunate side won out. Julianne Mercer's corpse, bleeding onto the sidewalk on a hot summer's day, was a grisly reminder of where he might have wound up.

Three cameras had captured footage of Julianne Mercer's shooting. Hetty, Granger, Eric, and Nell watched all the video in the Ops Center, on the biggest screen they had. Multiple times.

"I say it's a good shoot," Granger said finally. "Callen didn't have any other option. If he hadn't shot her when he did, she'd have taken out Martin, and who knows how many innocent motorists."

"I am inclined to agree, Owen," Hetty said. "Impressive, too, from that distance. Certainly a shot *I* could have made, but I'm not sure I would have wagered that Mr. Callen could make it." She turned around to face Eric and Nell, who stood a few paces behind the others. "What can you tell us about Ms. Mercer that you couldn't have told us an hour ago?"

"An hour ago, we were spending all our time trying to find Kelly Martin and the bank robbers," Eric replied. "We didn't know that Mercer was someone we should be checking out."

"I'm simply asking, not criticizing," Hetty said. "Although, since you bring it up, everybody involved in any active investigation should be subject to scrutiny, as I'm sure you know. That said, I know there are only two of you, and that there were competing priorities."

"What really tipped us off—" Eric began.

Nell cut him off. "Eric was scanning for the face of the bank robber we caught on that cellphone video. He got a hit when the crew stopped for gas, and—"

"If it's Eric's story, perhaps he should be the one to tell it," Hetty suggested.

"Oh, sure. Sorry."

"Anyway," Eric said, "they stopped for gas. The one guy whose face we had in the system happened to look right up at a camera as he was going into a convenience store at the gas station. That gave me a better image to work with. Eventually I found more footage of him, with three other men, six days ago."

"They were eating in a restaurant," Nell said. "There was a camera over the cashier's station, and they happened to be seated within view of it, and—oh. I got carried away. Sorry again."

"It's okay, Nell," Owen said. "Go on, Eric."

"That's pretty much it," Eric said. "I was checking out that footage, hoping we'd be able to capture the rest of their faces, when someone else came and sat down at the table with them."

"Julianne Mercer!" Nell said. She glanced at Eric. "I'm not sorry, that time. Anyway, it's my turn now. Before she sat down, though, she gave that one man a kiss. More than a friendly kiss. That told us that she hadn't been honest with us from the start, since she obviously knew those guys. So while Eric kept scanning for more times they were together, I started digging into Mercer's past."

"And you found what?" Hetty asked. "Which was, after all, my original question."

"Someone with a rap sheet as long as your arm."

"My arm is not particularly long," Hetty said. "Is there perhaps a more specific measurement?"

Nell ran it down for her. Mercer's first arrest had come at nineteen, when she had been known as Brianna Kondik, though that was probably an alias. No known parents could be located. As Kondik, she had served a couple of years on a minor drug possession rap. Since then, she had cycled through different identities—Dana Flint, Abby Wagner, Joan Clement, and Ruth Morrison among them—and different correctional institutions in different states. She had been pretty and smart and utterly without conscience, all of which helped her get away with lighter sentences than someone else might have earned. On one occasion, she had managed to avoid punishment altogether by starting a heated affair with the much older, married district attorney charged with prosecuting her. Once the charges had been officially dropped, she had disappeared, only to resurface in another city under another name.

The crimes she'd been convicted of had not been violent ones, and she never spent much time behind bars. She was a skilled enough actress to pull successful cons on a variety of unsuspecting marks—almost always men—which made her a decent living.

"There are a few gaps I haven't been able to fill in yet," Nell said after describing the rest. "But she's been in Los Angeles for four years, as Julianne Mercer. She's probably been involved in a few scams here and there, but mostly she's been doing legit modeling and acting. I don't know if she's tired of the criminal life, or just making good enough money that she doesn't need it, but—"

"Or," Hetty interrupted, "simply lying low while working on a major score."

"Or that," Nell agreed. "Anyway, I'll keep digging, as time permits. I mean, if you want me to. What with her being dead and all."

"Yes, I want you to," Hetty said. "Her mortality does not affect my curiosity. We need to know how she came to know those bank robbers, and what they're up to. There's more going on here than a simple bank robbery, I'm certain, or there would have been no need to steal Kelly Martin's assumed identity."

"We'll stay on it," Eric said. "And on the robbery crew, too. If they're still in the city, we'll find them."

Hetty paused, meeting each of their gazes in turn, as if to emphasize the importance of the moment. "See that you do," she said.

11

"You're Kelly Martin," Sam said.

Martin's expression was antagonistic, his tone stubborn. Sam couldn't really blame him. "That's right. You want my rank and serial number, too?"

Sam tapped a file folder on the table in the Boatshed's interrogation room. "Got those. I don't imagine Mitch Bostic has a rank or a serial number."

"I don't know what you're—"

"Don't insult us," Callen interrupted. "We know about the El Paso bolthole, about the Bostic identity. We also know that the identity appears to have been compromised."

"Sounds like you know pretty much everything you need to. And then some."

"Here's something we don't know," Sam said. "What is the relationship between you and Julianne Mercer?"

"Who?"

"The woman who just tried to shoot you," Callen said. He was letting his exasperation show. Sam felt the same way. They had just saved this guy's life, and he was treating them like they were the enemy.

He opened the folder, took out a picture of Mercer, and slid it across the table.

"Never seen her before. Except, you know, today when she pulled a gun on me."

"You haven't thanked us for saving your ass," Callen said.

"How do I know you did?" Martin asked. "I never saw any of you before, either. It looked like some of your people were there with her. Maybe brought her there. You should be apologizing to me for setting me up. Can I go now?"

"You'll be here a while," Sam said. "You might as well get comfortable."

"I have business to take care of." Martin nodded toward the door. "Out there."

"Business with bank robbers who shot a cop," Callen pointed out.

"And stole your identity and your car," Sam added. "Anything else?"

"Did some serious damage to my bank account," Martin said.

"I'm assuming your bolthole was a closely held secret," Sam said. "I get it; I was a SEAL, too. I understand why you'd want it, and why you'd be pissed if somebody got to it before you did."

"You say that, but you're holding me here instead of letting me deal with it."

"Did you miss the part where they robbed a bank and shot a cop?" Callen asked. "And tried to kill you on at least two occasions that we know of?"

"Two?"

"We've connected Julianne Mercer to them," Sam said. "We're not sure yet how they link up, but we know she was with them shortly before she came to us, claiming to be your girlfriend."

"And we saw the fight at the Sea Vue, live on

streaming video," Callen added. "We've tried to tamp that down, but for all we know, it's gone viral by now."

"Look," Sam said. "We're not trying to jam you up. There's something going on here, and it involves you, and you're still Navy. We think it also involves Bobby Sanchez. You know what happened to him?"

Martin's expression softened for the first time. He nodded glumly. "I heard."

"So help us help you, man. Tell us what's going on."

"I'm only guessing on a lot of it," Martin admitted.

"That's cool. So are we. Between what you know and what we do, maybe we can make sense of it."

"Start at the beginning," Callen said. "Who else knew about the Bostic identity?"

Martin took in a deep breath and eyed his two interrogators. Then, as if indicating that he'd reached a decision, he let it out and began. "Just Bobby."

"Sanchez was tortured," Sam said.

"That's what I heard on the news."

"Do you know why?"

"I think I do now. At first, I wasn't so sure. I just figured that if it happened to him, I might be next. Bobby was a fighter. I wouldn't want to go up against him. So anybody who could do that to him was serious trouble. I figured it might be a good idea to disappear for a while."

"Logical conclusion," Sam said.

"I think there's a 'but' coming," Callen said.

"But…" Martin continued.

"There it is."

Martin ignored him and kept going. "…when I got to El Paso, I could tell somebody had already been in the house. The car was missing from the garage, and some of my ID paperwork was gone. I checked my bank balance online, and found that the account had been drained. If Bobby had been found right away, I might have made it there first, but instead whoever killed him had a head start."

"How do you think someone got onto it?"

"There's only one possible answer to that. Bobby caved. I never thought he would, but he's been in pretty bad shape lately. PTSD, depression. He's a great guy, and he's been trained to resist torture. But everybody has a breaking point, and his resistance might not have been the best, considering."

"So you came back to L.A.," Sam said. "Why?"

"By then I wasn't scared, I was just pissed. I wanted to get my hands on whoever had hurt Bobby and taken my ID. When my car was called out as the getaway vehicle, I caught the first flight back here. I couldn't stay in El Paso, anyway."

"How did you find them at the motel?" Callen asked.

"A post on an internet personals page," Martin said. "It said, 'Mitch Bostic we have something of yours' and gave the address."

"That's pretty specific."

"I knew it was a trap. The whole point of using my car—letting it be seen and identified—was a trap to draw me into range. But I thought knowing that would give me an edge."

"You don't seem to have any stray holes in you," Callen said. "So I guess it did."

"Yeah, well, they didn't get me but I didn't get them, either. I call it a draw."

"Maybe a little better than that," Sam said. "Since it was four to one."

"But I'm a Navy SEAL."

"Good point," Sam said. "What about downtown?"

"I was meeting a friend. Guess you guys have blown that for me."

"You still have friends you trust?" Callen asked. "Even with everything that's going on?"

Martin shrugged. "A couple. Maybe one less, now."

"Which brings us to the next big question. Do you know who they are?"

Sam could read Martin's thoughts by the way his lips tightened and his eyes shifted to the left. "We really are on your side, Kelly," he said. "We want to find those guys before they hurt anybody else."

Martin's face remained frozen a few seconds longer. He was thinking it over. Finally, he shifted his gaze to meet Sam's. "It's all I've been thinking about for days. I think I might know," he said. "Not *who* they are, precisely. But why they're after me."

"That's a start," Callen said.

"It's mostly just a guess at this point, but I think it's the likeliest one."

"We all make enemies in this business," Sam said. "You're in the best position to know who yours are."

"Yeah, I guess there are plenty of people who'd like to take me out. But I'm pretty sure I can narrow it down in this case. When I was in Ramadi, back in oh-seven, Bobby and I came across four private security contractors who had just slaughtered six or seven Iraqi nationals outside this museum. They said they'd been ambushed, and in those days, in that place, that wasn't hard to believe. We thought they were acting a little strange, and there were parts of their story that didn't hold up. But we had just wrapped a pretty hairy mission ourselves. We went back to our base and hit the sack, and didn't think much about it for a few days."

"What happened then?" Sam asked.

"Nothing," Martin replied. "Nothing at all. We didn't see any official investigation of the incident. It was like the military brass never heard about it. But on the Iraqi side, it turned out people were talking about it. Only they were blaming al-Qaeda for the massacre. And the theft."

"Theft?" Sam hadn't been sure there was anything about this story that would be surprising, instead of just sad. But this had come out of nowhere. "What theft?"

"I said it was a museum, right? There were all these ancient artifacts in it. I never even heard what they all were, but one that the locals were upset about was a stone tablet that showed how to translate Sumerian into Akkadian, or something like that. Almost like a Rosetta Stone thing, I guess."

"But from the people who invented the first writing system," Sam observed. "I can see why they'd be unhappy about losing it."

"Did you report what you knew?" Callen asked.

"We didn't really know anything. All we had were suspicions. For all we knew, the contractors really had been ambushed. A couple of the people they'd killed were wearing uniforms, not like police uniforms, so they could have been museum guards. But the guys might have taken off right after us, like they said they were going to. At that point, anybody could have gone into the museum and lifted whatever they wanted. We didn't even know who the contractors were or where they were based, so we couldn't exactly tell anyone to go search their bunks."

"And you hadn't raised the alarm right off the bat," Callen pointed out. "So you didn't want to call attention to that."

"We had our own crap to worry about," Martin snapped. "Ramadi was crawling with AQ, mostly operating out of a neighborhood called the Ma'Laab. We were trying to make it safe for our guys to put up a barrier. There was an op, called Operation Murfreesboro, which was intended to weed out the AQ presence there. It worked, too, but it wouldn't have if we hadn't cleared the way."

"I remember it," Sam said. "Ramadi was a lot quieter after that."

"Bet your ass it was. So yeah, maybe we made a mistake. But we had a mission, and we did it, and it saved a lot of lives. American and Iraqi."

"Nobody's questioning that," Sam assured him. "I'm just trying to figure out the connection. If you've kept quiet all those years, then why would those guys be after you now?"

"That's what I can't figure out," Martin said. "After the firefight at the motel, I'm more convinced than ever it was them. They just fought like guys who'd been in the sandbox, you know? But I have no idea why they're trying to kill me. That part's just a gigantic question mark, far as I'm concerned."

Sam was going to answer, but the big video monitor behind him blinked to life with a buzz. He turned around to see the screen. Hetty.

She didn't waste any time. "Sam, I believe I can make Mr. Martin's question mark go away."

12

Kensi parked the Escalade in front of the Westwood apartment building where she had dropped Julianne Mercer off. It seemed like a week ago, or a month, but it had really been a matter of hours.

"Nice place," Deeks said as he climbed out. "Ritzy."

"You don't know the half of it. The elevators magically know where you're going."

"Magic? I like it."

"Well, the security guard in the lobby might have something to do with it."

"I like magic better, but it's all illusion, right? Prestidigitation. Sleight of hand."

"What did you have for breakfast, a thesaurus?"

"You know what I had for breakfast, Kenselina," Deeks replied. "You gazed lovingly at me while I ate it."

"Maybe I was gazing lovingly at your Frosted Flakes."

"It was a Belgian waffle, as you well know, and it was delicious."

They passed through the big front doors, into the cavernous lobby. The security guard looked very small at the far end of the room. Deeks didn't think he seemed very intimidating, but who knew what he had behind that high counter? A faraway security guard with a flamethrower or a bazooka could be plenty scary.

Kensi's heels echoed as she strode across the marble floor. "Excuse me," she said, even though the guard's attention was already riveted on her. "Do you remember me? I'm a federal agent. I was here last night with Julianne Mercer."

"I remember," the guard said. He was probably in his sixties, but fit, and he didn't look like someone who missed much.

"Ms. Mercer is deceased," Kensi said.

"I heard."

"We need to take a look in her apartment."

"Then I'm sure you have a warrant."

"We can get one, if it's necessary. We were hoping to do it the easy way, before anybody else gets in there and compromises any evidence. You know she trusted me."

"I know you went up in the elevator with her. You didn't look like close friends. For all I knew, she could have been under arrest."

"Are you going to be a hardass about this?"

"That's why I get the big bucks. The tenants here value their privacy."

"I'm sure they do. Okay, we'll play it that way. I'll go get a warrant. Deeks, stay here and make sure nobody goes near Mercer's apartment."

"Gladly!" Deeks said, considerably louder than was necessary. He spun toward a sitting area. "Are those leather? I love leather!" Before the guard could respond, Deeks rushed over, hurled himself onto a couch, and put his sneakers up on a glass-topped coffee table. "This is cool, right? My shoes are almost new. Hey, do you have a snack machine? Or microwave popcorn? I love that stuff. Kens, you'll be gone long enough for me to order in a pizza, right?"

He caught the guard's seething glare. "Do you like pepperoni? You look like a guy who wants the works. That's cool, we can do that. Take your time, Kens. Charlie and I will get acquainted. That's your name, isn't it? Charlie?"

"It's Bryce," the guard said.

"Bryce? That's a kid's name. You look like a Charlie to me."

"Make yourself comfortable, Deeks," Kensi said. "I'll see you in a few hours."

"All right," the guard said softly.

"Excuse me?"

"You win. Go on up."

"Got a key?"

"I'll let you in," he said.

"See?" Kensi said, extending a hand to help Deeks to his feet. "Magic."

13

They went up.

"Don't you think it's weird?" Deeks asked as the magic elevator whisked them skyward.

"What, that you could so thoroughly grate on someone in a matter of seconds that he couldn't wait to get rid of you? Not in the slightest."

"That a successful professional model who makes enough to live in a place like this would spend time and energy setting up a Navy SEAL, then be the one to draw on him."

"Are you saying women can't be stone killers?"

"Baby, I sleep with you. I know they can, under the right circumstances. Just like men. But when *you* pull the trigger, it's in the service of a higher ideal. God and country, and all that."

"Okay, yes, it's a little weird. Your typical female killer is more apt to use poison than a gun, and the ones that do use guns are more often doing so in self-defense, or in the commission of some other crime. There aren't many hardened female assassins, I grant you. Some, but not a lot, proportionate to males. It's still kind of a guy thing."

"So what would drive her? She'd have to know his capabilities. And she knew we were right behind her. But she went for it anyway."

The elevator door slid open soundlessly, and Kensi stepped out with her hand resting lightly on the butt of her SIG. The last time she'd been here, she had thought somebody might be lying in wait for Julianne Mercer. This time, it was too late for that, but she still wouldn't take any chances. Mercer was mixed up in something, and the harder they looked at it, the bigger it got.

"That's what we're here to find out," she said. "Sounds like maybe it was about love, although we know she's a skilled liar, so that kiss Eric caught on camera could have been phony, too. Could be politically motivated. Could be money—this place doesn't come cheap, after all, and she's no supermodel. Without a steady paycheck, it's got to be hard to make the rent."

"Truth."

As they approached 1127, the door buzzed, clicked, and popped open. "The magic continues," Deeks said.

Kensi reached the door first, because Deeks was admiring the plush carpeting, the wallpaper, and the light fixtures mounted along the hallway. She shoved it the rest of the way open, and stopped. "Deeks, what's the best magic trick there is?"

"I don't know," he said. "Maybe cutting somebody in half?"

"How about a disappearing act?"

The apartment was empty. Not just of personal items. All the furniture was gone. The drapes had been removed from the windows, the carpeting torn from the floor. There wasn't a visible speck of dust or an apparent smudge on a wall.

Deeks gave a low whistle. "Heck of a maid service they have here."

"This place hasn't just been cleaned," Kensi said. "It's been *sterilized*."

"We could scope it with alternative light sources," Deeks suggested. "Maybe turn up a fingerprint, a spot of DNA."

"Deeks, we have her body. We have her fingerprints and DNA."

"I meant from someone else."

"We can have somebody else look at it. I don't have time for that, and I doubt that you do."

"I go where you go, Kens."

She went farther into the apartment, checked the other rooms. Empty. The place could have just been built.

"Maybe a miniature black hole opened up in here and sucked in all the matter," Deeks suggested.

"Or professionals did a thorough job making everything go away."

"Or that. You think Charlie noticed?"

"I think we should ask him."

"Excellent idea," Deeks said. "If he'll bother to send another elevator for us." He glanced toward the ceiling, scanning the corners. "Probably watching us now."

"I doubt that the apartments have cameras."

"Yeah, but you didn't think the joint would be cleaned out, either."

"Touché." She waved, just in case.

The elevator came, though they had to push the DOWN button this time.

When they reached the lobby, Kensi started storming toward the guard and talking at the same time. "You might have mentioned that she'd moved out. Sometime in the last twenty hours or so."

"You didn't ask," the guard said, trying hard to stifle a grin. "I told you, our tenants value their privacy."

"Mercer forfeited hers when she tried to kill somebody in front of us," Kensi said. "I need everything you have on her. Rental application, credit references, who did her windows, who emptied out that apartment in no time flat. All of it, and now."

The guard reached for something behind the counter. Kensi's hand dropped to her sidearm, but he just came up with a business card, which he slapped noisily onto the countertop. "I watch the doors," he said. "You want any more than that, you'll have to talk to the office."

"Is there anyone in there now?"

"You could try."

"Is it on the premises?"

"It's in Hong Kong."

"You're really an annoying guy, Bryce," Deeks said. "Anyone ever tell you that?"

"Coming from a master like you," Bryce said, "I'll take that as a compliment."

Back in the SUV, Kensi pounded a fist against the wheel. "Who is this woman? She didn't have a phone or any ID on her when Callen shot her. She seemed to live here, but then she didn't. We saw her at work, but Nell checked out the park, and the shoot's over. For all we know, everybody involved has left the country, and since we never found out anybody's name, they'll be hard to find."

"They had to have a permit to shoot there, right?"

Deeks said. "It was city property. And Mercer had to have an agent, to set up her gigs. We should be able to find out who her agent was, and learn more about her that way."

"So far, she's our only solid link to the bank robbers—and presumably the people who murdered Bobby Sanchez. We've got to get something on her, and we have to do it fast."

As they turned from Westwood onto Santa Monica, Kensi looked to her left. "Is that smoke over there? In the hills?"

Deeks craned his neck. "Sure looks like it."

He tuned the radio to an all-news station, and a female voice was saying, "…wildfire in Franklin Canyon Park is growing fast, and residents of the area are being told to evacuate. Meanwhile…"

"Good eye," Deeks said. "Hot and dry as it's been, I'm surprised there haven't been more of those."

"It's early in the season, still. I'm sure we'll have some big blazes going before long."

"You're probably right."

She shot him a grin. "When will you learn that the 'probably' in that sentence doesn't apply?"

"*Probably* right around the time that you learn that a guy needs some space around the sink for his things, too."

"Oh. In other words, never. Good to know."

14

"First of all," Hetty said from the monitor, "I would like to offer you our most sincere apologies for letting Ms. Mercer get anywhere near you."

"Stuff happens in war," Martin said with a shrug. "The only thing that doesn't seem to happen anymore is wars coming to an end. They just roll on and on."

"A valid observation," Hetty said. "Welcome to our little organization, Mr. Martin. I am Henrietta Lange."

Martin's jaw dropped open. "*The* Henrietta Lange?"

"The only one of which I'm personally aware," she said. "Your career is an impressive one, Mr. Martin. Multiple joint SEALs–CIA operations, multiple commendations. Thank you for your service to our country."

"Thank you," Martin said.

"I'm going to show you some photographs." She disappeared from the screen, replaced by several photographs of the same man, from different angles, taken on different occasions. In none of them did he seem aware that he was being photographed. He was shown in various locations, from a restaurant to a luxurious living room to what appeared to be a marble swimming pool overlooking an ocean. Three of the pictures showed him in the company of various beautiful women, all decades younger than him.

The man looked to be in his mid to late sixties. He was heavyset but solid, with blond hair going steel-gray slicked close to his head, a strong chin, and a bulbous nose jutting out over prominent lips. His eyes were blue-gray, small and suspicious. In most of the pictures, he wore finely tailored suits, suggesting Savile Row, but in the poolside one, he wore only striped trunks, and his flesh had a dark, leathery texture that reminded Callen of European nudists. It bothered him that he had that frame of reference in his memory banks, but there it was.

"This man," Hetty said, "is Slava Belyakov. He's a Russian petro-billionaire with a fondness for fast cars, expensive homes, young women, and overpriced vodka. He collects all of the above, and more. He is, shall we say, ethically challenged. Various reports have tied him to the Russian underground, as well as to figures at the highest levels of the Russian government."

"Is there a difference?" Martin asked.

"No comment," Hetty said. "Regardless, his tentacles—figurative ones, mind you—run throughout every sector of the Russian economy, and extend quite a ways outside of Russia, too. Billionaires tend to have grandiose ideas about their place in the world, and Mr. Belyakov is no exception in that regard."

"I've never heard of him, much less met him," Martin said. "What's he got to do with me?"

"I'm getting to that, Lieutenant Martin," Hetty said. She had that crisp tone in her voice that came when she was interrupted. If Martin wasn't afraid of her yet, it was only because he didn't know any better.

"One of his many collections—perhaps the one

he's proudest of, in fact—is a collection of antiquities. Not just your standard relics of the ancients, but real museum-quality finds; the sort of cultural touchstones that nations usually prefer to hang onto. Belyakov likes to outbid national museums, to amass artifacts that should belong to the world, so he can keep them in one of his homes."

"Selfish," Callen said. "So he's the only one who gets to see them?"

"He and his friends, I suppose. Though for all I know, he charges them admission."

"I still—" Martin began.

Hetty shut him down. "Mr. Belyakov is in Los Angeles. He is ostensibly here on oil company business, but the truth is that if he's in the United States, he's buying. Naturally, many of the items he purchases on these jaunts aren't exactly legal to own or sell, so he's secretive about it."

Callen could see understanding bloom in Kelly Martin's eyes. It was almost like one of those light bulbs coming on over somebody's head in the cartoons. "So you think—"

"What I think," Hetty continued, "is that, given your story about the contractors probably looting a museum, combined with the torture and murder of Mr. Sanchez and the attempt on your life, the logical conclusion is that they've been holding onto something—likely that tablet you mentioned—and finally the opportunity to sell it for the right price has come along. But it happened to be in your backyard, and they didn't want to take a chance on you and Mr. Sanchez interfering."

"If they'd just left us alone, we'd never have known they were out there."

"Yes," Hetty said. "That is a reasonable view. But put yourself in their tactical boots. They've had this tablet—the revelation of which could send them to prison for decades—on their hands for years, waiting for the right time to unload it. They stand to make millions of dollars—many millions, most likely—which they hope will repay all the effort they put into stealing it, smuggling it into the country, and hiding it. But they're dealing with an unknown quantity, a notoriously unpredictable Russian billionaire who could as easily have them killed as buy what they're selling. Everything they've done since Iraq has led to this one point. They are desperately afraid that something will undo it all. You and Bobby Sanchez are the greatest threat to their ultimate reward. Of course they want to eliminate that threat."

"And we know they don't mind killing for it," Sam observed. "That's how it all started, after all."

"Or robbing a bank," Callen added. "They didn't do it for the money. They just knew it was the best way to let you know that they had stolen your identity, no matter where you were. You were bound to hear that you'd become the object of a citywide manhunt. And you did."

"I guess when you put it that way…"

"I do," Hetty said flatly.

"Makes sense to me," Callen agreed.

"So, what do we do now?" Martin asked.

"That," Hetty said, "is what we have to figure out. And quickly. I don't have to remind you that our relationship with the government in Iraq—such as it is—is a little strained these days. If it became known that Americans had stolen this treasure, that would surely make things worse rather than better."

Before anyone could respond, two new images popped onto the screen—a military ID card from 2002, with the name Harold Shogren on it. He was a clean-shaven, good-looking guy with a shaved head. His most prominent feature was a pair of brilliant green eyes, like cut emeralds.

"Explain, please," Hetty said.

A moment passed, and then Eric Beale's voice sounded. "That's Harold Shogren," he said. "Goes by Hal. He's a former Army Ranger. He left the service in 2006 to join Lionheart Security Services, a security contractor with some significant Department of Defense contracts in Iraq and Afghanistan, among other garden spots around the region. He was in Iraq in 2007."

"And you're showing him to us because?"

"Because facial recognition finally popped his ID from that video image I captured this morning. He's also the man we saw meeting with Mercer in a restaurant. Based on analysis of body size and type, and gait, Shogren is the one who shot Officer Scarlatti. He's a lifelong resident of Los Angeles County. Trouble is…"

"Yes?" Hetty urged.

"He's dead."

"Then he can't be the man who just shot a cop, can he?" Callen asked.

"Let him finish," Hetty said. "Eric, this would be an opportune time for clarity, not for mystery."

"Hal Shogren was killed in action in Iraq in 2007. His body was recovered and shipped back here. Since he wasn't military, it wasn't on an official DoD transport plane, but on a private plane leased by Lionheart."

"That's definitely one of the guys who was there that night in Ramadi," Martin said. "He was the one Bobby and I talked to. I'd know those green eyes anywhere."

"Again—" Callen began, but Sam cut him off.

"Inside a coffin would be a good way to smuggle a priceless artifact into the country," he said. "As long as the ID was right, who the body inside belonged to wouldn't matter. It's not like customs officials in that situation would open the box to compare the corpse's face to the ID card."

"And if you wanted to keep it hidden for a long time, six feet under would be a pretty good place to do it," Martin added.

"Agreed," Hetty said. "Eric, find out where Mr. Shogren was buried. And find out who else was working for Lionheart in Iraq in 2007."

"Will do," Eric said.

"What do we know about Lionheart?" Callen asked.

"They have a pretty crappy reputation," Martin said. "They call themselves security contractors, but they're really mercenaries. Some companies were hired to do things like run dining facilities for the troops over in the sandbox, or to drive supply trucks, or install and maintain communications systems, things like that. All Lionheart did was provide security services for those other companies. Their people are gunslingers and adrenalin junkies. A couple of years after my last tour—around twenty-ten, I guess—some of their guys were mixed up in a controversy over the killing of some village elders. The Iraqis wanted to charge them with murder, but they were spirited out of the country before any action could be taken. The DoD stopped using them after that. Last I heard, they were still in the business, but mostly they sell their services to various African and Latin American governments."

"That is my understanding, as well," Hetty said. "It

doesn't sound at all out of character for Mr. Shogren and friends."

"No, he'd be a perfect fit," Martin agreed. He stared at the image of Shogren on the screen, and Sam thought he was glad, at that moment, that he wasn't Shogren facing down Martin in real life. His fellow SEAL looked like he wanted to do the mercenary some serious damage.

Nell's voice broke the brief quiet. "Here's another one. The room at the Sea Vue was loaded with fingerprints, of course, and DNA samples that you don't want to hear about and I sure don't want to talk about. But a good print was captured on the toilet flush handle, and it matched up to a man who was working for Lionheart in Iraq at the same time as Shogren."

A second set of photos appeared onscreen, again a military ID and a more recent driver's license. The name on both was Wendell Brower. In the military photo, he was rail-thin, with cheekbones that looked like they could cut through his flesh at any moment, a jaw that came to a point, a jutting nose, and dark eyes that looked almost dead, like those of a shark. He had put on some weight in the interim, and his short-cropped hair had grown into a tightly curled red mop.

"Details?" Hetty said.

Eric took over again. "This is Wendell Brower. Goes by Wen or sometimes Wendy to his friends. Delta Force, four tours in Iraq and Afghanistan before he left the service and joined up with Lionheart. There were some discipline issues in his last couple of years with Delta Force, but nothing serious enough to get him thrown out or busted down in rank. We have an address for him in the Valley."

"I'm certain that since you've identified those two,"

Hetty said, "you've also found everybody else who worked in Iraq with them."

"Photos coming up," Nell's voice replied. "Everyone who was on Lionheart's payroll in-country in 2007, while Shogren and Brower were there."

As she spoke, images began to appear on the screen in neat rows. When they stopped, there were thirty-six in all.

"Any of them look familiar, Kelly?" Sam asked.

Martin studied them. Sam alternated between studying him and the photographs. They were all men, mostly white but with a sprinkling of African-American and Latino faces. With few exceptions, they'd been in their twenties and thirties when these pictures had been taken. Several of them looked older around the eyes—they'd lived hard, and they'd seen terrible things. Done terrible things in some instances, Sam was sure. That was what war did to you. Very few came out of it as whole as they went in.

"I can't tell," Martin said. "It's been too long. Almost any of these guys could have been them, but except for that one, Shogren, I never had a really good look at the others."

"Thanks for trying, anyway."

"Wish I could—wait," Martin said.

"What?"

He tapped the screen on the photograph of a man with thin dark hair and a narrow face. "This guy—I don't remember him from over there. But I'd swear he was the guy at the motel, the one who set me up and came at me from behind. He was pretending to be high, but I'm sure it's him."

"Name, Nell?" Hetty asked.

Nell's voice filled the room. "That one is Jon

Wehling. Believe it or not, he still works for Lionheart, though in a more executive capacity these days. I have an address near Marina Del Rey."

"Let's have it," Sam said. "I think we need to pay these guys a little visit."

Callen and Sam left Kelly Martin at the Boatshed. They would let him stay in the equipment room, rather than locking him in the considerably less comfortable interrogation room. On the way, Sam gave him the rules of the road. "You've got to let us handle this from here out," he said. "You lay low. We'll leave you at the Boatshed while we drop in on Wehling, then we'll pick you up again and get you into a safehouse."

"Understood," Martin said.

"I mean it. You're a target. Let us bring these guys in. We know how to do these things the right way. Let's keep you alive and out of prison."

"Works for me."

"Good. We wouldn't usually leave someone in the Boatshed unaccompanied, but you're a professional, and a brother SEAL. Also, you'll be watched the whole time."

"Good to know," Martin said. "I won't pick my nose or scratch my ass."

"If you have to," Callen put in, "there aren't any cameras in the bathroom." He thought for a second, then added, "Are there?"

"Your guess is as good as mine," Sam said. "I'd like to think not. But I wouldn't swear to it."

15

"Slight detour," Deeks said, lowering the phone from his ear.

"How slight?" Kensi asked.

"Pasadena."

"*Pasadena?* It's a good thing we're reimbursed for mileage."

"Look at it this way, Kensilicious. You get to spend another forty minutes or so alone inside an enclosed vehicle with the man you love."

"It's a good thing we're reimbursed for mileage," she repeated.

"Could you say that again, in the robot voice?"

"Don't push your luck. Why are we going to Pasadena?"

"Because that's where Julianne Mercer's parents are."

"Her parents?"

"Am I mumbling? Because I could enunciate more."

"I can hear what you're saying, it just doesn't make any sense. Which, I know, I should be used to by now. I thought Mercer was an orphan or something."

"More of a runaway than an orphan, I think. Or at

least, the existence of living parents would seem to indicate that. Betsy and Hugh Peabody."

"Peabody? Nobody's named Peabody."

"Like that classic cartoon. 'I'm Mr. Peabody, and this is my boy Sherman.'"

"Now I know I'm not hearing you right."

"The internet is a wonderful thing."

"So is silence, Deeks. Sometimes it's the most wonderful thing."

"Sure, sometimes, but—"

She shot him a glare he could feel down to his toes.

"Silence," he said. "Sounds good."

The Peabodys lived in a comfortable, upper-middle-class house, in the kind of neighborhood where nobody had to ask if the schools were good or the playgrounds were safe. It was a well-preserved Victorian, probably from early in the twentieth century, with the usual gingerbread touches, a combination of peaked and domed roofs, and from the street, it seemed to face three directions at once.

"This wouldn't be a bad place to live," Deeks said.

"Long way from work."

"Yeah, but it's nice. Wide, tree-lined streets, big yards. A person could raise a family out here."

"A person could?"

"Or, you know, a couple."

"Let's not have that conversation again, Deeks. We're here to see the Peabodys."

"Sure, let's see them."

Kensi opened her door and started to get out.

"If they have a dog, I hope he's named Sherman," Deeks said.

Kensi might have slammed her door a little, or it could have been the wind.

Hugh Peabody opened the screen door before they reached it, and stepped out. He was in his seventies, probably. In reasonable health, from the looks of him, but a little stoop-shouldered, and he peered down the stairs at them through glasses thick enough to be double-paned windows. He wore a blue cardigan, despite the heat, and under it a neatly pressed white dress shirt, with gray pants and house slippers. His hair was wispy and snow-white.

"Can I help you?" he asked.

Kensi was in the front. She showed him her badge. "We're federal agents," she said. "I'm Agent Blye."

"And I'm Marty Deeks of the LAPD," Deeks said.

"LAPD? But she said federal…"

"It's complicated," Kensi said. "And really, not worth your time to worry about. May we come in?"

"What's this about, may I ask?"

Kensi brought a photo of Julianne Mercer up on her phone and showed it to the man. "It's about your daughter."

"Our…" He didn't finish the thought. His knees started to buckle, and Kensi caught his elbow. Suddenly he looked about twenty years older, and just this side of the grave. *Guess I could have handled that more discreetly*, she thought.

"Let's go inside," she said. "Is your wife home?"

"Ye-yes," he stammered. "In-inside."

Kensi opened the screen door and helped him inside, Deeks following. She tossed him a glance, and he nodded—if the old man fell, Deeks would catch him.

"Elizabeth!" he called as they entered. His voice was as shaky as his knees. "Bets!"

A female voice answered from upstairs. "What is it, you old coot?"

Kensi held back a chuckle. She steered Hugh Peabody toward the living room, where the furniture seemed like it might have originally filled the house. "Let's have a seat," she suggested.

Footsteps sounded on the stairs, and then on the hardwood floor. Kensi helped Hugh to the sofa, then looked up to see a tiny sprite of a woman coming toward them. She had a cap of close-cropped silver hair, lively eyes that sparkled with mirth or mischief, and a broad smile. She wore a magenta tie-dyed tee shirt with a peace sign on it, with blue jeans and bright pink sneakers.

"Why didn't you tell me we had company?" she said. The tone of her voice was almost joyous, as if the visit was the most exciting thing that had happened in years. She hurried to Kensi, sticking out her hand to shake. "I'm Betsy Peabody," she said, gripping Kensi's in both of hers.

"Kensi Blye."

"*Agent* Blye," Hugh corrected. Color was starting to return to his cheeks. "They're federal agents, or something."

"Marty Deeks," Deeks said, shaking the woman's hand.

"Federal *agents*?" The woman's excitement level had increased dramatically. "To what do we owe this honor?"

Before Kensi could answer, she said, "Oh, where are my manners? Please, sit. What can I get you? Iced tea, coffee? Probably not a drink, if you're on the job. There are some sodas in the icebox, I'm sure."

"Nothing, thank you," Kensi said, certain that Deeks was about to ask for something. She wanted to get through this fast. Painless would be nice, too, but she knew that wasn't an option. She sat, and Deeks did the same.

"If you're sure," Betsy said.

"Yes, thanks," Deeks said. "We're fine."

She dropped down beside her husband and put her hand on his knee. "All right," she said. "Here we are. What is it?"

"It's about Susan," Hugh said.

Betsy's hand went to her mouth. "Susan?"

Kensi passed her the phone. "If that's Susan."

Betsy took it and stared at the photograph for almost a minute. "It could be. Yes, I think it is. Was this taken recently?"

"Yes, it's from a modeling shoot last month," Kensi said. "Under the name Julianne Mercer."

"Is she—has something happened to her? If you're police… or agents, or whatever."

"Yes, ma'am," Kensi said. "I'm very sorry to have to tell you this."

"Don't be," Betsy said. "With a start like that, I think I know what you're going to say. And I'm ashamed to say that we gave up on Susan a long, long time ago. Or she gave up on us. I guess that came first, come to think of it." She sounded casual, but her fingers were probably leaving marks in her husband's knee. His mouth was tight as he tried not to wince. "We've never stopped trying to figure out where we went wrong with her—"

"We didn't," Hugh interrupted.

"Well, we must have. The way she turned out."

"We didn't do anything wrong. We gave her a good home, love, support. We were involved in her school, we knew her friends. We protected her but weren't overprotective."

"I know all those things, Hugh, but there must have been something—"

He cut her off again. "Some children are just born bad. I don't know what it is, but there was nothing we could have done to make her different. It is what it is, Bets. She is what she is."

"Or is she?" Betsy looked at Kensi again. "How did it happen?"

All the way to Pasadena, Kensi had been mulling over how to tell them. She hadn't known what to expect, but the Peabodys—especially Betsy—defied her expectations anyway. She decided the woman would appreciate the direct approach. "She was shot," she said.

"Shot?" Hugh echoed. His face paled again.

"We're so sorry for your loss," Deeks said. Kensi breathed relief and let him take up the story. "She was involved with something—we're still trying to figure out exactly what it is—and she tried to kill someone. One of the people we work with shot her. Warning shots and shooting to wound are fiction, I'm afraid. He shot to stop her from committing a murder, and his aim was good."

Betsy took a deep breath and held it for at least thirty seconds, then let it go. "Thank you," she said. "For respecting us enough to tell it like it was. I couldn't have taken it if you'd tried to beat around the bush."

"It's obvious that you're a very upfront person," Kensi said.

"I call them like I see them, and I like others to do the same. This coworker of yours. Is he in trouble?"

"There were plenty of witnesses," Deeks said. "Including us. We all saw what happened. It was what we in the LAPD call a righteous shoot."

"And our daughter was the target," Hugh said. He

wasn't taking it as well as Betsy. Kensi had worried about the mother, on the way over, but the father turned out to be the fragile one.

"I'm very sorry," Kensi said again. "It couldn't be helped."

"Can you tell us what it was all about?" Betsy asked. "Who she was... trying to kill?"

"As my partner said, we're still not entirely sure." She took her phone back and scrolled to a photo of Shogren. "Do you know this man?"

Hugh Peabody glanced at it and shook his head. Kensi showed it to Betsy, who took the phone. "Those eyes," she said. "Is this who she tried to kill?"

"No," Deeks replied. "But this man is involved in it."

"Hugh, it's Dinah and Woody's boy. Susan knew him when they were children. They had a place just down the block. What was their name? It was like that Japanese book, with the samurai."

"Shogren," Hugh said. "Dinah and Woody Shogren."

"That's right."

"Yes," Kensi said. "This is Hal Shogren."

"That's it!" Betsy cried. "I knew it. He had those unforgettable eyes."

"He was a friend of Susan's?"

"He was the reason things started going bad, I think. That was when things went downhill. He was always in trouble, and that was irresistible to her."

"The more we told her to keep away from him," Hugh said, "the more she wanted to be with him."

"That's pretty basic child psycholo—" Deeks began. Kensi shot him a look and he changed course. "I mean, according to the more recent theories."

"We weren't perfect parents," Hugh admitted. "We

tried. We read the books, from Mr. Spock—"

"*Doctor* Spock," Betsy corrected.

"Right, yes—to Adele Faber, and everything in between. We watched the right videos, played Mozart and Bach and Pete Seeger for her in utero. But we were busy, too. Working, trying to stay ahead of the bill collectors, trying to have a marriage as well as a family. It's hard."

Kensi hoped Deeks was listening. Some time, sure, a baby would be great. But to try to fit it into their lives right now would be tough. Maybe disastrous. "I'm sure it is," she said. "Nobody's criticizing your parenting skills. Like you said, sometimes kids just turn out the way they do, and there's nothing that could have been done."

"I can't believe that," Betsy said. The mirth was gone from her eyes, replaced by as profound a sadness as Kensi had ever seen. "There had to be something. Something we missed, something we could have tried, if only we had known."

"I might not be the world's greatest parenting expert," Deeks said. "Or, you know, always as diplomatic as I should be. But I know this—the best you can do is the best you can do. You can't kick yourself for not doing something you couldn't have known about, or something beyond your human capabilities."

"I think I see where you're going, Agent Deeks," Betsy said. "But—"

"What I'm saying is that we'd all like to undo the Holocaust, and Nine-Eleven, and maybe a few presidential assassinations, along with lesser, more personal catastrophes and disappointments. But the past is the past and we can't change it, unless you've got some technology in the basement we don't know about. So if you did your best—your best in the moment, not necessarily your ideal, when-everything's-going-just-right best, but your human-being best at that time—there's no reason to beat yourself up. You tried. None of us are godlike. Trying's the best we can hope for."

Kensi realized she was staring at Deeks, and that furthermore, her mouth was hanging open. Had he been replaced by an exact double only with twice the sensitivity? Or was it more like ten times?

"Thank you," Betsy Peabody said. She bit her lower lip and blinked away sudden moisture in her eyes. "You might even be half right."

"Once a day, like a stopped clock," Deeks said.

"That's twice a day," Kensi said.

"Not if it's only half right." He sat back with that grin that drove her nuts—and that she loved.

That was more like it. Like the Marty Deeks she knew.

"Do the Shogrens still live in the area?" Kensi asked.

Betsy looked toward the ground. "We lost touch a long time ago."

Kensi fished out a business card and handed it to Betsy. "We believe Shogren is the key to what Juli—Susan—was mixed up in. If you think of anything that might help us find him, please let me know right away. It's very important."

"We'll try our best," she said. "And I mean our best. No promises—we're not godlike, as we've just been reminded—but we'll try."

16

"Wow," Kensi said when they were back in the SUV. "Where did that come from?"

"What?" Deeks asked. Playing her. As he did.

"That... that monologue. Or was it a soliloquy? I forget my high school drama class terminology sometimes."

"You don't need the terminology. You're a better actress than ninety percent of the Oscar winners in Hollywood."

"Only ninety percent?"

"Maybe ninety-five. But Meryl Streep—sorry, babe, but you can't touch her."

"You're dodging, Deeks."

"What? I've tried to tell you, I have unplumbed depths."

"Most of the time I think I need hip boots to wade through your depths, but that was pretty good."

"I'd like to plumb your—"

"Not at work, Deeks."

"We're in your car. Who's listening?"

"Who knows? North Korea? Anonymous? Congress?"

"You're straining the bonds of believability there, Kens. Congress couldn't plant a bug in your car. Or if they did, it wouldn't work."

Kensi tilted her chin toward the distant hills. "Fire's still going. Looks bigger."

"Fires do that. Especially on hot, dry, windy days. Some decent rains over the winter, too, so there's a lot of fuel to burn up there."

"Yeah," Kensi said. "Lot of valuable real estate up there, too."

"The urban-wildland interface. People love to live close to nature. But they hate the consequences when nature strikes back."

"Pithy," she said. "That's what you are. You're just full of pith today."

"Sorry, full of…?"

"Pith! I said pith!"

"Just keep telling yourself that, babe. Maybe someday you'll convince yourself."

Hetty sensed his presence more than heard it. She looked up from her desk—even in the modern, high-tech world she inhabited, paperwork remained a burden—and saw him standing in the entrance to her office. "Have you been watching long?"

"Only for a minute," Granger said. "A little more, maybe."

"You're easily entertained."

"Not really. I'm a demanding critic. But I wasn't just standing there for the joy of watching you work. I was waiting for an opportune moment to interrupt you. And, honestly, I was taking a moment for myself."

"A moment of what?" Hetty asked.

"Stillness, maybe? Peace is probably too much to ask for, around this place."

"It's what we work for every day."

"What, peace? Yes, I suppose it is. But working for it doesn't bring us much, does it? It seems like we're always at war."

Hetty closed the file she'd been working on. This was clearly going to be more than a momentary distraction. Owen Granger was usually very buttoned up, so if he felt the need to unburden, she wanted to give him her full attention. "It's a complicated world, Owen. And while it's full of people who love us, who love this country, there is no shortage of people who would love to do it harm. So yes, we are, as you say, constantly at war. We take it upon ourselves, so they"—she waved a hand toward the outside world—"are protected from it."

He nodded, and she read the look in his eyes. "You know all this. Probably better than I do."

"It's an age-old story. Timeless. Probably been going on since the first amoeba grew legs and walked out of the sea."

"You know that's not exactly how it happened, right?"

"I'm exaggerating for comic effect, Henrietta. Hyperbole. Another old tradition."

"So if you didn't come in to ask me for a sociological treatise on all the shades of gray surrounding the intersection between law enforcement and defense…"

"I came in to tell you that I know it's a bad time, but I have to leave for a few hours."

"It's always a bad time. That is, after all, what we were just discussing, is it not?"

Granger sighed and ran a hand across his high forehead. "I think I told you I'm caring for a friend's horses while she's away for a couple of weeks. She keeps them up off Coldwater Canyon. I took the liberty of asking Eric and Nell to keep tabs on the wildfire burning up there, and it sounds like it's getting a little too close for comfort. I've arranged boarding for them in the Valley, but I've got to load them up and get them out now."

"She must be a good friend."

Granger just smiled. A good friend, then. "Go on," Hetty said. "You're right, best to take care of it before the fire gets any closer. We'll hold down the fort."

"I never had any doubt," he said.

"Just be careful. Those fires can move fast, and change direction without warning."

"I know about fire, Hetty."

"And you know about me, and that occasionally—very occasionally, I must say—I like to give advice to my friends, whether they've asked for it or not."

"I'm glad," Granger said, "to be included in that company. I'm sure traffic will be a mess, so I expect it to take hours and hours. I'll see you tomorrow."

"Be safe," she said to his departing figure.

She knew he would. One didn't rise as high as he had in their profession without learning how to take care of himself.

Still, it was a dangerous world. And when you added nature's dangers to those wrought by human beings, the danger level rose exponentially.

17

It wasn't true that the sun always shone at the beach. Sam had seen cloudy days in Santa Monica, in Malibu, and even in Marina Del Rey. Some summer days, June gloom socked in the shoreline and didn't let up until late in the day, by which time disappointed tourists from points inland had either given up and gone to the mall or persevered, grumpy and bitter about the price of airplane tickets, hotel rooms, and rental cars. But as he steered the Challenger down Venice Boulevard toward the coast, the sky was gloriously cobalt, with only enough puffy white clouds to offer some contrast, and the sun blazed like it had something to prove.

More small boats were permanently berthed in Marina Del Rey than anyplace else in the world, and that sun and sky were big parts of the reason why. The Southern California myth still reigned supreme there. No matter what happened in the economy or in the news, you could find people polishing their boats, sitting on their decks, even sometimes taking those beloved crafts out into the open sea. Close by was a strip of beach fronted by expensive homes, and Sam had no doubt that on this hot summer day, the beach was packed.

He preferred Atlantic beaches, personally. The water was warmer and the locals less turf-conscious. But he was a SEAL, and among the things they shared with their animal namesake was a love of the water. Warm or cold, crystal-clear or dark and soupy, he was almost as at home there as he was on dry land. He cracked the window as they approached, letting ocean-scented air rush in.

"We don't have time for a swim," Callen said. "We have a bank robber to visit."

"Alleged bank robber," Sam reminded him. "And if it was me and I'd just killed a guy, robbed a bank, and planned a failed ambush, I probably wouldn't be hanging around my own house. I'm just saying."

"Chances are slim," Callen agreed. "But we aren't getting anywhere with their phones or Kaleidoscope."

"Guys are pros."

"Right. Which means old-fashioned shoe leather. Like our cop forefathers."

"Were your forefathers cops, G?" Sam asked.

"Yeah, I don't think so."

Sam turned up a residential street and braked in front of an unpretentious detached home. The street was lined with palms, and quiet early on this weekday afternoon. The ocean was invisible from here, with only a faint tinge of saltwater in the air. The more pronounced the scent, the higher-priced the real estate. Jon Wehling did okay, judging by the neighborhood, but this wasn't the kind of house a multimillion-dollar score would buy him.

"This is the place," he said.

"Modest," Callen said.

"Just what I was thinking."

There was a little patch of yard in front that had probably had grass once, but the grass had been taken up and gravel put down. A common choice in drought-ridden California—easy maintenance and no tickets or nasty notes from the neighbors when the spray from the sprinkler reached the sidewalk.

"You want the front or back?" Callen asked, opening his door.

"Doesn't matter to me."

"Okay, front's all yours. I'll go around."

The two had done this often enough that Sam knew how long it would take Callen to get around back. If the crew was inside and still spoiling for a fight, having one man in front and one behind would be risky, but Sam doubted that they were. There were no vehicles in the driveway or immediately in front of the house. There was a garage he couldn't see inside, but the house had an empty feel to it. He couldn't explain it better than that; it was just a sense he had, derived from years of experience. Sometimes he was wrong, but not often.

When he was sure that Callen was in place, he drew his SIG and pounded on the front door, standing off to the side just in case. "Federal agents!" he called. He waited a couple of seconds, and hammered some more. They didn't have a warrant, so breaking in was legally questionable without exigent circumstances.

No sound emanated from within. He stayed put beside the door for a few more seconds—you never stood directly in front of a door if you thought there might be armed bad guys behind it, unless you were angling for a short life expectancy—then put his head against it. Listening.

Nothing.

"Hey, Sam?"

Callen, from around back. Sam stepped away from the door and went to the side of the house, where he saw his partner coming toward him. "Yeah?"

"Place is empty."

"Empty like nobody home?"

"Empty like nobody lives here."

"Really?" Wehling had made phone calls from here three days earlier—before the bank robbery, but after Bobby Sanchez's murder. Electricity had been used in the last several days, and water. The house's physical presence gave every sign of having been recently occupied.

Callen tilted his head toward the back. "French doors," he said. "Take a look."

Sam walked into the backyard. There was a small brick patio, with a fire pit, a cheap propane grill, and a sliding glass door into the house.

He looked inside. He could see a kitchen and part of a room beyond it, a dining room, he figured. There were no appliances visible, nothing on the counters or walls, and not a stick of furniture. "It's empty," he said.

"Do you have to independently confirm everything I tell you?" Callen asked. "If I said, 'Don't move, there's a black widow spider on your neck,' would you have to see it in a mirror before you believed me?"

"You told me to take a look, G. I was humoring you."

"Humoring me? I told you to take a look because I knew you would anyway."

"So I was humoring you while you were humoring me. Sign of a healthy working relationship, or something."

"Or something," Callen echoed.

"Also? If you see a black widow spider on my neck,

don't bother telling me not to move. Just brush it off, okay? Just knock it off there before it bites me."

"Are you afraid of spiders?"

"I wouldn't say that. I wouldn't say I like them, either. But poisonous spiders on my neck? That's a whole other deal, man. I'd knock a poisonous spider off *your* neck if I saw it."

"Well, thanks. I appreciate that."

"Wouldn't go telling you about it and not doing anything. What kind of friend is that?"

Callen gestured toward the house. "What do you think? Want to go in?"

"I'm pretty sure the crew didn't take everything out of the rooms we could see just to hide in the bathroom. House looks empty, it's probably empty. Same way Julianne Mercer's apartment was empty."

"These guys definitely have a plan," Callen said. "Kill the only two people who might possibly get in the way, sell the tablet, and skip town. Don't leave anything behind that might indicate where you went."

"They're pros," Sam pointed out. "Maybe Special Ops, maybe military intelligence. Before they decided to go for the big bucks in contracting. And then the bigger bucks in murder and theft of national treasures. They come up with a plan, they don't do things halfway."

Sam and Callen were heading back to the car when a man came out of the house across the street. He was tanned and fit, with sun-bleached hair and teeth a few shades whiter than was natural. He wore a Hawaiian shirt and board shorts. Sam was surprised he was home, but maybe it was low tide. "You guys looking for Jon?"

"Do you know him?" Callen asked.

"Just to say hi to, you know. We've been neighbors for a few years. Not really tight or anything."

"Know where he is?" Sam asked.

"No idea. It's just—day before yesterday, a moving crew showed up. Jon wasn't around, but they must have had a key. They loaded everything up and took off."

"You know where he was moving to?"

"Last time I saw him was about a week ago. He said something about a job in Virginia. I guess the company he works for is headquartered in Washington, D.C., and he wanted to be close to that. I didn't get the idea that he was going immediately, but then this truck came, so I guess he was. Sorry I didn't get a chance to say goodbye."

"Do you remember what company the truck was from?"

The guy grinned. "How could I forget? The truck had these gorillas painted on it, and the name was Two Gorillas Will Move You. There were just two guys in the crew, and they could have passed for gorillas. Big, strong guys, know what I mean? Like, bigger than you."

"Two Gorillas, huh?" Sam said.

"That's right. They worked fast, too. Not that Jon ever had much in there, that I saw. He travels light, I guess. Me, it'd take dynamite to get all my crap out of my house."

"Well, I guess there's no point waiting here for Jon," Callen said. "Thanks for letting us know."

"Sure thing. If I see him, should I tell him you came around?"

"That's okay, thanks," Sam replied. "I have a feeling we'll see him before you do."

Only one of the gorillas was in the office when Callen and Sam got there, but it was easy enough to see where the company name had come from. The guy was a brute, with no neck, huge, sloping shoulders, and long, well-muscled arms. The last time he'd been able to buy clothes off the rack, Callen figured, he'd probably been in seventh grade and shopping in the big and tall department. Adding to the effect was the matting of tightly coiled hairs all down his arms and puffing out the open collar of his blue work shirt. The name embroidered on the shirt was "Timmy," which seemed like a misprint.

"You moved a guy named Jon Wehling recently," Callen said. He gave the address.

Timmy nodded. "That sounds right."

"Can you tell us where his belongings went?"

Timmy looked surprised. "Of course not. What do I look like, the information lady?"

"I don't know who the information lady is," Sam said, showing his badge. "Do you know what a federal law enforcement agent is?"

"Why didn't you say so?"

"I didn't know we'd need to. You're not a psychiatrist or a priest."

"Hey, movers find out lots of intimate secrets about people," Timmy said. His voice was high for such a big man, and Sam guessed that it even skewed toward girlish when he was excited or laughing. "Some things can't be hidden, and if we're packing—well, you'd be amazed at some of the stuff we have to handle. If we went around blabbing about our clients, we'd be out of the business in no time."

"Excuse our ignorance," Callen said. "We had no idea. But like my partner said, we are federal agents, and we are in a bit of a hurry. If you could get us a delivery address—"

"You read Chinese?"

"A little," Callen said. "Why?"

"Because that's what language it's written in. We loaded Wehling's stuff into a container, and delivered the container directly to the docks in Long Beach. It's on a container ship right now, headed for China."

"Maybe a photocopy," Sam suggested.

"Sure thing, hang on."

He stepped into a back office. Callen took advantage of the opportunity to look around, but there wasn't much to it: a chest-high counter with a couple of messy desks behind it, photographs of moving trucks on the walls, a cardboard cutout of two real gorillas standing beside a water cooler with paper cups stacked on top. The chances of finding clues to the bank crew's whereabouts laying around were slim to none, but studying his environs had become as habitual as breathing.

They heard a photocopier humming, and Timmy emerged bearing a sheet of paper with Hanzi—Chinese characters—written in the crucial spots. The agents thanked him and took their leave.

"Slow boat to China," Sam said as they got back in the car. "I guess we could catch a chopper, find the ship."

"Waste of time," Callen said. "If I had shot a cop and killed a SEAL and just sold a priceless treasure to a Russian oil baron, and everything I owned was being shipped to China, it would be because China was the last place I ever planned to go."

"He thinks he'll be able to afford new stuff," Sam said, nodding his agreement.

"He thinks he'll be able to afford a new life. And he might be right."

"I guess our job is to make sure he's wrong."

"And how do you propose we do that?"

"Well, Grisha Alexandrovich Nikolaev," Sam said, using Callen's recently discovered real name. "I guess you're going undercover. How's your Russian these days?"

"*Xopowo*," Callen said. "That means—"

"I know what it means. It means good. And I *know* how your Russian is. We were just there, remember? Do you even know what a rhetorical question is?"

"Sure," Callen said. "It's—"

"Again, rhetorical! Means it doesn't need an answer."

"Doesn't need one isn't the same as can't be answered. Maybe I'm just more polite than you."

"Maybe," Sam said. "And maybe you're such a pathetically lonely man that you have to take every possible opportunity to speak to another human being."

"I'm not lonely," Callen argued. "I have friends, I have coworkers—"

"You have coworkers who are friendly toward you. Not the same thing."

"Are you saying you're not my friend?"

"I'm saying I might be the best friend you've got. Which means when I tell you that you're lonely, you should listen to me."

"I'm listening," Callen said.

"Okay. You're lonely."

"I'm still listening. I just know you're wrong. I'm not lonely."

"Keep telling yourself that," Sam said. "Maybe one day we'll both believe it."

18

Their next stop was on Orion Avenue in Van Nuys, a peaceful street of single-story ranch homes with a lot of trees, by Southern California standards. Deeks checked the address on his phone, and pointed to a gray house with white trim. A low white fence surrounded the grassy yard, and a driveway curved toward an attached garage. A copper-colored Expedition sat in the drive. "That's the place," he said.

Kensi was already braking to a stop at the curb. "I can read street numbers," she said.

Deeks chose to disregard the inherent sarcasm. "Looks like somebody's home." Stating the obvious again, but sometimes there was nothing else to state. At least he hadn't said, "That house is mostly gray." Also true, but unnecessary.

"With any luck, it'll be Wendell Brower and his friends, and they'll all surrender when we reach the door."

"You mean Wendy," Deeks said. "He must have taken some serious heat in Delta Force, with that name."

Kensi shook her head. "It's probably the first test. If you're tough enough to wear a girl's name, you can go on to the next level."

The front door was standing open, and it was obvious before they reached it that the house was empty. A dark-haired woman in dress pants and a pink blouse with a bow on it turned as they approached, putting on a big smile. "You can't be here about the house," she said. "I haven't even listed it yet, or put out the sign."

"It's for sale?" Kensi asked.

Also obvious, Deeks thought. He knew better than to say it. Although if they had been alone, he probably would have said it despite knowing better.

"It's really a fantastic deal, and you could have the jump on everybody," the woman said. She stepped forward, extending a hand. Kensi and Deeks both shook it, and the next thing Deeks knew, he was holding a business card with the woman's face on it. "I'm Maria Orecchio."

According to the card, she was a licensed realtor. Deeks didn't know of any other profession in which people put their faces on their business cards and on every ad. He never saw bus stop benches with accountants' photos on them, or plumbers', even though both of those professions sometimes advertised there. On Maria's card, her face took up fully a third of the space.

"I'm afraid we're not in the market," Kensi said.

"Yet," Deeks added. "We might be soon, though. I'll keep your card."

Maria's forehead wrinkled and her smile faded, leaving her open-mouthed. "Then what—"

They showed their badges. "We're looking for Mr. Brower," Kensi said.

"Oh." The look of confusion didn't go away. "I'm afraid you missed him by a couple of weeks."

"Missed him?" Deeks echoed.

"He's taken a job in Spain," the realtor explained. "He left two weeks ago."

"Spain," Kensi said.

"That's right. He left the key with me, but just completed the paperwork via the internet, so I could list the house for him."

"Do you know where in Spain?"

"Barcelona, he said. Some sort of executive security position, I gathered. He didn't go into a lot of detail."

"I'll bet he didn't," Deeks said.

"What do you mean?" Maria asked.

"Never mind. It's just been that kind of day."

"You said you might be looking," Maria said. "If you want to see the house—"

"We're kind of in a hurry now," Kensi said. "We'll let you know if we want to see something down the line."

"Well, you have my card."

"Sure do," Deeks said. *With your smiling face all over it*, he added mentally.

They were barely back in the car before Kensi said, "You might as well throw away her card. There's no way we're living in Van Nuys."

"Why? This looks like a nice street."

"Maybe. But it's Van Nuys. Ninety percent of the American porn industry is located here."

"Ninety? Exactly? That's really—"

"*Approximately* ninety. Maybe not that much. But a big, big piece of it."

"I'm not sure 'big piece' is a phrase you want to use when you're talking about the porn industry," Deeks said.

Kensi ignored him. In that instance, he would have done the same. "Anyway, we're not moving someplace where our neighbors might be porn executives. Or porn actors."

"They're probably perfectly good neighbors," Deeks offered. "Stable incomes, take care of their yards. Their backyard barbecues might get a little wild, but—"

"No," Kensi said firmly. "Van Nuys is off the table."

"Off the table?"

"Off. Way, way off. End of discussion."

"Got it," Deeks replied. More discussions should end that way, he thought. Left no room for ambiguity. No *are we finished talking about that? Should I say something else? Is she waiting for me to?* Just *end of discussion*.

Still, having porn stars for neighbors couldn't be that bad.

Could it?

He decided to let it drop.

At least, for now.

Back at the Ops Center, Hetty had another pair of photos for them. "Eric and Nell cross-checked the photographs of the three security contractors we've identified, and the computer found multiple recent instances of them with one other former Lionheart employee. That would be this man, Denis Faulk. He's ex-MARSOC, joined Lionheart in 2006, and worked with the others in Iraq."

"So we know all four now," Kensi said. She studied the pictures. There wasn't much difference between Faulk's military ID and his driver's license. He had a head like a cannonball, squared off only by a short crew-cut. His blue eyes were set wide, over an almost flat nose and a thin, lipless mouth. His neck looked as thick and solid as a tree trunk. He wasn't smiling in either shot;

Kensi wasn't sure from the photos that he knew how.

"Do we have an address?"

"Eric and Nell already checked it out," Hetty said. "He rented an apartment in Santa Monica. It's empty. He left no forwarding address, even though he has a thousand-dollar security deposit coming to him."

"So we have four guys who were in Iraq together," Deeks said. "One of them's dead, and—"

Hetty cut him off. "That's the other thing we learned while you were out. I had Mr. Shogren's casket exhumed. He was not at home."

"What was in it?"

"Currently, nothing at all. But when I contacted the cemetery, I was told that it had already been dug up. Seventeen days ago. There's a police report on it, but no suspects. It happened at night, and a groundskeeper found it in the morning."

"That's where the tablet was, then," Kensi said.

"Almost certainly."

"Okay," Deeks amended. "Four guys, all presumably living."

"And one woman," Kensi added. "No longer living."

"Right. All of whom have disappeared from their homes in the last few days or weeks. We know who they are, we know what they look like, we can even link them using facial rec. But we can't find them now."

"That sums it up nicely," Hetty said. "And we believe we know what their goal is. Now all we have to do is prevent it from happening, and make some arrests in the process."

"It sounds so simple when you put it like that," Kensi said.

Hetty smiled. "I'm sure, Agent Blye, that it will be anything but."

19

Callen studied the file that the Ops team had amassed on Slava Belyakov. His father had been a mid-level Party functionary in Belgorod, but Slava had been born during an extended assignment across the border in Kharkiv, Ukraine.

Kharkiv, Callen remembered, had been the first Ukrainian city occupied by Soviet troops, back in 1917. The third largest city in the Soviet Union, it had been a target for German forces during World War II, and in the course of being captured twice by the Germans and liberated twice by the Soviets, most of the city had been destroyed, its people either enslaved—*Ostarbeiter*, or Eastern worker, was the polite word for it in German, but the euphemism didn't change the reality—executed, or starved. When Belyakov was born there in 1947, his father had been one of a small army of Soviet officials sent to oversee the rebuilding. Apartment blocks and factories went up, jobs returned, and before long Kharkiv was a leading center of science and industry, third in the USSR only to Leningrad and Moscow.

By then Slava Belyakov was back in Belgorod, which

was undergoing its own rebuilding. His family had an upper-floor apartment with a view of the Seversky Donets River, and lived a comfortable existence. At their son's birth, Belyakov's family had adopted the Ukrainian style of speech, so pronounced Vs as Ws, making the boy Slawa Belyakow. Callen imagined that had prompted more than a few fights with his fellow Russians.

His father's position in the Party got him into a decent university, where he married a girl whose father was even higher up the Party ladder. These connections resulted in a management position with a company that manufactured pipe. When *perestroika* created opportunity for entrepreneurship, Belyakov gathered funds from a few investors and opened his own, competing pipe-manufacturing business. He drove the first one under, then took over its factories and client base, which included several major oil companies. His new, larger company extended credit to a struggling oil company, and when they couldn't pay it back, he took over that company, too. Little by little, he amassed more oil companies drilling more and more wells, until he had his own small empire and a net worth in the billions. Only estimates of his total wealth could be made, because it was assumed that, given the usual patterns of corruption among Russia's wealthy, he had hidden millions if not billions of dollars in offshore accounts.

Now he owned palatial homes in London, Sochi, and Moscow, a fleet of private planes, a railroad in Ghana, and a media business in Sweden. His varied interests kept him on the move. His romantic life was just as diverse: he had divorced that first wife in 1993, and had since been linked with a rotating cast of models, actresses, and other world-class beauties.

Rumors of darker habits were many; at least two of his homes were said to contain dungeons, and people whispered that three or four willing women who had gone into those had never come out.

A billion dollars crossing palms here and there bought a lot of forgiveness, Callen supposed. He harbored no expectations that he would like Belyakov, and the more he learned, the more confident he was in that assumption. The man was a ruthless opportunist, apparently unburdened by anything resembling a conscience.

Fortunately, he didn't have to like the man. He just had to get the man to like him.

"You, Mr. Callen, will be Grisha."

"That should be easy enough," Callen said. It made sense, too. He was getting used to the name, but almost nobody used it. The people he worked with still went with G, or used his last name. He had internalized it, though, so if someone called him Grisha, he would respond naturally.

Hetty handed him a flash drive. "Your last name is Koslov," she said. "Learn this. Your identity is more than adequately backstopped, but you don't have much time to memorize the details. We're going tonight."

"Tonight?" Deeks asked. "I was kind of hoping to, you know, get some sleep tonight. Since we didn't last night."

"Sleep is overrated," Hetty said. "I once went for nine days on only seven hours of sleep."

"On purpose?"

"Had I slept any more than that, a large portion of Boston would probably still be radioactive."

"Well, then I'm glad you didn't."

"If we could get back to the business at hand," Kensi said, "where is this going down?"

They were all gathered in the bullpen. Callen, Deeks, and Kensi sat at their respective desks, Hetty, Nell, and Eric were standing, and Sam was perched on the corner of his desk. Nell turned toward Kensi, her cheeks starting to redden. "We've learned that the Belyakov party will be enjoying the pleasures of the Tops & Tails club, on Olympic."

"Tops & Tails? Isn't that a strip club?"

"They call it a gentlemen's club, but yes."

Kensi turned to Hetty. "If you're expecting me to go undercover as a stripper—"

"Not at all, Agent Blye. You'll be undercover as Agent Deeks's date. I trust that's not too big a stretch."

Kensi shot Deeks a glance. "I guess I could pull that off. With a little practice."

"What about me?" Sam asked.

"You're a bouncer."

"Typecasting again," Sam said. "Okay, I'm down with that."

"What about us?" Eric asked. "Are we going in?"

"You're needed here," Hetty replied. "Sorry, Eric."

"You wouldn't like it anyway," Nell added. "All that female flesh on brazen display."

"Oh, yeah," Eric said after the words registered. "Who'd like that?"

"Exactly," Nell said.

"Get busy, people," Hetty said. "You have to be on scene in seventy minutes. Here's how it's going to go down…"

20

Traffic was a nightmare.

The 405 freeway was a parking lot, thanks to a semi full of chickens that had collided with a luxury SUV and overturned, so Granger took surface streets to Sunset. But Sunset was just as bad as the freeway had been. Smoke from the fire in the hills tinted the sky a dusky gray-brown, and the line of cars headed westbound, away from the fire, looked like a mass flight from some apocalyptic disaster. Some were still thick with ash, though it sheared off with the wind of their passage. Headed eastbound, the cars were also lined up, but going nowhere.

Granger drove Stacey Quan's old Dodge pickup, creeping along at five miles per hour. When he was able to hit ten, he felt like he'd achieved a triumph of some sort, though it was short-lived. Past Greenway and around the bend he crawled, past the Maltz Park and its silly sculpture, going slow enough to study the bits of houses that could be spotted from the road, the ones that, at the usual Sunset pace, were essentially invisible behind walls and screened by trees and shrubbery. He gained a little speed after Whittier, because people ahead of him gave up and turned south there, likewise at Roxbury, but after Bedford even five miles an hour became an unreachable goal.

Now he moved along a car-length at a time, stopping longer than he was able to inch forward. He watched the sun sink in his rearview. On the faces of other motorists he saw panic, disbelief, frustration, and rage, and he suspected others saw much the same on his. Mostly, what he felt was an unfamiliar sensation that he eventually pegged as powerlessness. He didn't like it. He was the assistant director of the Naval Criminal Investigative Service. Getting there had been a hard climb, and he'd had to do and see and endure things that would have broken most people. What he wanted now was to flick a switch, illuminate a light bar and wail a siren and flash his badge and get past all the vehicles blocking his path.

But Stacey's truck wasn't equipped for that. A steel box contained some tack and a few tools, and there was a plastic water jug in the bed, but that was about it. It didn't have a siren or a light bar, and even if it had, he would have refrained. Every person in every vehicle no doubt felt the same, had his or her own reasons for wanting to drive the wrong way, heading toward the conflagration instead of away from it. Granger felt that his mission was the most important, but that was only because it was the only one he knew. In the long run, it wasn't—whatever the OSP team was up to in his absence was undoubtedly more crucial to national security. All he was trying to do was rescue some horses that weren't even his, and the urgency came only because Stacey's father had saved his life in Da Nang back in '78.

Granger had been trying to extricate Nguyen Bao,

a South Vietnamese scientist who'd been helpful to the Americans during the war, and whose agricultural research would continue to benefit the West, if he could be liberated from the reeducation camp to which he'd been sent. And where so many had died, after the Americans bailed and the South fell. Quan Huong had been an agent of South Vietnam's intelligence service, and after the war he'd been spirited out of the country with his wife. But he had volunteered to go back for Nguyen Bao, and his presence had made the difference between freeing the scientist—by then suffering from beriberi and a skeletal shadow of his former self— and utter failure. The three had escaped the country together, and Granger's debt to Quan was lifelong.

Once stateside, Quan had Americanized his name, becoming Huong Quan instead of following the Sino-Vietnamese custom of surname first, then given name. His children, Stacey, Jack, and James, had been given American-style names at birth. Granger tried to watch over all three, but Stacey had stayed in Los Angeles and she was the one Granger knew best. At that moment, she and the now elderly Quan were on a kind of pilgrimage back to Vietnam, so he could show her the places he'd known growing up, before the South's fall to the Communists. When she'd asked Granger to look after her precious horses, he could hardly refuse. And with an out-of-control wildfire tearing up and down the hills, he had to do whatever was necessary to get them to safety.

When Granger reached the intersection of Beverly and Lexington, the traffic stopped again. This time, uniformed sheriff's officers were to blame. Granger recognized what was happening, and pulled his badge out. When he finally reached the officers, he rolled down the window—no electric windows in this old beast of a pickup—and showed it to the harried-looking young man. "NCIS," he said. "I need to get up into Coldwater."

"Sorry, sir," the officer said. "Only residents allowed beyond this point. And that won't last much longer. We're trying to evacuate everybody, not let people drive into harm's way."

"I'll only be a few minutes. It's important." He stopped short of claiming "national security," though he considered it. But people whose jobs really did affect national security learned early on not to cheapen the phrase by throwing it around lightly.

"No can do. I'm really sorry, but we've got a bad situation up there. You could be the ghost of J. Edgar Hoover and I'd tell you the same thing."

Granger glanced at the line of vehicles behind him, and the steady stream coming past from the direction he wanted to travel. "I'm kind of stuck going this way, now."

"We'll break the traffic so you can turn around, sir. I wish I could cut you a break, but if I did that, I'd—"

"Never mind," Granger said wearily. "I understand. Can I just turn left onto Lexington?"

"Sure, we can arrange that. Thank you, sir."

Another officer stopped the oncoming traffic long enough for Granger to make the left. There couldn't be roadblocks on every street, he figured, and there was more than one way up into the canyon. He took Lexington back to Hartford and made a right on Cove. Here, traffic was lighter. The evacuation route seemed to be confined to the main streets out of the hills, Beverly and Benedict Canyon, so he wound up on smaller streets, making frequent turns. Approaching

Coldwater Canyon Drive on Shadow Hill, he saw that Coldwater was barricaded by sheriff's vehicles. Nobody was getting through there.

Instead of trying, he backtracked to a narrow dirt road he had passed a few minutes earlier. He turned onto it and headed up into the hills, counting on Stacey's truck's four-wheel drive to handle the rugged terrain. It was almost full dark now, and thick smoke blotted out the sky.

And he still had a long way to go.

21

Betsy Peabody sat on the dusty attic floor. Her back ached and her knees were complaining about all the ups and downs. Although the sun had set and the attic had vents on each end, the day's heat was trapped inside and she was sweating like she had on steamy summer days in North Carolina, where she'd lived until her thirteenth year. Arrayed before her were cardboard boxes, some of them decades old, the cardboard so dry and brittle that it tore instead of bending. They'd been stacked in a corner, behind Hugh's old Army footlocker and a dressmaker's dummy she hadn't used in ages and should probably try to sell or give away. Her fingers weren't as nimble as they'd once been, and her eyesight seemed to get a little worse every week. Sewing was one hobby she'd had to give up on.

She had known that some of the boxes contained old photos; that was why she'd come up the folding ladder to look at them. Hugh had protested that she was in no shape to be climbing ladders, but she had ignored him and come up anyway. He hadn't been up that ladder in the last seven or eight years, at least. He was three years older than her, but seemed considerably frailer, as if his height made him more vulnerable to gravity. She was closer to the ground, had a shorter distance to fall, and consequently worried less about it. And she had no problems with her balance, while he sometimes had to check himself against a wall as he was walking from one room to another. She knew in her heart that she would outlive him, and she could hardly bear the thought of going on alone. Losing Susan—albeit not to the grave—had not taught her resilience in the face of loss; it had only taught her to fear it.

She hadn't intended to stay up here so long. A quick rummage through the boxes was all she'd had in mind. But she found that once she opened an album or one of the shoe boxes contained inside the larger cartons, she was drawn to page or thumb through everything. Some of the pictures were meaningless now—for instance, there was a set of five black-and-white snapshots featuring a couple, nicely dressed, the woman blonde and statuesque and wearing a strand of pearls so white they almost jumped off the paper, the man shorter, with thinning dark hair and black-framed glasses and an easy grin. They were at a restaurant or a nightclub, and they seemed to be enjoying themselves. But Betsy had no idea who they were or where the place was. She was certain she hadn't been there. Relatives of Hugh's perhaps, who she'd met in passing and then forgotten? There had been a lot of those; he wasn't a man who kept up with family, not the way that she did.

Others, though, transported her to times and places of her past. Her seventh birthday party, on the back lawn in Durham with its gentle slope to the line of autumn-brilliant trees and the creek that whispered along behind them. The pictures were black-and-white but she could see the colors, the deep reds and rich golden yellows of the trees, and she could hear the burble of the creek passing over rounded stones, and even though the photos had been taken during the day, she could almost make out the croaking of frogs and the flutter of moths against the screen, almost see the intermittent flicker of fireflies that she and her sister Jean tried to capture in Mason jars.

There were pictures from her college days at USC, others from her long courtship by Hugh, and what seemed like album after album of shots of Susan as a baby, a toddler, and a child. Most of those had been taken in this very house, and Betsy was captivated by the changing décor, the painted walls giving way to wallpaper, furniture and appliances worn out and traded away for newer. There were glistening Christmas trees and early morning Easter egg hunts and Susan's birthdays. Betsy had forgotten that she had allowed others to smoke inside the house, long ago, but she found three photos of a dinner party she and Hugh had thrown for one of his coworkers at Boeing, who'd gone to Europe for six months and returned with a French wife and a taste for smelly French cigarettes. He and the wife—Amélie, she recalled, though she couldn't remember his name—were both puffing away in one of the shots, and in another he was holding a cigarette and a cocktail in the same hand, talking to Hugh's supervisor George Marks, who had a lit pipe clenched in his teeth.

The rattle of the ladder startled her. "Hugh?" she asked.

"Who else would it be? The Boston Strangler?"

"You scared me."

"Sorry," he said. She didn't think he was climbing;

his head would have shown in the trap door by now. "When are you coming down? It's past eight."

"It is? I had no idea."

"If you'd wear your watch—"

"Let's don't start that again. I don't see any need to wear one in a house you keep full of clocks."

"Except in the attic."

"The old cuckoo clock you won't let me throw out is up here. It's laying on top of your footlocker."

"That's an antique," he said. "Who knows what it's worth?"

"*You're* an antique. The clock's junk, the cuckoo bird's been dead for years, and it's not worth anything if you don't sell it to somebody."

"What in heaven's name are you doing up there, anyway? You're missing your program."

"I don't care about the show. We have a DVR, if you're worried."

"I don't know how to use the damn thing, you know that."

"Anyway," Betsy said, "I told you. I'm looking for pictures of the Shogren boy. In case there's anything in them that would help those agents." His memory was slipping more often these days. She didn't think it was dementia, not yet, but she couldn't help being worried just the same.

"Pictures from twenty years ago? I can't see how knowing what he looked like then would do them any good. They could just look up 'juvenile delinquent' in the dictionary; his picture is probably there."

"He couldn't have been that bad. They let him join the Army."

"They were clearly desperate. And the fact that he never went to juvenile hall only means that he never got caught doing whatever. It doesn't mean he didn't do it."

"I have two more boxes to look at, Hugh, then I'll come down, all right? I'm just... I'm enjoying some reminiscing as I go."

"Reminiscing is fine," he said. "Just remember that you live in the here and now, and here and now it's almost eight-thirty. You know you like to be in bed by nine."

"I know. I also know the longer you talk to me, the longer this will take."

"Fine," he said. "If you're not down by ten, I'll holler again."

"By ten you'll be snoring loud enough to wake the dead. I'll feel the floor shaking and I'll know it's safe to come down."

She waited for a response, but all she heard was the ladder rattling briefly, and then his footsteps as he walked away from the opening.

She turned back to the boxes, and pulled out another album.

22

Tops & Tails had a reputation as the most upscale gentlemen's club in Los Angeles County. Which, Sam knew, was a pretty low bar. But he was surprised when he arrived. The valets were neatly dressed and courteous, the club appeared clean and relatively brightly lit, and the dancers—those he could see—were attractive and seemingly healthy. He gave his name to the cashier and was escorted into the club manager's office, where he met Jerry LaDue.

LaDue had a firm handshake, and he made good eye contact; Sam suspected it was something he'd learned, maybe in strip club management school. He had carefully trimmed auburn hair and a neat beard. He was forty-something, and he wore a dark suit and tie. With the exception of his decidedly flashy Patek Philippe timepiece, he looked more like a Midwestern funeral director than a strip club executive. The chronograph told Sam one more thing: a high-end strip club manager could make some bank.

"It's a pleasure to meet you, Agent Hanna," he said when Sam had taken a seat across the desk from his. "We're always happy to help out law enforcement. You guys don't get enough credit, you ask me. Your job is dangerous and necessary."

"Yeah," Sam agreed. "Tonight—"

"And you're with NCIS, right? Are you a vet?"

"Navy SEALs," Sam admitted.

"Oh, wow! I'm doubly honored. Thank you for your service, sir."

"You're welcome," Sam said. He was never quite sure how to respond to that line, which always came from people who hadn't served. Often people who could have chosen to do so, but had decided the other way.

"So you want to be security-for-a-night?"

"That's the idea." Sam touched the lapels of his tuxedo jacket. "Is this okay?"

"It's fine," LaDue said. "A lot of people don't expect a gentlemen's club to be such a high-class joint, but we spare no effort. Everybody's comfortable here: men, women, and, uhh, just everybody."

"I'll try to uphold your standards," Sam said.

"I'm sure you will. It won't get busy for another couple of hours, so I'll have you shadow Jason for a while, until you learn the ropes."

"I pretty much throw out people who are misbehaving, right?"

"But in a classy way. And on the DL—try not to make a scene."

"I'll do my best," Sam said. But a scene would be made, and he would be in the middle of it. That was pretty much the point, after all.

The work, it turned out, wasn't particularly demanding. Sam took a shift checking people's IDs at the door, to make sure they were at least eighteen.

After that he was a roamer, mostly walking around the club letting people know he was there, so they wouldn't try anything untoward with the dancers—who Jason called alternately "the girls" or "the merchandise"—and the dancers, conversely, didn't suggest anything untoward to the customers. The club had two private rooms, the more expensive of which was labeled the VIP room. The security man at that door was expected to make sure that anyone accompanying a dancer inside had paid the hundred dollar entrance fee, and otherwise to stand with his back to the room so that whatever took place within was unobserved. Unless, Jason explained, anybody who looked like a cop was in the place, in which case security had to walk through every few minutes. That could be complicated, Sam thought, since he was in fact a cop.

Every industry had its rules and customs, Sam knew, but he was a little surprised that this one's were so rigidly formalized. Basically, the philosophy seemed to be that the dancers could handle themselves, and if they engaged in any illegal activity, that was on them, unless it looked like it would blow back on the club. The dancers, he learned, were all independent contractors, not employees, which limited the club's liability to some extent.

Waiting for the club to fill up, he was chatting with a dancer who said her name was Brandii, "with two Is."

"How long have you worked here?" he asked.

"About eight months, I guess. I work here and at Panthers in Hollywood, and sometimes in Las Vegas."

"Do you like it?"

"It's okay, I guess. In another year and a half, I'll like it better."

"What changes then?"

"I have to work fully nude now, because I'm too young to work topless."

Her statement caught him by surprise, and it took him almost a full minute to parse. "Oh," he said when he'd figured it out. "Because—"

"They don't sell alcohol at fully nude clubs, but they do at topless ones. So when I'm twenty-one, I'm switching over to topless. I'd be more comfortable that way."

"So would I." He looked away from her—knowing her age, even though she wasn't currently fully nude or topless, he wasn't remotely comfortable with the quantity of skin she was displaying. He had a daughter. If Kamran was nineteen and wanted to work as a stripper, he thought he would try to be supportive of her decision. But the temptation to brutally slaughter whoever had put that idea in her head would also be strong. And he'd have to lock Michelle into a cell to keep her from ripping the head off anyone who saw their daughter nude.

He didn't want to make judgments about this girl's parentage, but he figured there was a pretty wide gulf between them and he and Michelle, in some very important areas.

Gradually, the place filled with patrons, and as it did the music got louder and the energy more intense. He was kind of glad it was a fully nude club in one respect: the addition of alcoholic beverages to the mix of mostly male clientele and mostly naked female workers would have made for a potentially explosive situation. Which would have made his work as a bouncer more complicated, preventing him from doing what he was really here for.

He'd been at it for almost two hours when Callen

came in, wearing an expensive suit with a dark shirt and no tie, too much gold jewelry, and *way* too much cologne. He was using his Russian-accented English, which he was almost as good at as his own natural accent. It always sounded a little off to Sam, but only because he knew Callen so well. If he had heard him for the first time tonight, he would absolutely believe he was a Russian citizen visiting the U.S., or one who had just moved here.

Sam signaled Callen which seat to take. Callen sat and watched the dancers, either enjoying their performances or doing a convincing job of pretending. Every now and then he tipped one, lavishly, but he turned down offers of lap dances.

Twenty minutes later, Kensi and Deeks came in. Deeks wore his own clothes and looked like Deeks. Kensi was more heavily made up than she would normally be, and wore a tight skirt with a slit up the side and a low-cut blouse. Some of the patrons momentarily forgot there was a dancer on the stage wearing nothing at all. Again, Sam showed them where to sit with the subtlest of hand signals. Keeping those particular seats empty all evening had been the hardest part of the job so far.

But the night was young, and he was pretty sure that wouldn't last.

23

It was ten-thirty before Belyakov showed up, along with a retinue of five. Sam wasn't sure if the proper description was bodyguards, thugs, or enforcers, but something along those lines, from the looks of them. Eric and Nell had been tracking Belyakov's phone, and had reported that they'd gone to a Russian restaurant on Ventura in Studio City. Sam didn't know about the food, but it was immediately apparent that the vodka had flowed freely.

Belyakov looked just like his pictures, if a little grayer and thicker through the face. The others were all considerably younger, all male, all solidly built. Two of them had flushed faces and laughed too easily, two were pretty quiet, and one looked like a guy with a chip on his shoulder and a perpetual mad-on for the world at large. He stuck close to the boss, and was the first one to the table, standing beside it and checking out the rest of the room, as if to make sure they weren't walking into an ambush.

Which, of course, they were. It would be a pretty lousy ambush if the victims could see it coming.

They settled back in their seats watching Carly—

Sam knew all the dancers' names by now, even their real names in some cases—who was in her mid-twenties, lean and athletic, and gave a gymnastics performance on the pole that would have been impressive even if she hadn't been wearing only a pair of plastic-soled shoes with seven-inch spikes. He supposed it was unlikely that pole dancing would ever become an Olympic sport, but if it did, he'd watch it.

Three more dancers came on. The Russians downed their drinks, complaining from time to time that no alcoholic beverages were available. Once, Sam went to the table and asked them to tone down the complaints. They were making the waitress nervous, he said, and the law didn't allow full nudity and alcohol to be served up together. If they wanted hard drinks, he could direct them to a topless club not too far away, but if they chose to stay, it was soft drinks or bottled water, and no amount of griping would change that. He was respectful but stern, and he spoke directly to Belyakov, as if acknowledging the older man's place in the pecking order. Belyakov responded by telling his crew to shut up and enjoy the show.

Finally, the moment he'd waited for all night came. One of the ruddy-faced Russians asked a dancer named Marcella, a curvy brunette with an amazing smile, for a lap dance. Before she could oblige, Deeks lunged from his chair, and grabbed Marcella's wrist. "My lady wants a dance," he said, pointing at Kensi. "We've been here a lot longer than these guys. They're not even American!"

"I can get her next," Marcella said, trying to ease her arm from Deeks's grip.

His voice elevated by several decibels. "It's taken her all night to be ready for it, but she's ready now! One dance, come on!"

Sam started toward the commotion, making sure the other bouncers knew he was the closest. He intentionally took a path that was blocked by other patrons, watching the scene, and that slowed him down.

Deeks turned his attention to Belyakov, balling his hands into fists. "Look, guy, tell your punks to let the woman dance for my lady."

At that, the bitter-looking guy rose. He was a little shorter than Deeks, but built, and with the confident air of a stone killer. "Sit down," he said in thickly accented English. "Before you start something you cannot finish."

Deeks held his ground for a good thirty seconds, then shrugged, said, "Fine, whatever. Come on, baby, this place sucks."

"I like it," Kensi whined. "I just want Marcella to dance for me."

Sam watched from his position eight or nine feet away. It looked like the situation was settled, and the other bouncers relaxed.

Then Deeks spun around, whipping a leather sap from a pants pocket. He charged toward Belyakov. The Russian thug who'd backed him down before was off-balance, starting to sit behind one of the low tables. Marcella blocked the other nearest one.

But Callen launched out of his chair as if shot by a cannon. He intercepted Deeks, who swung the sap at him. Callen threw out a forearm, stopping the weapon, and drove his other fist into Deeks's midsection. Callen followed that with a snap kick to Deeks's knee, knocking him off-balance, then an uppercut that dropped Deeks to the floor.

By this point, all the Russians except Belyakov were on their feet, and the one who'd confronted Deeks had drawn a small pistol from somewhere.

Sam and the other bouncers converged on the scene. The whole place had come to a standstill. Music still played, but the dancer on stage stood at the edge, amid tossed dollar bills, watching. None of the patrons were looking at the girls, and even those dancers who'd been engaged in lap dances had stopped their writhing to observe the action.

Sam got a grip on Callen's shoulder. "You need to come with me," he said. He eyed the Russian thug, who had already made the gun disappear. "You, too," Sam said. "And you, sir. We apologize for the inconvenience, and I'm sure we can reach a resolution that's satisfactory to all involved. Please, five minutes in the office and we'll get this all straightened out."

While that was going on, another bouncer had helped Deeks to his feet. Blood trickled from the left corner of his mouth, and he was going to have some bruising. He shook off the bouncer's hand and said, "Babe, it's really time to go. I'll buy you a dancer someplace else, where they cater to Americans. Come on."

The bouncer tried to lay hands on him again, and Deeks swatted him away. "Hands off!" he said. "We're leaving, don't worry. And we would never come back to this hole, so you don't have to worry about that."

Kensi whined something else—she was disturbingly good at whining, it turned out—but she took Deeks's hand and led him toward the door, followed by two bouncers who would make sure they didn't turn around and come back for more.

Belyakov muttered something to his thug, and then nodded. "Five minutes," he said to Sam. "I have never been treated with such disrespect in America."

"I'm so sorry, sir," Sam said. "We'll get it all worked

out back here." He went first, glancing behind him to make sure they were following. He pushed through the Dancers Only door, and led them down a hall tinted with pink lights, past the dancers' dressing room and into Jerry LaDue's office.

LaDue was gone, but four LAPD officers waited inside, weapons drawn.

"What is this?" Belyakov demanded. "We will leave now."

"Not so fast," Callen said. He had brought up the rear, and blocked the door to prevent anyone from exiting. He kept up the Russian accent, though. "We have some things to work out still."

"What things? If this is some kind of trap—I have many good lawyers. The best. I will own this place, and all of you besides."

Sam put his hand on the Russian thug's shoulder. "Let's have that piece," he said. "Nice and easy, too."

"I do not know what you mean."

"The little nine-mil," Sam said.

The thug looked to Belyakov, who frowned and gave a nod. The man took the gun out between two fingers and handed it to Sam. Sam passed it over to one of the cops. "ID now," he said.

The thug drew a passport from his inside jacket pocket. Sam glanced at it and handed it over to the cop. "Don't suppose you have a concealed carry permit, Anatoly Pankin?"

"Your Second Amendment—"

"Doesn't apply to visiting Russian tough guys. And you're in California, where the laws are relatively strict even for locals. Maybe you should have gone to a strip club in Arizona or Texas."

"Do you know who I am?" Belyakov demanded.

"You're Slava Belyakov," Sam said, intentionally pronouncing the Vs. "You're rich. Big deal. We have billionaires here, too." He gave Pankin a shove toward the cops. "Get him out of here."

"Anatoly Pankin," one of the cops began as his partner cuffed the Russian. "You're under arrest. You have the right to remain silent—"

"You'll be out by morning," Belyakov said in Russian.

"Don't count on it," Sam added, also in Russian.

The cops took Pankin out through the back door, leaving Sam and Callen in the office with Belyakov. "Now it's just us," Sam said. "And you're down one man. Lucky for you this man here—what's your name?"

"I am Grisha Koslov," Callen said.

"Lucky for you Mr. Koslov is on the scene. He saved your ass once tonight already. I think he deserves a little something for that, don't you?"

"If this is a shakedown—" Belyakov began.

Sam cut him off. "Not a shakedown. You're going to offer Mr. Koslov a job. You're going to tell your guys that Pankin got arrested, but that you were impressed with Koslov's reflexes and you offered to bring him on as a replacement until Pankin's back."

"Guys who can handle themselves, I can always use."

"Good. Now this next part's a little more complicated. You're expecting to make a deal for a precious artifact, from Iraq."

Belyakov's eyes widened and one heavy eyebrow arched up, but he offered no other signs of surprise. Sam continued. "I know you want to add it to your collection, but that's not going to happen."

"The future is hard to predict, no?"

"Not this time. You can buy it, but you're not

keeping it. If you say anything to anyone about this conversation, or if you try to lose Mr. Koslov here, or do anything at all that's contrary to what I'm saying, you won't like the consequences."

"Which are?" Belyakov asked.

"Let's just say most of the Patriot Act is still in force, and Gitmo's not closed yet. It'll be decades before you see Mother Russia again, and in the meantime your businesses will have to struggle along without you. And without whatever assets you might have parked in this country."

Belyakov gave a dry chuckle. "So much for the home of the free, eh?"

"Nobody's violating your rights, Belyakov. We could send you away right now, but instead we're giving you a chance to prove you're a law-abiding visitor to these shores. Do we have an understanding?"

The Russian didn't look happy about it, but he nodded his agreement. "*Da*," he said.

"Good. Go back out there and introduce Koslov to his new coworkers. Good luck, Mr. Koslov."

"Thank you," Callen said, still using his Russian accent. "You are pretty decent guy, I think. For tool of oppressive capitalist state." He tossed Sam a grin, then followed Belyakov back to the floor.

24

Granger had finally admitted that he was lost.

He had tried to bring up a map on his phone, but the signal was so bad he couldn't connect. He couldn't call Ops, either. He guessed that everybody in the vicinity was using mobile phones and tablets at the moment, or the fire had taken out some cell towers. Or both, most likely. At any rate, currently the phone was effective as a flashlight or a paperweight, neither of which he had any use for.

He was sure he'd set off on the correct dirt road. After a few miles, though, it turned out to have more branches than a river, many of which didn't even show on the satellite view he could bring up on his phone then. He tried to intuit the way to go by studying the condition of the roads he saw, seeing which ones were more traveled, or which seemed to angle in the right direction. He was thrown off, too, by smoke filtering the day's last sunlight, and the dust of the few other vehicles that tore past him, hurrying out of the hills. A couple of the drivers shot him surprised looks, no doubt not expecting to see anyone climbing toward the fire, but none slowed to answer questions. He tried to flag a couple down, and got only a dust-caked face for his trouble.

Granger had a superb sense of direction, and an almost uncanny ability to navigate urban landscapes. He was generally almost as good in the wild, but as the years had passed, he'd found himself needing those skills less and less. Consequently, he was a little rusty. He knew where he needed to be, he was just having a hard time finding a pathway to that place.

Every now and then, when the angle was right, he could see flames higher up in the hills. Smoke was everywhere. Airplanes and helicopters buzzed overhead constantly; the choppers, he guessed, mostly belonged to news organizations or incident response teams trying to gauge the situation from the air. The small planes were probably dumping loads of fire retardant. He hoped not to drive through a cloud of that. Already, his eyes stung from the smoke, and he felt like the smell of the fire was seared forever into his nostrils.

The truck's radio still worked, so he was able to follow the news. Coldwater and Benedict Canyons had both been evacuated, he'd learned. The fire was believed to have started by accident, probably by a campfire that hadn't been adequately contained or extinguished. It had almost reached the crest of the Hollywood Hills, and though fire spread uphill more easily than down—because the heat raced upward, drying out the fuel above and creating perfect conditions for its advance—that didn't mean the San Fernando Valley was out of danger. At the same time, it continued moving down the canyons toward West Hollywood and Beverly Hills on this side. There were plenty of homes up in the canyons, lots of them expensive, but if it reached Beverly Hills the property damage estimates could spike into the hundreds of millions in no time.

Granger wasn't too concerned about that. Those people had insurance. They'd have plenty of time to get out of the way, even to grab some choice possessions, if they could pick between their Hockneys, their Warhols, and their Monets. No, his concern was for the people who lived in the canyons who weren't mega-wealthy, who had small homes on dirt roads, where everything they owned could go up in flames with almost no warning.

And his concern was for Stacey Quan's horses. There were three of them. Mutts, she called them. She prized them for their personalities, not their bloodlines. Their names were Salt, Pepper, and Allspice. Cooking was her other favorite pursuit, one that had led her to open the restaurant down in the Valley that had paid for the Coldwater Canyon land and the horses she kept there. Appropriately enough, Salt's coat was almost pure white, Pepper's was a charcoal gray, and Allspice's was mottled, with grays, blacks, and browns in almost equal parts.

Granger's presumed obligation for three weeks had been to feed, water, and groom the horses, and to occasionally let them out to exercise. He had expected to muck out the stables once, and to get in a trail ride or two. The idea that he might have to race a wildfire had never entered into the discussion.

But he'd told Stacey he would "take care" of them, and taking care, to him, included not letting them burn to death. So he kept pushing up the hill, trying to keep edging right. At some point, he needed to reach Coldwater Canyon Drive, and he would need to cross it. He hoped that this high up, it would be open, and he'd be able to take pavement to the actual dirt road off which Stacey's gate stood. There was a four-horse trailer parked near the stable, and her truck had a tow hitch. If he could get there, then getting out wouldn't be a problem.

As his mother had been so fond of saying, however, "That's a pretty big 'if.'"

Callen accompanied Belyakov back to the table, where his entourage waited with varying degrees of anxiety. Most were at the edges of their seats, and on their feet when they saw the boss coming. One was otherwise occupied, finally getting his lap dance from Marcella. She looked like she was enjoying herself, but Callen knew that was part of the act, necessary to bring in the kinds of tips that could make the gig bearable. Since she'd had to endure two guys—including Deeks—yanking at her limbs, he hoped the Russian would tip extra.

He also hoped he hadn't hit Deeks too hard. Sometimes the guy got on his nerves, and he might have let that affect the force of his punch.

Belyakov leaned in and explained what had happened to Pankin. The "official" version wasn't so different from the truth, so he didn't embellish and he sounded convincing. There was always the chance that Belyakov and his men had some sort of prearranged code word that would tip them off about Callen's real loyalties, but if there was, he didn't notice it, or see any unexpected reactions. Pankin wasn't that popular with the other guys—a couple of them offered variations of "good riddance."

Callen took that as a sign. Even among Russian

thugs, it didn't pay to be too dour and grouchy. He would play it the other way, then. He pasted on a smile and was upbeat from the start. "It's a strange way to get a job," he said in Russian, when Belyakov introduced him. "But I'm glad to get to work with you guys. I've heard of Mr. Belyakov, of course, and always admired his accomplishments."

"Where are you from?" one of the men asked. That was always the beginning of one of the riskiest parts of any undercover. No matter what he said, someone in the group would know somebody from there.

Fortunately, Callen had done his homework, and he'd been more than adequately backstopped. "Originally? Novgorod," he said. "But I've been here for more than ten years. Closer to fifteen, really, because most of the last ten were spent at USP Lompoc. It's been a while since I've been able to speak Russian." He let loose a hearty laugh. "It feels good!"

He could tell by the expressions on their faces that at least a few of the men knew what USP Lompoc was. The United States Penitentiary there was a medium security prison, with a maximum security Special Housing Unit. Serious people did serious time there.

He'd been thoroughly briefed on what the organized crime situation had been in Novgorod fifteen years earlier, and the Lompoc stretch gave him an excuse for not knowing all the current players. A couple of guys offered names of people they'd known, back then, and Callen was able to respond believably. He was fluent in Russian, and spoke like a native, but the time in the US would also explain any slipups he might make.

Certainly, not all of Belyakov's men were necessarily connected to the Russian crime scene. But the chances were good that several were. Russian capitalism had grown up like a weed, suddenly and without having the ground prepared for it. Those who prospered, with few exceptions, operated in the shadowy turf that joined the government and the criminal underworld. Belyakov moved easily in that realm, and it made sense that he surrounded himself with people who had connections in both places.

Belyakov ran through the men's first names. Callen memorized them, but decided he would pretend he hadn't. He didn't want to come across as smart as he was. They'd be more likely to underestimate him if they thought he was a little slow. Just a happy, kind of dumb guy whose skills tended toward violence: that was the impression he wanted to give.

The man named Evgeni was finally finished with Marcella, or he'd run out of cash. Either way, she gave him a quick hug and a kiss on the cheek, spun around in case anyone else wanted a dance, then wandered off to earn tips somewhere else. He had a head like a cinder block, with a bad haircut that made it look even squarer. Vadim was slender and dark, wearing a black leather jacket over a black silk tee shirt and black jeans. Yegor had a proto-beard—three or four days of growth—and a tattoo of a dagger that entered his right collarbone, "disappeared" under the skin, and emerged again at the left. Callen knew that one—it meant the man was a convicted killer. He couldn't see how many drops of blood might surround the dagger's tip, which often correlated to the number of years on his sentence or murders committed. Pasha was quiet; Callen got the impression that he was shy, but he was big and his nose had been broken a couple of times. He had fists the size of canned hams, and it wouldn't be wise to underestimate his violent proclivities.

"We should go," Belyakov said. "Get Grisha settled in the house. Tomorrow will be a busy day."

A couple of the guys grumbled, but everyone knew who the boss was. Belyakov put a hundred dollar bill on the table as a tip, and they left the club with Pasha in the lead, then Belyakov and the rest. Evgeni sidled up alongside Callen, shoulder to shoulder. "You will like the house," he said in English. He spoke with his head tilted down, only his eyeballs looking up. "Big pool, with girls always there."

"I can't wait," Callen said in Russian.

If nothing else, he had learned where Evgeni's interests lay.

25

Belyakov had a pair of matching black Navigators, and everybody piled into those. Callen made a point of taking a long look at the junker Toyota he'd driven to the club, then pulled the keys from his pocket and threw them at the car. They hit the front passenger door and dropped to the pavement.

"You're just leaving it?" Vadim asked. "Isn't there paper?"

"Not in my name," Callen said with a grin.

As soon as they were inside the SUV, Belyakov lit a cigar. As if that equaled permission, Vadim and Yegor lit cigarettes. By the time they reached the house in Brentwood, the interior was thick with smoke. Callen thought about the fire in the hills—Hetty had said Granger was running an errand up there—and figured this was how it must feel to be trapped inside it.

Evgeni was right about one thing. He did like the house. It spoke to Callen of old Hollywood money. The property was hidden behind a high wall, and seemed to be full of trees. The house itself was rambling, as if instead of being built all at once, it had grown organically from the soil. The walls were adobe, the roof an undulating sea of red tiles. Inside, the walls had been whitewashed, and bright Mexican tile accented them in unexpected places; on the risers of stairs, above windows, edging curved niches. The floors were Saltillo tile. The doors were wood, heavy, with black iron hardware. The furnishings were surprisingly modern and bland, not much more elaborate than what a medium-end hotel might offer; Callen figured they were rented for the occasion, and would be trucked out as soon as Belyakov was gone.

Evgeni turned out to be right about something else, too. In back there was a pool rimmed with Mexican tile, brightly lit, and there were several women in it. They were nude, and every bit as attractive as the strippers, which made Callen wonder why the men had bothered going to the club. Change of scenery, he guessed.

"What do you think, bud?" Evgeni asked in English. "Want a drink? A dip? If you know what I mean."

He liked speaking English, it seemed, but Callen replied in Russian. "Not tonight," he said. "I'm tired. Where do I sleep?"

"Upstairs," Evgeni said. "Pick a room. If the door's not locked and nobody's stuff is in it, take it. You got clothes? Suitcase?"

"At the motel I've been staying in. I'll pick them up tomorrow."

Evgeni grabbed his crotch with one hand, jerked his thumb toward the pool, and laughed. "Those girls, man, they're wild."

"Enjoy," Callen said. He went back inside, wandered through the downstairs until he found the staircase again. Vadim and Belyakov were headed outside, Belyakov with a towel wrapped around his substantial middle, Vadim carrying a pair of champagne bottles. No glasses, Callen noted.

"You're not coming out?" Belyakov asked.

"Not tonight," Callen said. "But thank you, Mr. Belyakov. I appreciate the chance."

"I had no choice," Belyakov said. Callen was surprised, thinking he was treading perilously close to the truth in front of Vadim. But Belyakov recovered. "Your reflexes? I couldn't resist."

The staircase wound as it rose. At the top, Callen paused, getting his bearings. The hallway forked in both directions, and he picked the left, then focused on the doors on his right. He wanted to be close enough to see the pool and the deck around it. Not because he particularly wanted to watch what the Russians might do with their water nymphs, but he liked the idea of knowing where they were. The first three rooms he checked were occupied—the bed sheets were a mess, or there were clothes on the bed, shoes on the floor. Pasha was sitting in a chair in the fourth. He looked up when Callen opened the door. "Sorry," Callen said. "Looking for a room."

Pasha simply nodded once. Callen closed the door, and skipped the next room. The one after that was empty, as neat as the hotel room the furniture suggested. He checked the window. Good view of the pool. Belyakov sat at the edge, legs dangling in the water. There was a woman in front of him. Callen couldn't tell for sure what she was doing, and he didn't want to know. The point was he knew where all the men were. Pasha in his room, staring at the walls, and the rest at the pool. They looked like they were there to stay for a while, though he couldn't be sure of that.

Still, no time like the present.

Hetty was convinced that Belyakov hadn't made the buy yet. If he had, she said, he'd already be on his way back to Russia with the goods. His buying habits were well documented, and there was no reason to think he would change his pattern now. Still, knowing was better than believing. He didn't think the man would leave something so valuable lying around in the open, but in a rented house where he was only staying for a week, at the most, chances were he didn't have a very sophisticated hiding place.

He took off his jacket and threw it on the bed, so if someone glanced inside, they'd know the room was occupied. He checked out the window again, confirming that they were all there.

Time for a quick look around.

Sam opened the Boatshed, half-expecting to find Kelly Martin asleep somewhere. But only half, because Martin was a SEAL, and Sam knew that if he were in the other man's shoes, he might have grabbed a nap at some point, but when the door opened, he would be awake and ready for anything.

"It's Sam Hanna!" he called, to ward off any potential surprise attacks. "Sorry it's been so long."

"It's cool," Martin said. He was sitting at the table, looking relaxed. "I've just been pocketing everything I thought I could pawn."

"Makes sense. Ordinarily we wouldn't leave anyone in here alone, but this was kind of a unique case. And you being a SEAL—"

"I get it," Martin said. "Thanks for trusting me."

"It's clear that you're the victim here. And we did almost let you get shot."

Martin touched a spot on his ribs. "Wouldn't be the first time." He looked at Sam, his eyes widening.

"You have glitter on your neck."

"I do?"

"And you smell like cheap perfume."

"Undercover assignment," Sam said.

"You went undercover as a stripper?"

"Bouncer. My clothes stayed on."

"No wonder you let me cool my heels here longer than you promised."

"Yeah, I said I'm sorry. It's been a… complicated day."

"Aren't they all?"

"Pretty much, yeah. You ready to go to the safehouse?"

"Is it an actual house? Or a motel room?"

"It's a house. Not a big one, but it'll work for a couple of days."

Martin looked skeptical. "You expect to have this wrapped up in a couple of days?"

"Less than that, I hope."

"You and me both," Martin said. "I'd like to get back to my life. And get to work building a new bolthole somewhere, since my old one is screwed."

"Understood," Sam said.

"Did you ever have one? A bolthole?"

Sam considered for a few moments. "Not as such. I had contingency plans, but I didn't go so far as to get a place and a separate bank account." He left unsaid that at NCIS, almost every day was its own bolthole. He was constantly trying on new identities, to the point that sometimes it was hard to remember who he really was. Sometimes in his dreams, he couldn't keep track of his own name. His face changed from moment to moment, so he couldn't recognize himself even when he was standing in front of a mirror. A couple of times, he'd turned to Michelle upon awakening, and for the first few awful seconds, couldn't come up with her name.

Often, the false identities he assumed were as elaborately detailed as his real life; if he needed to disappear, he could become any number of people.

"Come on," he said. "I'll take you to the house."

"Can I get some food?"

"It's stocked with groceries," Sam replied. "But if you want to stop on the way, we can do that, too."

"Cool," Martin said. "You look tired."

"Like I said, it's been a day."

"Those strippers will wear you out every time."

"Don't I wish?" Actually, he didn't. He was deeply in love with Michelle, and she was all the woman he would ever need. All he could handle, for that matter. All the strippers in the world couldn't equal what she was to him.

"Just tell me where you want to stop," Sam said, stifling a yawn. "Then we can both get some shuteye."

26

Callen moved quickly past Pasha's room. He didn't want the big man to come out and catch him back in the hallway, though he could always use the old "looking for the bathroom" excuse at least once. Since his time was limited, and since Pasha would be able to see him in the upstairs hall, he went back downstairs. He'd tried to scan the rooms he'd passed en route to the pool and the stairs, but he hadn't been able to look closely at any of them. He doubted the tablet—if it was here yet—would be out in plain sight.

He soon found out that the house was even bigger than he'd first thought. He turned left at the bottom of the stairs, a direction he hadn't seen earlier. He found himself in a formal dining room anchored by a table long enough to sit ten or twelve on a side. He checked the corners, opened the doors and drawers of a huge sideboard, but the thing was empty. Just for show, he figured. Ordinarily in a house like this he would expect a lot of artwork on the walls, maybe sculptures on pedestals carefully lit from above, but this house had almost none of that. A handful of motel-quality framed prints had been hung here and there, and when he found one he lifted it to look underneath for a safe.

That room led into a smaller serving room, then into an enormous kitchen with a good-sized pantry attached. Callen looked inside the refrigerator—mostly beer, American and otherwise, and some of the cabinets—mostly vodka and other adult beverages. The oven didn't look like it had ever been used, even for storage. The pantry held an assortment of packaged foods, but no ancient Sumerian antiques.

A door on the other side of the kitchen fed into a breakfast nook, then into other rooms less easily identified, although eventually he figured out that he'd entered the servants' quarters (which included another, considerably smaller kitchen, another series of bedrooms and bathrooms, and a second staircase leading up).

Still no tablet. Finally, he reached the end of the house and a door that opened into a side courtyard. He checked out the window, then made his way back through the series of rooms. There were still plenty more he hadn't explored on the other side of the staircase.

Before he got to those, he noticed a small door underneath the staircase. He opened it and peered into the darkness, and after a few seconds, realized he was looking at an armory. He didn't have time to count, but estimated that there were probably two dozen long guns in there, mostly Kalashnikovs, it appeared, along with stacks of magazines and boxes of ammo, and miscellaneous other weaponry. These guys were ready for war, if it came to that.

He closed the door and was headed for a sitting room he'd passed through before, on the far side of the staircase, when Belyakov and Yegor emerged from the darkness, bottles in their hands and naked women on their arms.

"Grisha," Belyakov said. He plucked the stub of a cigar from his mouth with the hand that also held a bottle of champagne. "I thought you were going to bed."

"Couldn't sleep," Callen said.

"If you're going to the pool, you're overdressed."

"I don't have trunks."

Belyakov squeezed the side of the unashamedly nude blonde next to him. "Not necessary here."

"If I looked like her, I wouldn't mind being naked."

"Well, you don't, so I'm taking her upstairs. You're on your own." Belyakov started up the stairs, his blonde and Yegor and friend trailing behind.

"Thanks again, boss," Callen said.

"No problem, Grisha. Get some rest, though. Big day tomorrow."

From the looks of things, it would be a while before those four got any rest. But for all Callen knew, they'd slept until six in the evening.

He hadn't.

Anyway, if the party at the pool was breaking up, he ran the risk of bumping into the other guys. If Belyakov had come along thirty seconds earlier, he'd have found Callen looking into the gun cupboard under the stairs.

Time to call it a night. He made a U-turn and headed back to his room.

That bed had actually looked pretty comfortable.

Kensi went into the living room, carrying another ice pack for Deeks's knee. The kneecap was swollen and, by morning, she expected, the bruise would be lovely shades of purple, indigo, and black. The one on his chin didn't look much better.

"You doing okay?" she asked, sitting beside him on

the couch and pressing the ice pack to his knee.

"My teeth hurt," Deeks said. He rubbed his jaw with his left hand and took the ice pack in his right.

"Good excuse to see your dentist." She shook her head, sadly. Deeks enjoyed trips to the dentist more than anyone she'd ever known. She supposed it was an acquired taste. Some people paid to be beaten with paddles, too. Different strokes, and all that.

"I mean, I get that Callen had to make it look real," Deeks went on. "He needed to get on the inside in a hurry, and some phony-looking fight wasn't going to do the job. But I was ready to go down. He didn't have to be quite so convincing."

"Probably not," Kensi said. "But remember the circumstances. It all had to happen fast. He was supposed to show off his reflexes, not just his fighting skills. Probably if you guys'd had time to practice once or twice, or if he could have slowed down a little, it would've gone a little smoother."

"Yeah, maybe. I think there was more to it than that."

"Like what?"

"I don't think Callen likes me that much."

"To be fair, Deeks, nobody likes you that much."

"Ouch. Talk about adding insult to injury."

She'd regretted the words as soon as they had left her mouth. She and Deeks teased each other, a lot. Maybe too much sometimes. But she loved him, and she knew he loved her. It was a reversal of gender expectations, she guessed, but he found it easier than she did to express his sensitive side—to say the mushy stuff that could be awkward, but that was nice to hear in a romantic relationship.

She supposed it had to do with her upbringing. Her father hadn't longed for a son, necessarily, but he hadn't quite known how to bring up a girlie-girl. As a result, he'd treated her like one of the guys, teaching her what he considered survival skills. At his side, she'd learned to track, to hunt, to shoot. She could hotwire a car or rewire a house with the best of them, thanks to him. Her mother had been out of the picture until after Kensi's father had died, during her fifteenth year, so she'd grown up without a traditional female role model.

It wasn't just that, though. Her father's influence had led her to study criminology, certainly, and to pursue a law enforcement career. But that field, not so long ago, had been an almost entirely male domain. Even now, there were few women working in it, as evidenced by the fact that she was the only female field agent at the OSP. That dynamic fed her determination to be just as tough as any of the guys, to tamp down any traditionally feminine traits and emphasize the other side of her personality.

It helped her function on the job, but she recognized that sometimes, Deeks might appreciate some nurturing once in a while. Maybe sensitivity, at a time like this, as opposed to sarcasm. It didn't come naturally to her, and that made it feel forced and artificial when she tried. But that was how habits were formed, right? By forcing it until it did come naturally?

Worth a try, she decided.

"I'm sorry, Marty," she said. "I was just joking. You know I love you, and so do the rest of them. Not the way I do. But Callen does like you. More importantly—in his world—he respects you. I'm sure he wasn't trying to hurt you on purpose. It was the moment, and the fact that he was trying for realism. And that you hadn't practiced. I know I don't say it enough, but you're a wonderful man, and everybody thinks so. Even Hetty, and when I first met her, I didn't think she liked anybody, ever."

Deeks just stared at her, open-mouthed.

"Did I say something wrong? I was trying to be sensitive."

"Who are you?" he asked. "And what have you done with Kensi Marie Blye?"

She laughed, and punched him on the arm. Probably hard enough to hurt. "Give me some credit for effort!"

"You called me Marty. Kensi never calls me Marty. I want her back. You're scaring me."

"Now you know why I never talk that way. All I get is grief."

He leaned over and gathered her into his arms. "I'm sorry, babe. I guess I just wasn't prepared for it. I did like it, kind of. Maybe I could get used to it."

"Don't bother," Kensi said.

"Maybe just a little?" He drew her closer, took her chin in his hand, and pressed his lips against hers. Held them there. She loved the way they felt, the tickle of his facial hair, the warmth that passed between them when they kissed. Kissing and making love brought them together, made them almost one, in ways that words never could.

Then he released her, suddenly, and pulled back. "Ow!" he said. "My teeth."

She laughed again, but resisted the urge to land another punch, harder than the last.

It took almost all the willpower she had.

27

June 16

Granger's eyes flickered open when the first hint of smoke-filtered sunlight touched them.

A little gray bird—the sort dubbed LGBs by birdwatchers because they were so commonplace and nondescript—was perched on one of the truck's windshield wipers, apparently more curious about the man inside the pickup than he was about it. Granger eyed it for a second, then uttered a soft "Boo," sending the LGB into panicked flight.

He had pulled off the road last night and parked under a spreading oak. Not only could exhaustion lead to poor decision-making, but driving all night without a definitive plan could lead to an empty gas tank. In an isolated canyon in the middle of a raging wildfire, that could be just as fatal.

It didn't take a lot of time in a combat zone to develop a knack for grabbing some sleep whenever circumstances allowed it, and that was a habit Granger had never lost. He had been a little nervous about sleeping when he didn't know what course the fire might take during the night, but assumed that if it came close, the noise and the heat would wake him before he was engulfed. With the sound of the choppers and planes and wind roaring around him, he had drifted off. Now he felt somewhat refreshed, and with the rising sun, would have enough light to continue his mission.

He checked his phone. Still no service. That probably wouldn't change until whatever towers the flames had felled were restored. At the best of times, there were spots deep in the canyons where cell service was slim to nonexistent. That didn't affect the GPS, but it did affect the ability of the phone to download current map data. And as he'd already found, the maps were a little lacking when it came to these dirt roads—sometimes barely more than wheel tracks through the brush. The satellite view was marginally more helpful than the map view. But even that was operating on cached images that weren't necessarily up to date.

If he had realized this trip would turn into such an adventure, he could have brought a satellite phone and more sophisticated GPS technology. He hadn't expected a simple drive up the hill would become so complex. Now he had to hope Stacey's horses had survived the night, and that he could find his way to them without many more delays.

He got out of the truck and stood in the bed, trying to get his bearings. He knew from the position of the sun where due east was, and that gave him the rest of the compass points. He still needed to move northeast—probably east-northeast, but that depended on his precise position now, and he didn't know that. Once he got to Coldwater Canyon Drive, he'd be able to figure that part out, though. So east was his main goal. The road he'd been traveling on when he finally gave up for the night had started out heading that way, but then had veered to the north, and eventually a little northwest. That was when he'd decided to get some rest, before he went too far in the wrong direction.

From the truck bed, he could see thick white smoke higher up in the hills, churning into the sky. There it mixed with the layer of smoke that already hung over everything, giving the sky a brownish-gray cast. A thin layer of ash coated the truck and the trees and the ground that surrounded him. Southern California had seen some devastating wildfires—the Cedar fire in 2003, down in San Diego, still held the record for sheer destructive fury, with almost three thousand structures destroyed—but Los Angeles had seen its share as well. The Station fire in 2009 had been a bad one, as had the Topanga a few years earlier. Fires in Ventura, Orange, and San Bernardino Counties had cast their pall over L.A., too. This one, Granger was certain, would find its place in the record books.

The meteorological circumstances had been perfect. Hot, dry, windy days were ideal fire weather. The past couple of weeks had been nothing but; days when touching anything metal could lead to a hair-raising electric shock—*not that I have much to worry about in that regard*, Granger thought. With plenty of fuel choking the hills and canyons, it wouldn't have taken a very big spark to ignite an inferno. Once it was touched off, the landscape would have contributed to its success. The ups and downs of the topography gave the flames the momentum they needed to spread quickly, and the isolation and ruggedness made it hard for crews to get in and control the blaze. Homes were a particular problem. Besides the loss of property and sometimes life, they often contained additional enhancements, like propane tanks or natural gas lines, that could lend extra oomph to even a fading fire. There were just enough of those in the canyons to ensure that the conflagration would continue to rage.

It looked like most of the fresh smoke was billowing up from higher elevations than he needed to travel. He got back in behind the wheel, cranked the engine, and backed out from under the tree, cutting a trail through the white-gray blanket of ash. He would continue in the direction he'd been going last night for two more miles, he decided, watching for a spur that led off to the east. If he didn't find one by then, he'd backtrack to where he had turned onto this path in the first place, and try another fork.

Calm, rational, logical. People died in fires because they panicked, like the LGB. They couldn't keep their heads, make the right decisions.

Owen Granger didn't intend to repeat their mistakes.

"Do we have a visual yet?" Hetty asked.

"Nothing so far," Nell replied.

"We have access to the most sophisticated electronic surveillance equipment in the history of the world," Hetty observed. "We have satellites that can count the spots on a ladybug on a leaf from low earth orbit. How can it be so hard to see a man in a big red truck right here in Los Angeles?"

"That might be a slight exaggeration," Eric pointed out. "About the ladybug, I mean. As for the man and the truck, there are multiple factors. The smoke, primarily, which is obscuring everything at ground level. Then there's the sheer amount of air traffic over those hills, which blocks some of what the satellites can see."

"I was, perhaps, speaking hyperbolically about the ladybug, but not by much. And I do recognize the limitations of our technology, as well as the difficulties involved, Mr. Beale. My overall point was that we know where Owen's mobile phone is, thanks to the GPS chip in it. I would like to confirm that Owen is with his phone. It's not like him to go this long without checking in, and given his stated destination and the current situation there, I'm worried about him."

"Do we know if he's even in the country?" Nell asked. "I mean, I know he said he was going up Coldwater Canyon. But... people... have disappeared from here before, without saying anything, and wound up in all kinds of places."

"It's polite of you not to name names," Hetty replied. She knew Nell was talking about her, after all. "All I have to go on is the GPS reading, and what Owen told me before he left. And the fact that I saw him driving that ghastly red truck yesterday. Since I have no reason to suspect otherwise, my assumption has to be that he did indeed drive that vehicle into those hills to rescue his friend's horses. That should keep the visual search parameters sufficiently narrow that even with the obvious limitations, you'll be able to see him."

"We're trying," Eric said. "And—"

"We won't quit until we do," Nell interrupted. Eric shot her a look, but it dissolved into a warm smile. She might never break the habit of finishing his sentences, but if he grew to like it when she did, that might not matter.

"Very well," Hetty said. "I'm going to my desk, where I'll pour a cup of Lapsang Souchong and wait to hear from you."

"We'll let you know—" Eric began, then stopped.

Nell glanced his way, expecting him to continue. When he didn't, she grinned and added, "Just as soon as we have anything concrete."

"See that you do," Hetty said, and left.

Those two were so cute, it was just this side of sickening.

28

As it turned out, the bed was almost too comfortable.

Callen wasn't used to that. He had slept on couches, on floors, in cars, jail cells, tents, war zones, on beaches and cliffs and occasionally in the arms of someone warm and soft and smelling faintly of shampoo. A luxuriously soft king-size bed was rare for him, and for the longest time he felt like some kind of trespasser in it.

Which, of course, he was. Not just in the bed, but in the house and in Slava Belyakov's retinue. That part—undercover work—was not at all unfamiliar to him, of course. But undercover work didn't often involve sleeping in a bed made of angel feathers and hope, which seemed to be the constituent parts of this one. At first, he couldn't fall asleep. Once he had, he never wanted to wake up again.

When he finally did, he lay there for a few minutes, wondering if he could parlay this assignment into a full-time gig. That didn't last long, though, before he remembered what a piece of work Belyakov was, and how damaging it would be to the nation's already fragile relationship with Iraq if it was learned that the tablet had been stolen by Americans supposedly working on behalf of the government.

Maybe this assignment wasn't as critical as stopping terrorists armed with dirty bombs or biological warfare concoctions, but that didn't mean it wasn't important. The Middle East, after all, was fraught with tensions. Some dated back thousands of years, while others were more recent, the agonizing throes that came with tossing aside decades of colonial rule and redrawing national boundaries imposed by outsiders. Those tensions—combined with factors like widespread poverty and a lack of jobs for young males—contributed to the terrorist threat, without which those dirty bombs and bioweapons wouldn't even be a concern. So while a stolen antiquity might seem like small potatoes, its impact could be substantial indeed.

Having convinced himself, Callen rolled reluctantly out of bed and took a quick, hot shower, then dressed in the same clothes he'd worn last night. A fresh pair of underwear would have been nice, but if discovered, might have exposed his ruse. He had told some of the Russians that he had more clothes in a motel somewhere, and if this undercover went on for much longer, he'd have to find a chance to go fetch some. If Belyakov insisted on someone accompanying him on that errand, it would be considerably more complicated, because there was no such motel. He'd have to try to call Ops and arrange for some of his belongings to be planted at one so he could go in and pick them up. Then his lack of a key would become an issue.

He checked the pool. Nobody, not even the women Evgeni had promised were "always" there. They might all have been in the rooms of the various men, he guessed, or even in rooms of their own. This house contained more than enough for everyone, after all. Walking downstairs, he wondered who it had belonged to in its heyday. And how it had looked then, when it hadn't been furnished in Contemporary Holiday Inn.

He wasn't sure what to expect downstairs, but whatever it might have been, what he found wasn't it. He followed the aromas of coffee and bacon into the kitchen, where Belyakov—with an apron wrapped around his middle, as last night he had worn a towel— stood by the stove stirring an enormous frying pan full of scrambled eggs. A plate nearby held a couple of dozen strips of crisp bacon, and more sizzled in another pan beside the first. On a nearby counter stood another plate with a stack of toast on it, and beside that was a bowl of chopped cantaloupe, honeydew, and pineapple, along with grapes and blackberries. It was a thoroughly American-style breakfast, Callen thought, or would be if there were some Cheerios or Frosted Flakes in sight.

"Good morning, Grisha," Belyakov said cheerfully. "Or whatever your name really is."

"It's Grisha," Callen answered truthfully.

"Have it your way. Hungry?"

"I hadn't given it much thought, but I am now. You're quite a chef."

"I try. Russian breakfasts, I'm afraid, aren't interesting to me anymore. Syrniki, porridge, kolbasa— I've grown tired of it all. Some pancakes with mince meat and sour cream, that's okay once in a while. But American breakfasts I find the perfect way to start the day. I hope it's good for you."

"Smells delicious," Callen said. "Can I have some coffee?"

"Help yourself. That's another thing. I grew up always having tea with breakfast. And lunch, and dinner. I find Russian coffee less than satisfactory, don't you? Compared to French or Italian. And here, one can get any coffee. That's Jamaican in the pot. Blue Mountain. It's my favorite."

"It works for me," Callen said. "It's been a long time since I've had a good Russian breakfast. But anything is better than prison food. Even the coffee in prison is terrible. But the water is worse, so I tried to drink coffee whenever I could."

"What were you in prison for, again?"

"I didn't say."

"Will you?"

"Aggravated assault," Callen said. When he was undercover, he liked to stay there. Belyakov knew it was a ruse, or had to suspect, anyway, given the fact that Callen had been foisted on him by law enforcement. But it didn't pay to slip out of character even for a moment. "And a weapons charge. And the guy might have died. But if he did, clearly that was by accident."

"Clearly. And your victim was?"

"A man in a restaurant. It was an occupational hazard. Hazard for him, occupation for me."

"So you've been a professional tough guy before."

"That's as good a way to put it as any, I guess."

"Yet now you have some sort of arrangement with the authorities."

Callen shot him a stern look. "We're not supposed to discuss that."

"Oh, everyone else is sleeping, and will be until I go and kick their beds."

"Really? I'd think there would be someone awake any time you are, to keep an eye out."

"You think my life is more dangerous than it is, Grisha."

Callen thought about all the firearms stashed under the stairs. "I'm not so sure about that."

"It's true, the men get upset if someone isn't watching over me," Belyakov said. "Not because they love me so, but because their incomes depend upon my continued presence on the Earth. They do not, however, get so upset that any of them are willing to wake up when I do." He stirred the eggs a little more, then, deciding they were done, took a large bowl from a cabinet and spooned them out of the pan into it. He sprinkled a little pepper over the top. "I've never slept much. The secret to my wealth, I think—I've always gone to sleep later and awakened earlier than my competitors."

"One of the secrets, anyway," Callen said.

Belyakov gave a knowing laugh. "Well, yes. One of them." He plucked the last strips of bacon from their pan and dropped them onto the rest. "One rule I have—I do insist that everyone joins me for breakfast. And now, it's time. Do you want to wake the men, or should I?"

"I haven't known them long enough to not risk being shot," Callen said. "I think you'd better."

"Done and done," the billionaire said. "Don't touch. Nobody eats until we're all at the table."

"Scout's honor," Callen said in English.

Belyakov stopped, arched an eyebrow at him. "Don't make that mistake in front of the other guys," he said. "Not if you want to live until lunch."

29

Sam was parked around the block from the driveway
to the house that Callen had identified, in the shade of
a willow tree. He watched said driveway on a tablet,
on video being fed by a couple of small cameras
he'd planted during the night. Sitting on the block
itself would be too obvious. For the same reason,
they were communicating only on anonymous
burner phones, not on radios. They were dealing
with professionals who knew many of the tricks they
did—albeit without having access to the same level
of technology. Or so he hoped.

Callen had sent one text, with the house's address,
but had otherwise maintained radio silence. His phone
was a burner, too, but nobody on the outside had any
idea what kind of privacy he might have to make or
receive messages. He'd be contacted when things
were going down, but otherwise left alone. He was the
one in the hot seat—the one surrounded by hostiles.
Nobody wanted to risk blowing his cover.

Because this was Brentwood, Sam had only been
there for about twenty minutes when a patrol cruiser
had pulled up behind him. He sighed as the officers

got out. The driver was a beefy, ruddy-skinned blond guy, mid-thirties, who looked like he hit the gym every morning. His partner was a few years older, and his uniform shirt gapped a little where a spreading belly strained it. The driver hitched up his belt as he approached the Challenger, but he waited at the rear quarter panel until his partner had reached the front passenger window. Sam had thumbed it down as they approached, but now he had both hands plainly visible on the wheel. He'd been here before. It was sadly a minority of black men his age who hadn't.

"Nice morning," the partner said.

"Listen, officer," Sam said. "I'm on the job. Can I show you my ID?"

The partner straightened up, his face disappearing from the window. "Says he's on the job," he said.

"Recognize him?" the driver asked.

"No."

"I'm not LAPD, I'm NCIS," Sam said. "If you'll just let me show you—"

"NCIS," the partner repeated.

"I heard. What's that, a cross between the NSA and the CIA?"

"Naval Criminal Investigative Service," Sam said.

The driver approached him now. "Step out of the car," he said. "Slowly, with your hands visible. Then you can show us what you got."

"Look, officers," Sam said. "You could be in the process of blowing an investigation that has serious national security implications. A low profile would be appreciated."

"It's up to you," the cop said. "You can casually get out, low profile, like you said, and show me your

ID. Or I can pull you out, put you facedown on the street, and cuff you. Your call."

"Okay, I see how it is," Sam said.

"What's that supposed to mean?"

"It means there are lots of good cops in the department," Sam said. "I've worked with some. But there are still a few who see an African-American man sitting in a car on a Brentwood street and think the worst."

The phony smile vanished from the driver's face, replaced with a look that vacillated between rage and disgust. "If you're calling me a racist—"

"I'm not the one jumping to conclusions here. I'm going to get out now, and show you my identification, and then you're going to get back in your car and get the hell out of here before you ruin a lot of hard work and potentially endanger the life of my partner. Am I making myself clear?"

The driver started to say something, but the words caught in his throat. He just nodded and made a grunting noise.

Sam opened his door slowly, showed his hands outside the car, and climbed out without using them. Once out of the car, he opened his badge case and showed badge and ID to the driver. The man caught his partner's eye and nodded once. "Looks real."

"It is real," Sam said. "You satisfied, or do I have to get your captain on the phone? Because I can do that with one call."

"Just making sure," the driver said. "You know how it is. Neighborhood like this, we have to take precautions."

"Do me a favor," Sam said. "Don't take precautions when you go by the couple sitting in a black Escalade on the next block. They're with me."

"We saw them," the partner said. "Didn't stop, though."

"Keep it that way," Sam said, letting the obvious go unspoken. Kensi and Deeks were white. "And if you guys can make yourself scarce, we'd appreciate it. We need you, we'll call you."

"Understood," the driver said. He touched a finger to his brow, the closest he could bring himself to a salute, then hitched his duty belt up once more and went back to his car. A minute later, they drove away.

Sam hoped the people in that house with Callen hadn't seen any of it. He'd rather have a better spot for a stakeout, but all the houses down the block were occupied, and somebody had to keep eyes on the driveway. He would wait a while, then change places with Kensi and Deeks. Keep switching things up in hopes of staying unnoticed as long as possible.

But if this was going to go down, he hoped it was today. Otherwise he'd have to train a whole new set of cops next time.

A few minutes later, Sam's burner phone rang. "Yeah?" he said. No names—they weren't using names on this op.

"Did you have a conversation with some of my old colleagues?" It was Deeks.

"Couple of LAPD officers in a cruiser," Sam said. "Yes, why?"

"Just curious," Deeks said. "They just drove past us. One of them pointed at us, and both gave us the stink-eye as they went by. I figured you must have been making friends and influencing people."

"I gotta say, it's pretty bad when *you're* a good example of the breed."

"Hey!" Deeks said. "Okay, I guess that's true. I wasn't the best cop ever. But I was better than a lot of them."

"I think I just met two of that kind," Sam said. "Anything else?"

"No, that was it. Unless you just want to shoot the breeze. You know, talk about sports, comics, anything like that. That new *Black Panther* series is—"

"Later," Sam said.

"Yeah, okay, later." Deeks ended the call, and Sam put the phone down, then checked the tablet. The driveway was empty, the street still.

He really hoped he didn't have to wait much longer. Sitting still in a car got old in a hurry.

30

When Kensi's phone buzzed, it wasn't the burner. She didn't recognize the number, but it was local, so she answered it. "Blye."

"Is this Agent Blye?"

A woman's voice. She sounded elderly, and it took Kensi a few seconds to place her. "Mrs. Peabody?"

"Yes, it's me."

Kensi hoped she wasn't in the mood to chat. "How can I help you?"

"You asked us to call you if we remembered anything about Hal Shogren that might be helpful."

"Yes. Did you?"

"I might have. I knew I had some pictures somewhere, but it took a while to find any. But I finally did."

"Pictures of what?"

"Susan went with the Shogrens to their cabin in the Hollywood Hills a few times, and she took some pictures. There's a big rock wall behind the cabin, with a unique shape to it. I thought you might be able to identify the location from that."

Kensi was impressed. So often, what civilians thought might be helpful wasn't, and the things they didn't bother to mention could be vital. Knowing about a tattoo on someone's left butt-cheek was useless unless they walked around with no pants on. But something as seemingly unrelated as learning that a suspect was a stamp collector might be the piece needed to complete the puzzle. Shogren had been living somewhere since returning from Iraq, purportedly dead. He'd been living under an assumed identity, but he still had to have a roof over his head and a place to stash his belongings. A remote cabin he was familiar with might be a likely spot.

"Can you text them to me? Or email them?"

"They're *pictures*."

She meant prints. "Do you have a scanner?"

"A scanner? I'm not entirely sure what one looks like, but I know we don't have one."

"Can you take a picture of them with your phone?"

"I'm afraid we're not very technologically sophisticated, Agent Blye. I'm calling you on a phone that's connected to the wall with a cord."

She wanted copies of those photographs, but she couldn't run over to Pasadena to collect them. And she couldn't risk having the Peabodys come here, not with the possibility of a firefight at any moment.

She had an idea, though. "Can you hang on for a second, Mrs. Peabody?"

"Of course, dear. But call me Betsy."

"All right, Betsy. One minute."

She pressed the MUTE button. "Mrs. Peabody has found some pictures of the Shogren family's cabin in the hills. She says there's a distinctive rock face in the background. Might help us find the cabin."

"And you think that might be where Shogren's been living?" Deeks asked.

"Maybe where they've all been hiding out since they abandoned their various homes."

"And I gather sending them electronically is out of the question."

"Yeah," Kensi said. "Apparently beyond her capabilities. I was thinking if she could meet us a few blocks from here, they'd be out of the line of fire if anything happened, but we wouldn't be so far that we couldn't get back over if the guys show up with the tablet."

"Worth a try," Deeks said. "Have her meet us at the intersection of Sunset and Barrington. There's an Italian restaurant there, and a Subway."

Kensi relayed the message. "She says they're leaving right now," she said after she'd ended the call.

"We'll give them about forty minutes, then head over," Deeks said. "Maybe a little longer. They're old; they probably drive slow."

"Works for me," Kensi said.

When Granger finally found Stacey's place, the fire was disturbingly close. It was a beautiful spot, ordinarily. A couple of ancient live oaks threw shade over the corral. The house was old but loaded with character, and the ramshackle barn and stables looked like something out of a Western movie. Photographers and filmmakers had come here to shoot in the rustic setting, multiple times.

But today smoke filtered the sunlight, giving the scene an eerie yellow glow. The horses were panicked, thrashing around in their stalls, snorting and squealing. Granger could see flames down the hill, marching toward the property. He'd thought the fire was all above this place, but there must have been a spur down below, or a wayward ember had floated down, igniting another blaze.

The horse trailer, dented and sun-faded, stood beside the corral, where Stacey had left it. Granger drove down the dirt trail, backed toward the trailer, shut off the truck engine then hopped out. Fuel was starting to be a concern, and although he was up the mountain now, he still had to get down again.

When the trailer was hitched and connected, he put a heavy stone on the brake pedal, to make sure the lights were working. This would be easier with two people, but that wasn't an option. Finally, he lowered the ramp at the rear of the trailer.

Success. The easy part was done. Now he just had to persuade the horses to go in the trailer. He'd been coming up to feed, water, and exercise them, so he wasn't a complete stranger. But in their current state of mind, he couldn't be sure they'd remember him. Horses were not dumb creatures—they were, after all, smart enough to understand that an approaching wildfire signaled trouble.

He'd start with Pepper. If there was such a thing as an alpha horse in this little herd, Pepper was it. He was a big stallion, and bossy with the other horses, though when Stacey was there, he became docile as a lamb.

Granger opened the door of the stable. The place was thick with the dust the beasts were kicking up, along with the musky smell of the animals themselves. He inhaled some and coughed a couple of times, but then tried to speak in low, even tones. "Easy now, guys," he said. "I'm going to get you out of here, and we'll find someplace to hang out until Stacey comes back. You all know me. I've been taking care of you. That's what I'm doing now; it's just a little more complicated. Okay? You all ready to roll? Get down out of these hills before they burn to the ground? Good."

He stopped by Allspice's stall. The animal's eyes rolled back in its head, wild. "I'll come back for you in a minute, Allspice," Granger said. "Just take it easy. Relax. Nothing's going to hurt you."

Allspice wasn't buying it. Granger gave up and went to Salt, telling her a variation of the same thing. She, at least, seemed to be listening, though she pawed the earth and snorted a couple of times during Granger's monologue.

He moved on to Pepper. The big horse reared back when Granger showed himself, then lunged forward as if to charge. "Easy, big guy," Granger said. "Calm down, now. You're the boss man, so you have to set a good example for the other two. We're going to get you all out of here, but I'm all by myself, and you're going to have to cooperate with me. Okay? Got it? You just take it easy, and we'll get this done in no time."

Pepper calmed. Granger held out a hand toward him. "Just wait here a second and let me get your halter," he said. "Just take it easy."

As soon as he turned away from the stall, Pepper snorted and kicked again. Dust rained down from the rafters as the whole building seemed to shake. "Chill, you big goof," Granger said. "You'll knock the place down."

He found a flat nylon halter and returned to Pepper's stall. "Okay, we're going to do this, and we're going to do it without a lot of drama. Right? Easy does it You ready, Pepper? I'm coming in."

He eased open the door. Pepper backed away, as if wanting to hide in a corner. Granger kept talking, saying nothing in particular, just trying to keep the horse calm with his voice. He moved slowly but with confidence as he slipped inside, then closed the door behind him so Pepper wouldn't decide to make a run for it. The animal's hooves were in constant motion, stepping, almost prancing with fear and anxiety.

When he approached the horse's head, Pepper jerked it away, snorting again and showing teeth.

"This doesn't have to be difficult, buddy," Granger said. "Just be cool, and we'll get out of here in one piece." He approached again. Pepper jerked his big head, almost slamming it into Granger. Granger reached out with his right hand, holding the halter in his left, and caught the horse under his chin, reaching around to cup Pepper's right cheek. "Easy, easy. I'm going to put this on you, and then things will get a lot better. Okay? You ready? Here we go."

Pepper's eyes stopped rolling in his head. He gave a soft blow, less agitated than a snort, and moved his head to the side a little, ears twitching. The horse's tail was pulled down, almost invisible from here. Pepper was still scared—*terrified* might have been more accurate—but willing to let Granger have his way. Granger looped the lead rope over Pepper's head, slipped Pepper's nose through the nose band. Pepper jerked his head again, but not hard enough to break Granger's hold. He eased the throat latch into place, positioned the crown piece behind Pepper's ears, and buckled it. Pepper stamped and tried to jerk away, but Granger got the lead rope in his hand and held the animal still while he checked to be sure the halter was tight enough, but not so tight that it would hurt.

All the time, he was talking to Pepper, reassuring, trying to generate calming vibrations.

"Okay," he said when he was satisfied that the

halter was snug. "That's step one. Now we're going for a little walk."

He tugged, but Pepper tugged back. Granger stepped forward, pulling harder. "Come on, Pepper. Time to go. You don't want to be here when the fire comes." He opened the stall door, bracing himself in case the animal bolted. Instead, the horse planted its hooves, as if trying to grow roots.

"No, Pepper. You can't stay. We have to get in the trailer." He tugged again. Reluctantly, pulling back every few seconds, the horse started to follow. Once clear of the stall, Pepper started pulling harder, bending his back knees, almost sitting. Granger stepped closer and pulled down on the lead rope, to lower the animal's head into a more submissive position. Then he made the horse take several backward steps, head down. Pepper didn't necessarily like it, but he obeyed.

"That's right," Granger said. "I'm in charge here. We go where I say we go, and we don't make trouble on the way. We clear on that? Good."

He started forward again. Pepper followed, relatively calm until they stepped out into wan yellow sunlight that smelled of smoke. Then he became agitated again, stamping and snorting and trying to jerk free from Granger's grip.

"Easy now," Granger said. "We're almost there. Hard part's done. Just work with me, here."

The hard part, of course, was just beginning. Haltering a horse was nothing compared to getting it into a trailer for the first time—Granger's first time with Pepper, not Pepper's first time. "I know, this is all strange," Granger said. "But you've probably done this a hundred times, with Stacey. There's nothing to it, really." He led Pepper to the trailer, the horse offering resistance all the way. When they reached it, Granger went in first. He clomped around, trying to imitate the sounds Pepper would make when he got in. Pepper's eyes rolled and he swung his head sideways, away from the trailer, almost yanking the lead rope from Granger's grip.

"Nope," Granger said. "Uh-uh. You're coming in, whether you like it or not." He tapped the sides, touched the roof. "It's pretty nice in here, really. Out of the elements. Shade, a nice breeze. You'll like it." He stepped out again, then back up on the right side, urging Pepper up the left. "Come on, Pepper. Just like downtown. Nothing to it."

It was obvious that Pepper was doubtful, but he sniffed at the trailer's door and floor. Probably, Granger thought, it smelled more familiar than the smoke-filled air did, because the horse calmed almost immediately, and stepped up as if he'd never had a problem with it at all. Granger went alongside him, up to the front, then stepped back and fastened the gate behind him.

One down. Two to go.

And the fire was closer than ever, so near that he could hear its roar, feel the hot wind it pushed ahead of it.

If he couldn't get the other horses on here in a hurry, they'd all be crispy critters.

31

Callen was playing poker on the big table in the dining room.

The stakes were low. Nobody wanted to lose much, or was too worried about cashing in. It was just one of those things guys did when they were waiting, and since breakfast, there had been nothing but waiting. He was a little surprised that Texas Hold 'Em had become popular in Russia, but the internet crossed all boundaries, it seemed, and that's what the guys wanted to play.

He was holding a pair of aces, and the turn card had been an ace as well. He upped the ante a little, but not enough to scare anybody out.

Then Belyakov came into the room. "Game's over, gentlemen," he said. "It's time."

Callen put his cards down somewhat reluctantly, stretched, and feigned a yawn. "Time for what?"

"Time to earn your pay," Evgeni said.

"Do I have a minute to take a leak?"

"If you're quick about it," Belyakov said.

"Shouldn't take long." He scooped up the small pile of cash he'd made, mostly dollar bills, and went into the bathroom. There, he took his phone from his pocket and texted "Go time" to Sam, Kensi, Deeks, and Ops. Then he flushed, washed his hands, and went back to the dining room.

It was empty. He found the other men in the foyer, taking long guns out from under the stairs.

"What's going on?" he asked. "Looks like we're going to war."

"We're just taking reasonable precautions," Belyakov said. "I'll be transacting business, closing a deal for a very valuable item. There will be a considerable amount of cash at hand, and I don't want it to go anywhere before I have what I'm buying."

Callen knew what he was talking about, and Belyakov knew he knew. So far, he had played along, as far as Callen could tell. At least he'd given no indication otherwise. Callen hoped he continued to do so throughout the negotiations to come. All he needed to do was buy the artifact, then turn around and give it to Callen. The sellers would be picked up outside, with the cash still in their possession. Callen wondered if Belyakov understood that the money would become part of the criminal case against the contractors—a case that could never be brought to trial, because it would mean admitting American involvement in the theft. The men would be tried for the bank robbery, and for shooting Scarlatti. Maybe for the shootout at the Sea Vue and the attempt on Kelly Martin. But the existence of the tablet, and the role that played in everything else, could never be acknowledged. He might get his money back, one day, but it would be years from now if it ever happened at all.

The atmosphere inside the house had changed almost instantly. Things had been casual, the men patiently waiting for something to happen without knowing precisely when. Now, in the space of a few minutes, it was tense, the air almost electric.

"Here you go, Grisha." Vadim handed him a Kalashnikov semi-automatic carbine and a couple of magazines. Callen gave the weapon the once-over, then shoved the first magazine home.

"Do we have reason to believe they'll try anything?" he asked.

"In this business," Belyakov replied, "it is only prudent to hope for the best but prepare for the worst." He eyed his men, each of them armed now. The smell of gun oil was suddenly strong in the room. "If everything is peaceful, then we won't use these. But if they give any indication that they're not accepting the outcome, we don't wait for them to start something. We start it and we finish it quickly. Is that clear?"

The men answered in the affirmative. "They'll know we're here, and armed?" Callen asked.

"They'll know," Belyakov said. "You'll be in plain sight. Don't point your guns at them, but let them know you have them and you're prepared to use them if necessary. They'll have guns of their own. Nobody will be pretending this isn't a dangerous business."

"How long until they get here?" Callen asked.

"Five minutes, perhaps," Belyakov said. "No more."

Belyakov's men had transformed from a bunch of thugs into a fighting force. Callen couldn't help feeling a kinship with them. They were on the wrong side, and he might have to turn against them, to arrest them, or worse. It all depended on what went down in the next few minutes. If Belyakov played his cards right, they might all be able to go home to Russia, having broken only some weapons laws in the United States. But if he didn't—or if the contractors objected strenuously to Belyakov's refusal to buy the tablet—then anything could happen. Callen might be fighting on the side of the Russians, against his own countrymen.

When armed men were put into proximity to objects of great value, and vast piles of cash, there was no telling what might occur.

Whatever it was, Callen would have to be prepared.

But prepared for what? That was the question.

And everything rode on the answer.

Sam watched a black Humvee drive past, slowly and deliberately. The windows were tinted almost to the point of being opaque, but he was pretty sure there were four people inside. Once it was out of sight, he checked the image on his tablet. The vehicle cruised up the street, and turned into the driveway of the house Callen was in.

It was on.

Deeks had already called, so Sam picked up the phone again. "They're in," he said. "Let's go."

"Roger that," Deeks said. Sam heard him say "Go" to Kensi, then heard the sound of their engine. "We're a few blocks away."

"I'm sure they'll be in there for a while," Sam said. "But hurry."

"We're on the way."

"See you soon," Sam said, then disconnected and dropped the burner into the passenger seat. He cranked the engine and pulled away from the curb. He fought the urge to race around the corner, instead taking it slow and quiet. The last thing he wanted to do was draw anyone's attention from the house out toward the street. He parked halfway across the driveway, not blocking it all, but ensuring that the car couldn't be seen from inside. The gate had been left open, probably because the visitors were expected, and he wasn't sure he'd be able to manually close it from here—or if trying to do so would set off an alarm inside.

A few minutes later, Kensi and Deeks came around the other corner. He motioned them across the driveway, nose-to-nose with the Challenger, blocking any potential vehicular egress. They got out and joined him, each carrying a Heckler & Koch HK416 that matched his. "Do you think we need more bodies?" Deeks asked. "Like maybe an army?"

"Be an army of one," Sam said. "I'm a SEAL, and Kensi's—well, she's Kensi Blye. Anybody dumb enough to mess with her deserves whatever he gets."

"You're not really expecting a firefight, are you?" Kensi asked.

They'd been over this several times, but once more couldn't hurt. "I doubt it," Sam said. "If there's going to be a fight, it'll be inside. Hopefully not, though. We just need to be in place to stop them once they're out of view from the house. They'll see that they're outgunned and surrender. Even if they don't, they won't be ready to shoot, and we will."

"I'm not complaining," Deeks said. "It's just that in the LAPD, we'd have brought in a lot of backup for an op like this."

"Yeah, but most of those people would be LAPD officers," Sam said. "You'd need a lot of them to equal the three of us. Especially if they were anything like the two who tried to roust me today." He gestured up the driveway. "Come on," he said. "Let's get into position. We want to get the drop on them as soon as they come outside."

"Sounds good to me," Kensi said. "Deeks?"

"Yeah, I'm right here. Let's do this."

Heads low, hoping no neighbors had looked outside and seen them with their assault rifles, they headed up the drive.

"I think that was them, Hugh," Betsy Peabody said.

"Who?"

"Agent Blye and her partner! In that car. That Jeep or whatever it is, the black one."

"Where?" Hugh asked.

"They were just sitting there, in front of the Italian place, like they said. Then they pulled out like a bat out of Hades."

"Maybe they didn't want to see you."

"Maybe they didn't think we were coming because you drive so dang slow."

"Guess we can go home, then."

"No, we can't go home. Follow them."

"Follow who?" Hugh asked.

"That black one!" Betsy pointed down the road. "It's right there."

"I don't see—"

Her vision had always been better than his, and even more so these past several years. At an age when many of her friends were dealing with cataracts or macular degeneration, she could still spot a white-breasted nuthatch in a tree at three hundred paces. "Use your eyes, you old fool! Or move over and let me drive."

"If I move over, I'll go out the door."

"That might not be the worst thing ever."

"Why are we following them?"

"Because we have pictures for Agent Blye. And because if she can find out anything about what happened to Susan, we have to know. I have to know. Just follow."

"Are you sure?"

Betsy sighed. She had loved Hugh since her teens. She still did.

But sometimes she wondered how she had put up with him for so long. How any woman ever put up with any man.

Probably, she thought, it was about as easy as it was for any man to put up with any woman.

"Yes, I'm sure," she said. "Go, before they get away."

32

A black Hummer pulled up the long, circular drive and came to a stop on the flagstones outside the house. Yegor watched from a window, sitting in plain view, his weapon just as clearly visible. Callen stood a few feet back, close enough to see but far enough to duck if it became necessary.

Four men got out of the vehicle. He identified them from the photographs he'd seen. Faulk, with that massive neck and shoulders and the shaved head. Dark, lean Wehling. Brower, with the sharp nose and red curls. And finally, Shogren, who'd let his brown hair and beard grow out since that old military ID photo had been taken, but who couldn't disguise his bright green eyes.

They were all wearing black tactical gear. They'd come for a business meeting but dressed for combat. Callen hoped that could be avoided. As long as Belyakov played his part right, it would only get tricky if the Russians witnessed the arrest of the contractors, or if Belyakov told them he wasn't being allowed to keep the tablet.

Pasha opened the door and stood aside, silent as

ever. Callen had never heard him speak, and wondered if he was mute.

The four visitors stepped inside. They didn't have weapons in their hands, but they were holstered at hips and ankles, clearly visible. Nobody was pretending the situation wasn't fraught. Ordinarily at the outset of a high-stakes negotiation, he'd expect to see smiles, however phony. There were none here, just grim faces.

Brower carried a black Kevlar bag, with something heavy in it. Vadim and Belyakov had already brought similar bags into the living room and set them beside the biggest chair. That would be Belyakov's chair, Callen figured—the closest thing available to a throne. Belyakov wanted everyone to know this meeting was ultimately about him, and what he wanted. The contractors were there to deliver his prize. Whatever he was paying them was worth more to them than it was to him, and that gave him the position of power.

"Welcome, gentlemen," Belyakov said, without a trace of good cheer. His English was Russian-accented, but fluent. "It's nice to finally see you face-to-face."

"Glad to be here," Shogren said. "We've been holding onto this item for a long time, looking for a good home for it. Looks like you're the lucky one."

"Luck has nothing to do with it," Belyakov replied. "Come, in here." He waved the men into the living room. "Sit."

Before they could, he crossed to his chair, flanked by the big bags of cash. The contractors followed him in. Evgeni and Yegor hadn't left the room; Callen, Vadim, and Pasha trailed the others in, then took their prearranged places against the walls while the contractors sat, two on a couch and two in separate chairs. There was a heavy wood coffee table in front of the couch. It didn't match the rest of the furnishings, so Callen guessed it had been brought in because it was sturdy enough to hold the tablet.

Among the Russians, only Belyakov was seated. Callen's station was at the doorway between the living room and the foyer. Probably, he thought, Belyakov wanted him there because if there was trouble, somebody was bound to shoot the guy standing between them and the way out.

"We all know why we're here," Belyakov began. "You brought the item in question?"

Shogren nodded toward Brower. Apparently the "dead" man was the designated spokesperson. "We have it. Go ahead, Wendy."

Brower lifted the heavy bag into his lap, unzipped it, and pulled out a package about seventeen inches tall and fourteen wide. With a tactical knife, he sliced through packing tape holding pieces of cardboard on each side, then peeled away bubble wrap to reveal a stone slab. Age had yellowed and stained it, and its edges were ragged, hewn from whatever its origins were by primitive tools. He put the bag on the table, then laid the slab on top of it, face up.

Callen was good with languages, but he wasn't up on his Sumerian or his Akkadian. He didn't think a stone tablet that allowed one to be translated into the other had much real-world utility these days—certainly there was an app for that, if anybody needed to do it. What made this thing valuable was not its function, but its age and its rarity. What made it particularly valuable at this moment was the size of Belyakov's fortune and his eagerness to possess things that nobody else could.

Callen didn't understand collecting. The only

certainty about life was that it would end, and when it did, what good was it to have amassed a bunch of objects one would have to leave behind? He never wanted to collect so much of anything that he couldn't stuff it all into a couple of bags and take off whenever it became necessary. Maybe that was his bolthole—not a rigidly defined place or identity, but the ability to go anywhere and be anyone, at a moment's notice.

When Belyakov looked at the tablet, his eyes almost gleamed. Callen was afraid he might start salivating. He rose from his chair and hovered over the table, examining the rock slab from a foot away. "It looks authentic," he said.

"It is," Shogren replied.

"You don't mind if I—"

"Pottery Barn rules. You break it, you bought it."

Callen was tempted to point out that Pottery Barn had no such rule, but he figured a Russian thug who'd just done a stretch at Lompoc probably wouldn't know that.

"Understood," Belyakov said. He crouched beside the table and lifted one end of the tablet. He studied the edges, then set it back on the bag and traced his fingertips over the etched-in symbols.

"There are several ways to date such an object," he said. "Most require a lab, which we do not have available to us here. And of course, we cannot take this particular artifact to any commercial lab. But there is another, only slightly less specific dating method, which requires only human expertise. I'm not being boastful when I say that I am as expert in the field as any other living human."

He raised the end again, then slid a hand underneath it and hoisted the entire thing off the table. He felt the weight in his hands, turned it over and eyed the back side, then put it down again. "I am satisfied," he said. "That is no forgery. It's the real thing."

"I told you it was," Shogren said.

"Of course. But then you would, wouldn't you?"

"We don't have all month. Do you want it, or not?"

Belyakov returned to his chair. He was smiling now, the grin of a little boy who has just found enough money in his pockets to buy the toy he's had his eye on. "I do."

"We agreed on a price."

"We agreed on a price range, pending authentication."

"You just authenticated, right?"

"Right. Now we must narrow the range down to a precise sum."

"We said fifteen to twenty. Let's just meet halfway. Seventeen-five."

Callen hadn't been sure until just then what kind of money the tablet might fetch. He was sure they weren't discussing thousands, though. And the language would be different if it was hundreds of thousands.

That left only millions. Was there twenty million dollars in those bags?

And if so, could either side resist the urge to keep both the money and the tablet?

"Not so fast," Belyakov said.

"What's the problem? You said it's real. It's what you thought it would be, right? What I said it would be."

"Yes, it appears to be. But there are other… concerns."

"Like what?" Shogren was getting angry. Maybe he'd expected, after all these years, that this part would be easy. Wishful thinking.

"Perhaps to you," Belyakov said, "the difference

between fifteen million dollars and seventeen million is an abstract exercise. Essentially meaningless, because the sums are too large for you to truly grasp. But for me—"

Shogren cut him off. "You'd spend that on a trip to the mall."

"My point exactly. You don't understand how much money that is. You have no basis for understanding it. The things it could do. Money isn't just for buying things. It has power. It does things. It changes things." Belyakov sat back in the chair and laced his fingers together. "It changes people."

"Hal—" Wehling began. Callen was surprised they were using their real names. He supposed as long as they were confining it to first names, it wouldn't be too dangerous. Still, he would have used code names, in their position.

In any event, Shogren interrupted him before he could say any more. "We didn't come here for an economics lecture," he said. "We came to do a deal."

"And a deal we shall do. On my terms."

"On mutually agreeable terms," Shogren corrected.

"I am the one with the money," Belyakov reminded him. "You're the ones with an object for sale that you've been holding onto for a long time. Costing you money without earning anything. You're more desperate to sell than I am to buy, and I am fully aware of your situation. I think that means I dictate the terms, don't you?"

Callen didn't like the sound of that. He was already on edge, but Belyakov's words spiked the tension even higher. If the contractors thought the deal was going south, they might just try to snatch the cash and run.

He was trying to read physical cues. Shogren and Brower were on the couch, and he could see both their faces. Shogren was the more relaxed of the two. He still thought this was a negotiation, and maybe it was. Brower wasn't so sure, though. He was biting his lower lip so hard Callen thought he might draw blood. His hand was twitchy, and kept inching toward the gun holstered at his side. Wehling was in a chair with its back to Callen, so he couldn't see much of the guy, just his feet and the top of his head. Only the balls of his feet touched the floor—he was ready to spring into action. Faulk sat in a chair beside the couch, so Callen could see about three-quarters of him. He looked relaxed on the surface, but his fingers were digging into the chair arm with almost enough force to rip through it. If things went sideways, Faulk was the one he'd worry about the most. On that side, anyway. On his own side, Yegor, with his dagger tattoo.

"You're not backing out, are you?" Shogren asked. "Because if you were, then we'd have a real problem here."

"I am not backing out," Belyakov assured him. "Simply trying to delineate the playing field."

"The field is, we got it and you want it."

Belyakov shook his head. "You misunderstand. You have what I want, but I can walk away without it. I have what you need. If you had other buyers, you would use them against me to raise the asking price. But you don't. I could offer you eight, and that would still be more money than any of you have ever seen in your life. Two million apiece, no? Would you turn that down?"

The contractors shot each other angry looks. Callen understood—none of them wanted to be the first to agree to a deal so much lower than what they'd been promised. But nobody wanted to walk away from two million dollars, either. They'd held onto the tablet so long, and now that the time had finally come to sell it, they'd murdered and robbed and put themselves at risk of long prison terms, or worse. To give up now, to leave empty-handed, was unacceptable. So was hanging onto the artifact and trying to find another willing buyer. Belyakov had them over the proverbial barrel, and he was letting them know it.

Callen even thought he understood why. He wouldn't be allowed to keep the tablet. If he could, he would probably hand over twenty million dollars without a fuss, but since he'd have to give it up, he wanted the purchase to cost him as little as possible. Callen couldn't blame him for that. He just didn't want the deal to be blown.

Or the meeting to erupt in gunfire.

Especially that.

33

Shogren came out of his chair wearing a furious scowl.

"This bastard thinks we don't have any other buyers," he said. "Let's go."

"Hal," Wehling whined. That single word gave away the whole game. It was Belyakov, or back to the drawing board.

"Sit," Belyakov said. "It's obvious that I am your only option. So the only question that remains is, what will you take for it? Two million is a lot of money."

"Two mil is *crap*," Shogren said. He wasn't sitting, but he wasn't leaving, either. The tablet still lay on top of its bag, on the sturdy table. He came from money, Callen remembered. Maybe not millions, but his family had lived in an upscale Pasadena neighborhood, and had a cabin in the Hollywood Hills, where low-rent districts were few and far between. It was just possible that two million dollars wasn't terribly meaningful to him. Clearly it was to Wehling. Brower looked like he was about to explode, too, but Callen couldn't tell if it was from anger or frustration.

Belyakov waved him back toward the couch. "I see

two million is not worth your time. Perhaps two and a half, then? An even ten, split four ways?"

"Fifteen was the bottom line," Shogren said flatly.

"I don't know," Brower said. "Maybe we should—"

"Maybe you should shut your damn yap!" Shogren said. "We agreed I'd make the deal, right? So let me make it."

"You might want to reconsider, before you wind up with a mutiny on your hands," Belyakov said.

Good advice, Callen thought. *Listen to him.* The longer it dragged on, the more he worried that it might fall apart.

Shogren planted himself in the chair again. "Twelve," he said. "Not a dime less. That's the final offer."

"Twelve," Belyakov repeated.

"Three for each of us," Shogren said. *He can do math*, Callen thought. *Wonders never cease.*

"Sounds good to me," Brower said.

"Me, too," Wehling added.

"Denis?" Shogren asked.

The big man shrugged. Callen couldn't see his shoulders, but the chair moved when he did it.

"Twelve," Shogren said. "Cash, right now. Count it out."

"I'm delighted that we could do business," Belyakov said. "Vadim, count out twelve million for our friends."

Vadim took one of the bags from beside the billionaire's chair and unzipped it. The money inside, banded hundreds, could hardly be contained; it threatened to spill out on the floor. He crouched beside it and started stacking bundles on the table.

"You got your prize, boss," Yegor said, in English. "I didn't think the spy would let it happen."

"Spy?" Shogren echoed.

Callen's blood froze. Yegor could only be talking about him. He didn't move a muscle, but he was already gauging possibilities in his head. How fast they were, how accurate with those guns.

How pissed.

For a second he thought Yegor would laugh it off. How could he know? He was probably joking.

Then he gestured toward Callen, standing at the doorway. "That one," he said. "He just came last night. Got something on the boss."

"It's a setup!" Shogren shouted. He yanked a Glock from the holster on his hip.

Then the room erupted in chaos.

The driveway was flanked by thick growth, almost jungle-like. Sam, Kensi, and Deeks had taken up positions among the plants, from which they could watch the drive and emerge at just the right time to surprise the contractors as they drove out, flush with cash. But when they heard gunfire from inside, their plans changed. "Callen!" Kensi called.

"Go!" Sam cried.

Charging toward a firefight without knowing who was shooting at whom was never a good idea, Kensi knew. Hell, it wasn't even a good idea when you knew full well. When bullets were flying, keeping out of the way was the wisest course of action.

Nobody had ever called Kensi Blye dumb—not more than once, anyway—but her reaction was ingrained. Callen was inside, where the guns were going off. Callen was OSP. Callen was family.

As she rounded the bend in the driveway, she could

see muzzle flashes briefly illuminating the windows. One window was already shattered. Nearing the front door, the acrid tang of gun smoke bit at her nostrils.

Sam reached the door first, she and Deeks right behind.

"We don't know what we're walking into," Sam reminded them.

"Doesn't matter," Deeks said. "Callen's in there."

Kensi wanted to kiss him. He and Callen weren't the best of friends. But when the chips were down, each knew he could count on the other to have his back. Callen had punched Deeks in the jaw the night before, kicked him in the knee hard enough to raise a knot, but Deeks hadn't hesitated for a second when it seemed that Callen was in danger.

That was the man she loved. Even if it was hard to say out loud, sometimes.

"We'll announce ourselves," she said. "Maybe the presence of federal agents will—no, never mind. Nobody in there would think twice about killing federal agents."

"Probably right," Sam said. "But we've got to get inside, and we've got to stop the shooting."

Deeks held up his HK416. "That's what these bad boys are for, right?"

Sam nodded. "Let's go."

34

When Yegor outed Callen and Shogren pulled his weapon, Callen didn't wait around to see who he intended to use it on.

There were too many guns in that room, and the emotions were running too high. Callen ducked behind the wall, then tore up the winding stairs, three at a time. He stopped when he was high enough to have plenty of staircase between him and the doorway, then waited with his borrowed Kalashnikov ready.

Brower was the first one through the door. He held a Glock nine-mil like Shogren's, and when he saw Callen on the steps, he raised it to fire. Callen shot first, a quick burst that dropped Brower like a hot rock.

Then he heard gunfire from inside the room, and someone cried out in pain. They were shooting each other now, and he couldn't tell who was being hit. A moment later, Evgeni dashed out, shooting behind him as he ran past the staircase, toward the kitchen and the series of rooms beyond that.

Callen heard the crashing of window glass. Shot out, or had someone jumped through to escape? He couldn't say. He was blind here. He was protected, but for how long? This house had more than one staircase, after all. What good would this vantage point be if someone came at him from above?

His first instinct had been that he'd be the main target, since he was the one fingered as a spy. Now, though, the two teams seemed to be after each other, maybe fighting over possession of the money, or the tablet, or both. Or just because they had guns in their hands and targets in front of them.

He moved down the stairs, employing considerably more caution than he'd used on the way up. At the bottom, Brower lay there, blood bubbling up from his mouth. His eyes were open. He was alive, still twitching, but not for long. A pool of blood was spreading around him. His Glock was close to his hand. Callen reached down, snatched it up, and tucked it in his waistband at the small of his back.

Leaping past Brower's dying form, he darted across the open space. On the far side of the door, he crouched and peeked around it.

Belyakov sat in his chair, arms splayed out to his sides. In the center of his forehead was a new hole, weeping blood. Cash was scattered all around him. The tablet still lay where Callen had last seen it, on the table.

Vadim was down, too, slumped against a wall, with a bloody streak painting an arrow from where he had been hit to where he'd landed.

The others were gone.

Callen tried to recall the layout of the house on that side. Another warren of rooms eventually led out to the pool. He thought there was another staircase over there, but he wasn't positive—he'd never managed to get all the way to the end, in that direction. The window he'd heard being smashed was clear enough that someone could easily have gone out through it.

So he had no idea where any of the combatants were. On this floor, above him, outside the house... probably all of the above.

He hadn't come here intending to kill anyone, although he had always known it was a possibility. Now, though, he had to assume that anybody he encountered was trying to kill him.

He heard voices outside, and whirled, finger on the trigger, just as the door banged open. "Federal agents!" sounded from multiple throats, and Callen froze his finger an instant before he squeezed it past the point of no return.

Sam, Kensi, and Deeks charged in, weapons at the ready, but they recognized him in time to hold their fire, too.

"Where is everybody?" Deeks asked.

"Got me," Callen said. "They were here, then they weren't."

As if to make a liar out of him, a couple of gunshots sounded, followed by an automatic weapon's burst. "That sounded like the pool area," Callen said.

"Nice pool?" Deeks asked. "Heated? Not that you'd need it heated in this weather, but—"

"I never went in, Deeks," Callen said. "Been a little busy."

The gunfire from that direction continued. "Go check it out?" Sam said.

"There's a dead guy," Kensi said, eyeing Brower. She moved to the doorway and looked in. "There's the tablet," she pointed out. "And what looks like an awful lot of money."

"And another dead guy," Deeks said. "Strike that. Two dead guys."

"Belyakov and Vadim," Callen said. "And somewhere in the neighborhood of fifteen million dollars."

"The tablet's what we want, right?" Kensi asked.

"Part of what we want," Deeks said. "We also want the guys who shot Tony junior."

"Yeah," Sam agreed. "The tablet's key, but we also need those guys."

"Guess we should find them, then," Callen said. "Pool's this way."

More gunfire sounded as they made their way in that direction. The pool was walled in, and the racket bounced and echoed off the walls and tiles, so it was hard to gauge just how many were out there and where they were. Callen had been told that beyond the pool was a trail that wound through some lush landscaping to a private tennis court. Another wall hemmed in the overall property, but Callen was sure it wasn't impossible to scale, so there was no guarantee that people hadn't gone over it and left the property altogether.

He held up a fist to stop the group as they approached the door out to the pool. Sunlight glinted off the water and carved shards of light across the wall. A patch of blood beside the pool caught Callen's eye, but he didn't see anybody. He made a forward gesture, and led the team outside. They moved like the cohesive unit they were; as they stepped out, he scanned forward, Sam spun around to check the windows above, and Kensi and Deeks swung their gun barrels to the sides, covering them that way. The odor of chlorinated pool water mingled with the smell of gunfire and the sharp edge of blood.

He had to take a few more steps toward the pool before he saw Evgeni's corpse floating facedown, tinting the water pink around him.

"One of ours or the Russians?" Deeks asked.

"None of them are exactly 'ours,'" Callen said. "That's Evgeni, the guy who took your stripper."

"Didn't recognize him from this angle," Deeks said.

"Not gonna say he deserves it?" Sam asked. "Dude took your stripper."

"I didn't really want her anyway," Deeks reminded them. "She was Kensi's stripper."

"That's a pleasure I can live without," Kensi said.

Callen was turning, ready to go back inside, when motion at the top of the pool wall caught his eye. "Down!" he shouted. At the same time, he dropped to the tiles, rolled once, and came up firing.

Wehling got off two shots before Callen's rounds raked across his hand and scalp.

Everybody picked themselves up off the ground. "Gross," Deeks said, tugging his shirt away from his body. "I hit the dirt in somebody's blood."

"Don't touch it," Kensi said. "You don't know where it's been."

"Okay, Mom," Deeks shot back.

"We're kind of sitting ducks out here," Sam said.

"Yeah," Callen agreed. "Back inside, I think."

"That guy was one of the Americans, right?" Kensi asked. "The one on the wall?"

"That was Wehling," Callen replied.

"So there might be more out that way."

"Could be. For all we know, they're all gone."

He said it, but he didn't believe it. The fight had started because of him, because he was exposed as an outsider who'd infiltrated what was supposed to be a private—and very illegal—transaction.

But the money and the tablet were still here. The people who'd cared about one or the other wouldn't have left without at least trying to take them along.

Even as he thought it, he mentally corrected himself. The tablet and the money had been here—before he and the others had been lured outside.

"The living room," he said. "The money."

When they made it back, Yegor was hoisting the unopened money bag onto one shoulder. He still had his Kalashnikov in the other hand.

"Drop it, Yegor," Callen snapped. He didn't specify which the man should drop. Both would be good.

Instead, Yegor turned slowly around, pointing the barrel of his gun down. "Don't shoot me, man," he said in English. "You got plenty money there, and that stone. Belyakov's dead. I don't want the stone, just enough money to get home, set myself up."

"You can't take that much cash out of the country," Callen said. "And I can't let you leave with it. We're federal agents, and you're under arrest."

"Arrest for what? Defending myself?"

"Just put them down," Callen said. "The money and the gun."

"You'll have to sh—" Yegor began.

The sound of a gunshot drowned out the rest of his sentence, and the force of the round blew a hole the diameter of a golf ball in his forehead, ejecting blood and brain matter as it passed through.

Yegor pitched forward, landing on the money bag and rolling off.

Behind him stood Faulk, with a Glock in his left hand and a Kalashnikov in his right.

"If that guy was green," Deeks said, "I'd think he was the incredible Hulk."

"Or the Jolly Green Giant," Kensi added. "Ho, ho, ho, indeed."

35

"Federal agents, Faulk," Callen said. "Put the guns down."

"Yeah, I heard," Faulk said. "You arresting me?"

"If you play your cards right, we are," Sam said. "I'd recommend you drop all that hardware before any of us feel threatened."

Sam could see the big man considering his options. He had a half-smile on his face, as if somebody had projected the Mona Lisa on a hairless giant. His eyes were shifting this way and that as he debated the merits. His guns were pointed toward them—if he squeezed the triggers, he'd hit somebody.

But he would almost certainly not hit everybody, and whoever was left standing would kill him.

He rolled his shoulders forward, almost as if he were weighing the guns along with his options. Then he leaned forward and put both guns gently on the floor. "I guess you win. Whoever the hell you are."

Callen moved forward, shoved the guns aside, then held out a hand to his companions. "Handcuffs? Maybe two pairs? I'm a little short."

"Right," Deeks said. "Undercover. Here." He handed

a pair to Callen, and followed it with some zip ties. Callen went to work cuffing the man. He looked like he could snap the chain with a single flex, but in less than a minute, Callen seemed satisfied. He shoved the man down in a chair. "Wait there, Faulk," he said. "Don't try anything stupid. Seriously. We'll be right back. You know where Shogren went?"

Faulk shrugged.

"His shrug moved the chair," Sam said.

Callen nodded. "Yeah, he does that."

"How many are left?" Kensi asked.

"There's—" Callen started.

A burst of gunfire cut him off. Rounds sprayed into the room, hitting Faulk in the face and throat, and making the others duck. Callen and Sam returned fire, but the shooter had bounded off the stairs and out the front door, firing as he went.

"—Shogren!" Callen finished. "Come on!"

He started for the door. "Anyone else?" Sam called as he chased after.

"Yeah," Callen said. "There's also—"

A second enormous man charged out of the opposite doorway. This one had a thatch of dark hair, a five o'clock shadow, and a glowering expression, and he wasn't quite as big as Faulk. Sam remembered him from the strip club. He had barely fit in the chair.

"—Pasha!" Callen cried.

The man bore down on him like an oncoming freight train. If he had any weapons, Sam didn't see them. But Callen was already racing at full tilt for the front door, and between his momentum and Pasha's, collision was inevitable.

Callen tried to veer away at the last second, but Pasha flung out an arm that would have made an ape proud, snagging him. They both went to the floor, Callen on the bottom.

Sam swung his HK416 like a baseball bat, catching Pasha squarely in the head. The blow rocked him a little, but not enough to get him off Callen.

"We'll get Shogren!" Kensi called. "Come on, Deeks!"

Sam nodded and they tore out the door. He threw an arm around Pasha's neck and tried to haul him away from Callen. No dice. The guy was not only gigantic, he was strong.

And silent. Sam realized he hadn't heard the man make a sound.

"Come on," he said, yanking again.

Nothing.

He had his hands on Callen's throat. Callen's face was turning purple.

"Man, I don't want to do this," Sam said. "Just get off him, okay?"

Callen's face was darker, and his hands were flailing uselessly at Pasha.

"Last chance," Sam said.

Pasha ignored him.

Callen wasn't looking good.

Sam put his gun on the floor, went into the living room.

And came back, carrying a coffee table made from heavy wood. He ran with it tucked under his arm, front end forward like a battering ram.

The impact knocked the huge Russian sprawling. For good measure, Sam tossed the table down on top of him, and he lay still.

"I'm not even *trying* to cuff him," Sam said, helping Callen to his feet.

"He's small time," Callen managed. His voice was a frail croak. "Shogren's the one we need."

He started toward the door, then stopped, turned around. Sam almost reached for him, afraid he'd had a dizzy spell, but Callen stepped back into the living room. "The other money bag's gone," he said. "Shogren's on the run, and he must have the money."

"Kensi and Deeks are on it," Sam said.

"I want to be there," Callen said. "Let's go. We'll call a cleanup team to come in and sweep up here."

Sam thought about arguing, but decided it was pointless. Callen was right. Everybody left in the house was either dead or hurt so badly they'd wish they were. Shogren was the mastermind, if anyone involved in this operation could be called that. And he was the only one who'd gotten away with what he'd come for.

"I'm with you," Sam said. "He can't be far."

Together, they raced out the door.

36

The black Hummer was gone.

Kensi and Deeks ran down the driveway, and found it at the bottom, stopped where the way had been blocked by Kensi's and Sam's vehicles. They approached it cautiously, guns ready. The windows were so dark that Shogren could be hiding inside and they wouldn't be able to see him from here.

Kensi took the left side, Deeks the right, and they reached the rear door at the same time. Nothing. Deeks peered inside, saw Kensi through the glass doing the same. No Shogren. They moved as one up to the next row of seats, then to the front.

Empty.

They met again in front of the vehicle. "You know," Deeks said as they walked to the automotive blockade they'd set up, "I never really understood why they called those 'Hummers.' I mean, it's a stretch from 'high-mobility, multipurpose wheeled vehicle' to 'Humvee' in the first place. But having made that stretch, why not leave it there. 'Hummer' has a certain sexual connotation to it, that—"

"You just answered your own question. The sexual

connotation is probably precisely why they went with that name." She changed the subject abruptly, as Deeks had noticed she often did when the subject was one he'd raised. "You think he's on foot?"

"Unless he had a getaway vehicle of some—oh, hey." A man sat on the pavement, and when he looked up at them, Deeks recognized him as Hugh Peabody. His glasses were broken, his nose and mouth bloody. What looked like a woman's purse lay on the ground beside him.

"Mr. Peabody?" Kensi said, rushing toward him. "What are you doing here? What happened? Are you okay?"

"You're pelting, Kensileena," Deeks said.

"I'm *pelting*?"

"Maybe one question at a time, that's all I'm saying." She helped Hugh to his feet. "Who did this to you?"

"It was that little wretch Hal Shogren," the man said.

"Not so little anymore," Deeks observed.

"What are you doing here?"

"We were almost at the place you said to meet you, Agent Blye, but then you took off. Betsy said to follow you, in case the photographs she found could help you. And in case you'd found out any more about Susan. I've never driven so fast in my life."

"What happened?"

"We caught a glimpse of you going inside. Betsy said we oughtn't bother you, but that we should wait until you came out so she could give you the pictures. We were just sitting in the car when Hal came screaming down the driveway in that black monster. He stopped when he saw how you'd parked, then saw us sitting across the street. He came over, yanked open my door, punched me right in the face, and threw me down on the street. Then he tossed a big bag in the back seat, got in beside it, pointed that big gun of his at Betsy, and told her to get behind the wheel and drive. Then she did the damnedest thing."

"What was that?" Kensi asked.

"Hal told her to pitch her cellphone, or something like that, so she threw her whole purse at me and drove away."

"She threw her purse at you?"

"Weird," Deeks said. "Most women never want to be away from their purse."

"And she doesn't even have a cellphone," Hugh added. Slowly, a smile spread across his face. "Unless…"

He opened her purse and rummaged inside for a few seconds, then came up with a fistful of photographic prints. "The pictures," he said. He handed them over.

"She thinks on her feet," Deeks said, impressed. "I love that in a woman. Or, you know, anybody."

"She's always been one smart cookie," Hugh said. "Smarter than me by a country mile. What's he going to do to her, Miss Blye? I don't know what I'd do without her."

"Don't worry, Mr. Peabody," Kensi said. "We'll get her back. We won't rest for an instant until we do."

Deeks got the car's license plate number from the man—he couldn't remember it, but Betsy Peabody had it written on a tag attached to her keychain—and called in a BOLO alert. Within minutes, every law enforcement officer in Los Angeles County would be on the lookout for the vehicle and Shogren and Betsy.

And, of course, the warning that Shogren should be considered armed and extremely dangerous.

He was just finishing that when Sam and Callen

came down the driveway. Callen was carrying the tablet in a black bag, and Sam had a money bag over his shoulder. "What's up, Deeks?" Sam asked.

"Shogren's gone. He's got a car and a hostage."

"A hostage? Who? How?"

"Who's that old guy with Kensi?" Callen asked.

"Pelting. It's the nation's singular shame," Deeks said.

"What?"

"Never mind. That's Hugh Peabody. Julianne Mercer's father. The hostage is Betsy, his wife. Julianne's mother. Except Julianne is really Susan Peabody."

"Was, anyway," Callen said.

"Is, was. I'm not picking sides here, but I'll just say, a lot of folks don't believe anyone's ever really gone. She might have shuffled off this mortal coil, but she's still Susan somewhere. She is to her parents, anyway."

"Too deep for me," Sam said. "You call in a BOLO?"

"Every cop in the land will be on the lookout," Deeks answered. "And the old man delivered some photographs his wife turned up, of the Shogren family's cabin in the Hollywood Hills."

"Those might come in handy," Sam said.

"Or the cabin might have burned to the ground by now," Callen added.

"Or that. Still, it's a place to start. Wonder if Owen's still up there?"

"Last I heard," Deeks said. "By which I mean, about three minutes ago, when I talked to Nell about the BOLO."

"He been in contact?"

"Not so far. She said his phone's still moving around, but they can't reach him."

"I hope he's okay."

"He's Owen Granger. He's not going to let some little thing like an enormous conflagration bother him."

"Deeks is right," Callen said. "If anybody knows how to take care of himself, it's him. We need to focus on Shogren."

"Yeah," Sam agreed. "Let's get this stuff to Ops, and see if we can locate the cabin in the old guy's photos."

37

By the time Granger had all three horses loaded into the trailer, the inferno was so close he could see individual embers floating ahead on the flame-generated wind. The horses were understandably nervous. So was he.

He climbed back into the truck's cab, and saw his useless mobile phone sitting there. Hetty would be furious that he hadn't checked in, or worried that he'd perished in the fire. More likely, both at once. He glanced over at Stacey's little ranch house, the exterior mostly covered in native stone, and the lines stretching from it to wooden poles. She probably had a landline in there, he realized. A little late to think about it, but better than after he'd driven away. He shut off the engine and ran to the house.

The front door was locked. He hurried around, found a back door with glass panes. Also locked. From the looks of it, the fire would be here soon, and he'd seen no sign that anyone was on the way to stop it. If the house was doomed, a broken window wouldn't matter. She had a couple of chairs and a little table outside the back door, on a kind of patio made from rough-edged bricks. Granger snatched up the table and rammed a leg through the pane closest to the doorknob, then used it to clear away the jagged shards clinging to the edge. Tossing it aside, he reached through and turned the knob.

The door opened into a kitchen. The house looked to have been built in the 1950s, and the appliances looked like the original ones. This was Stacey's getaway, not her fulltime home, so he imagined she didn't cook here often, and when she did she probably thrived on the challenge the practically prehistoric appliances offered.

The phone was on the kitchen wall, beneath a hanging cupboard. It was a Trimline phone, salmon pink, with a coiled cord that probably stretched twenty feet or more. He grabbed the receiver and held it to his ear.

No dial tone. He punched the plunger several times, to no avail. For all he knew, the thing was a period piece she kept around for the sake of irony, and hadn't been connected in decades. He hung up and went back out. No time left to search the house for another telephone. Anyway, chances were good that even if the phones worked, the lines were down.

He checked the refrigerator, and found four plastic water bottles. The power was out, but they were still relatively cool, and water was water. A quick look in the pantry revealed a half-full box of protein bars and a jar of peanut butter. He grabbed those and the bottles.

He raced back to the truck and keyed the engine. It started right away, but with a ragged stutter and a vibration he didn't like. He wondered if the thick smoke was interfering with the motor's air intake. One more thing to worry about. He was already concerned about running out of gas, since he hadn't driven the old truck enough to know how far it could go on a tank, and filling up out here would be impossible.

The road to Coldwater Canyon was dirt, carved out through thick brush and closely spaced trees— exactly the terrain wildfires loved to burn. It wasn't maintained by the county, and was pretty rough, but he'd negotiated it with ease on his way in. Coldwater would offer the quickest way down the hill, so he headed out the same way. It was about two miles to the pavement. He took it slower than he had earlier, because of the horse trailer, but he'd be there in a few minutes. Relief was already starting to settle in. Stacey's beloved mountain hideaway wouldn't make it, most likely, but the horses were more important to her, and he had fulfilled the obligation where they were concerned.

The dirt road curved toward the south, and here the smoke was so dense, it was like driving through a brown fog mixed with gritty snow. Ash and embers flew by, and Granger took to using the wipers now and then to keep the windshield clear enough to see through. After a quarter mile or so, the road straightened again, heading due west, until it ended at Coldwater. Almost there.

But when he rounded the last bend, he had to hit the brakes.

A burning pine had fallen across the road. Beyond it, the fire was already charging up the hill. There was no getting through here. Even if he could pull off the road and go cross-country, around the tree, he couldn't drive through those flames without risking his own life and those of the horses. Regardless, the brush was too thick to try that. He couldn't even pull off the road far enough to turn around.

There was nothing else for it. He had to back up—

with the horse trailer attached—for more than a mile. Reversing a trailer was never Granger's idea of a good time; the fact that he had never pulled this particular trailer until about ten minutes earlier made it worse. He knew the rules, though. He imagined that the top of the steering wheel was the trailer's front end, and the bottom its rear. Then he had only to steer with one hand on the bottom, in order to make the wheel's direction correspond to the direction he wanted the trailer to go.

In this instance, the other cardinal rule was the more difficult of the two: Don't hurry.

Rushing it would likely have one of three consequences. Either he'd jackknife the trailer, or he'd ram it into the truck, or he'd force it off the road and into the heavy brush. Going slow, however, was a challenge when the fire was closing in on him from the front.

He took a deep breath and shifted into reverse. Hand at the wheel's bottom, he started backing up, making the minute adjustments necessary to keep the trailer on the road. There were places where it was wide enough to accommodate two vehicles at a time, but not many of them, and as he neared each one, he gauged and determined that it was still too narrow to turn around. A little at a time, then, he backed the trailer up, all the way back to Stacey's gate. There, he cranked the wheel hard and backed through the gate, which he hadn't bothered to close. Then spun it the other way. The dirt road continued past Stacey's place. He didn't know where it went, or if it would dead-end or head straight into the conflagration, but it was the only option left to him.

The only option he would consider, anyway. He could, he supposed, abandon the horses and strike out on foot. Or he could stay put and wait to die.

Neither of those worked for him.

He didn't know where he was going, or if the road would lead to a way out of the hills.

He hoped it would, though.

And sometimes hope was all a person had left.

38

"What do you think?" Kensi asked. "Can you identify the site?"

"Well, the thing is," Nell said, "we don't exactly have a database of random rock formations. I know it seems like sometimes we can work miracles—"

"Because you do."

"—but what we do isn't really magic. We're fortunate enough to work with the latest and greatest technology—sometimes so new it hasn't even been offered for sale yet, and sometimes it's stuff developed in-house—but it's not like we can summon data out of thin air. The data have to go in before they can come out."

"Have?" Kensi asked.

Nell eyed her quizzically for a moment, then figured out what she was asking, and nodded. "Data is plural," she said. "Datum is singular. And really, pretty much useless. If you don't have data, plural—and the more, the merrier, as they say—you really don't have much of anything."

"Makes sense, I guess, but—"

"But it doesn't help you find Hal Shogren and his hostage."

"I thought you only finished Eric's sentences."

"Oh, no," Nell said. "I'm an equal opportunity sentence-finisher."

"She really is," Eric chimed in. "Especially if someone makes her nervous."

"Do I make you nervous?" Kensi asked.

"Oh, no, not you." Nell brought her thumb and forefinger together, then opened a gap about a millimeter wide. Then a little more. "Maybe just a tiny bit."

"But I'm here," Eric said. "And I make her nervous enough for both of us."

"I'm not sure I'd call it nervous," Nell said.

"I could speculate about other adjectives," Eric said. "But Hetty's been pushing those sexual harassment rules lately."

As if manifested by the sound of her name, Hetty appeared in the Ops Center. "For good reason, Mr. Beale," she said. "For one thing, we're employees of the federal government, and we need to exemplify the highest possible standards. For another, they're just the right thing to do. No one should be made to feel uncomfortable or threatened in the workplace. In fact, I wish they were a little more strict."

"More strict in what way?" Eric asked.

Hetty pursed her lips and touched her chin. "Well, I wouldn't mind if they prevented men from wearing kilts at all."

"That would be discrimination," Eric countered.

"Perhaps. But they do—in spirit, if not explicitly— ban the wearing of kilts commando-style."

Eric laughed, but he was blushing a little at the same time. Nell, on the other hand, was positively crimson.

Hetty swiveled toward Kensi. "No luck locating your cabin?"

Kensi shrugged. "Like Nell said, there's no database of random rock formations. And I'm sure those hills are full of them."

"No doubt. There are no clues to the location other than the formation in the background?"

"Not that we've been able to ascertain," Nell replied.

"The Peabodys thought the Shogren family owned the cabin, rather than rented," Kensi explained. "But from what they said, that would have been in the mid-nineties. A big batch of land records from that era were lost in a computer glitch—some kind of Windows NT four-point-zero crash, I guess. There are still lawsuits ongoing over who owns what. The Shogrens are both dead, so they aren't part of that, but we can't even find anything showing them as owning any land up there, so either they just rented, or their ownership is lost in that glitch."

"We'll keep analyzing the photos, and try to come up with some other angle," Eric said. "But nothing has presented itself yet."

"Do we know that Mr. Shogren and Mrs. Peabody went into the hills? The fire is still raging and the area remains under an evacuation order."

"We don't know that for sure," Nell said. "All we have is this."

As she spoke, she tapped some keys, and an image appeared on the big screen. It was a traffic camera still showing the Peabodys' Buick, making a right turn from Ventura Boulevard onto Valley Vista. Only Betsy Peabody was visible in the shot, her knuckles white on the wheel. In the background, smoke could be seen.

"That is fairly convincing," Hetty said.

"That's what we thought," Kensi agreed.

"Do whatever you have to," Hetty instructed. "But find them, and bring that poor woman home to her husband."

"You doing okay?" Sam asked.

Kelly Martin had his feet up on the arm of the couch. At least he'd taken his boots off, Sam noted. There was a tall, empty glass on the floor beside him, and a crumpled bag that had once held trail mix by that. Across from him, the TV was tuned to a reality show that seemed to involve people screaming at each other. Many of the words they used were bleeped.

"Couldn't be better."

"We're making progress. We have the tablet back, and only one of the contractors is still on the loose."

Martin sat up. "Really? Which one?" He read Sam's face in an instant. "Never mind, don't tell me. Shogren."

"Bingo."

"That guy's a real piece of work."

"You got that right."

"What are you doing to find him?"

"Everything we can. G and I are on our way to talk to someone who used to know him. Kind of hard to find people who know him now when the guy's officially been dead for years. Just figured since we were in the neighborhood, we'd stop in and make sure you're okay. Anything you need?"

"My life back? A girlfriend? A million bucks?"

Sam thought about the cash he had delivered to the OSP earlier. A million bucks was the most feasible of his requests. Still not something Sam was empowered to grant. But at least he'd had it in his hands, just hours earlier. He slapped Martin on the shoulder. "We're doing what we can, man. Hope to have you back in your own life soon, okay?"

Martin let out a sigh. "Yeah, I know. I appreciate it, brother."

"Just hang tight. Soon as we have this wrapped up, we'll let you know."

Outside again, Callen said, "Brother? I didn't know you guys were so close."

"We're both SEALs. That's a bond of brotherhood that doesn't end."

"Three of those contractors were Special Forces," Callen pointed out.

"Not SEALs. Makes a difference."

"So you trust Kelly Martin implicitly? Because of that bond?"

"With my life," Sam said.

Callen tilted his head and eyed his partner. The sun was high in the sky and the day was another scorcher, but the guy was hardly sweating. "Really? With your life? You don't even know him."

"Doesn't matter. You don't get to be what he is without having a core of steel."

"People change," Callen said. They'd reached the car, and Callen opened the passenger door. "People change, and they disappoint, and sometimes they seem to be something they're not."

Sam shot him a grin. "I trust you with my life, G. And you spend half your life being someone you're not."

"You're pretty good at it yourself."

Sam slid in behind the wheel, and Callen took his seat, buckling in. "What can I say?" Sam asked with a grin as he started the car. "We get paid to have ongoing identity crises."

"Better than being actors, I guess," Callen said.

"They have to do the same thing, but we get to shoot guns and chase bad guys."

"So do actors, sometimes. But it's all make-believe for them. At least we get to deal in reality once in a while."

Sam pulled away from the curb and started down the street. "Let's see what the reality of someone who served with Hal Shogren is like. Pretty dark, would be my guess."

39

Kelly Martin was beyond bored.

When he'd retired, with his full military pension, Bobby Sanchez had ridden him without mercy. He was a warrior, and when a warrior had no war, he had nothing. He'd play a lot of golf and get fat, Bobby had said. Or he'd sit on a couch, watching TV and drinking beer, and get fat. Somehow, Bobby's worst-case scenarios always involved Martin getting fat.

Martin had argued that he would stay busy—and stay in shape. He had plenty of buddies in the private sector, and some of them were raking in three and four times what the Navy paid. He could always get a job, if it came to that, and make his ultimate old-age retirement that much more secure. Or he could write a book—lots of Spec Ops guys were doing that, these days, and cashing some pretty nice checks. He could play sports. He could take classes, get an advanced degree. He could travel the world without having people trying to kill him in every port.

Okay, that part hadn't yet turned out to be true. In fact, most of it hadn't.

It had only been a few months, though. He worked

out every day. He took a few trips, saw some friends. He caught up on movies and books he'd missed. Once in a while, he provided security for a buddy who owned a nightclub, and that gig netted him a few under-the-table bucks and plenty of hot ladies.

But as the weeks became months, he'd started to think Bobby was right. More and more, he found himself staying home, fiddling around in the yard, binge-watching some TV series, scrolling through photos of his SEAL days. It didn't take much imagination to picture him winding up just like he was here in the safehouse: eating junk food and watching daytime TV, until it was night and the nighttime TV came on. A few hours of sleep, and he would get up and start another day just like the one before. The one after that would be more of the same.

It was no life for him. Hell, he'd have been better off letting those guys kill him at the Sea Vue than existing like this. The hours dragged by, painfully slowly and dull.

Being cooped up in the safehouse made it even worse. He'd been instructed not to reach out to friends, not to leave the house even to sit in the backyard. But he wasn't used to letting other people fight his battles. Bobby had been right. He was a warrior, and he wasn't good at anything else. He needed to stay in the game.

Sam Hanna had said that his team were professionals, with law enforcement authority. They'd treated him well. And from what Hanna said earlier, it sounded like they were good at their jobs. They'd found Shogren, Wehling, Brower, and Faulk—the guys who'd killed Bobby—and recovered the stolen Sumerian tablet, all in an impressively short time. It only seemed like forever because of his own circumstances.

They were good at their jobs, but not perfect. They'd let Shogren get away. And it had been clear, even back in Ramadi on that fateful night in 2007, that Shogren was the boss.

Which meant Shogren was the most responsible for Bobby's death.

Shogren was out there, and he was stuck in here, like a fish in an aquarium, without so much as a plastic diver or a treasure chest.

He glanced over at the TV and saw a red BREAKING NEWS banner at the bottom of the screen, and he watched the words scrolling by…

Betsy Peabody had never been so frightened.

There had been times in her life she had thought she'd experienced fear as bad as it could possibly be. The time she'd been pregnant with Susan and come down with pre-eclampsia, which her OB/GYN warned her could be fatal to her and the baby. They'd both survived, but it had been touch-and-go for a while. Then there was the time she'd had a late-night phone call from a police officer, informing her that Hugh had been in an automobile accident and was heading into the operating room.

But as terrified as she'd been on those occasions, she had been able to reassure herself with the fact that no one was actively working against her. Those had been uncontrollable events, but without human malice behind them. Even Hugh's accident had been due to a patch of black ice on the road. He'd lost control of the car and rolled three times, down an embankment. The only other people involved were the police, emergency workers, and doctors, and they had all been focused on saving Hugh.

This time was different, because she was at the mercy of an evil man with a gun, and she knew—down to the very core of her, she was certain—that he would rather find an excuse to kill her than a reason to let her live.

She had never liked Hal Shogren, from the first moment she'd met him. When she'd been growing up, boys like him had been called hoods. They were tough guys who favored white undershirts and leather jackets, who slicked their hair back, and probably carried switchblade knives. The first time she'd seen Hal, who'd come home from school with Susan, he hadn't been dressed like that, and she doubted he had a switchblade. A .45, maybe.

But the attitude had been the same. Even at that age, he acted like the world owed him something, and he had every intention of collecting. No matter who got in the way, or who got hurt.

She'd been afraid, then, that it would be Susan who got hurt, because it was obvious from the start that she was taken with him. Betsy didn't understand the appeal. He wasn't sensitive in the least. He was arrogant, narcissistic, and cynical far beyond his years. He spoke constantly about who had it in for him, who was out to get him, and what he'd do to them if they tried. Betsy had considered them nothing but fantasies, albeit extremely violent ones, full of vivid descriptions of what would amount to torture if he'd actually followed through. Somehow, Susan had found it romantic. She supposed Bonnie Parker had felt the same way about Clyde Barrow, and look where that got her.

She'd tried to warn Susan about him, but sometimes talking to a teenage girl about the danger posed by a boy only pushed her faster and harder into his arms.

And that scared her, too, because having survived Susan's gestation and infancy and at least the first part of her adolescence, she could see her only daughter drawn into his sphere of influence, like a dinghy being sucked into a whirlpool, and when everything she and Hugh had tried to do to dissuade her had failed, there was nothing left but surrender. Susan was tugged into the whirlpool, and the hand she'd extended had been batted away. Then there was nothing to do but watch and mourn.

Now her worst fears for Susan had come true. She lay on a slab in a morgue somewhere, and it was Shogren's fault, as surely as if he had pulled the trigger. As if that wasn't enough, now he did have an actual gun pointed at her, and his finger was once again on the trigger, and she knew it wouldn't take much to convince him to pull it. The moment she stopped being useful to him would be her last.

He told her where to drive, and she drove there. She tried to go fast, because he said to, but not so fast that she attracted the attention of the police. Every time she saw a police car, she was tempted to try to signal, even to crash into it. But that wouldn't save her. The car could be surrounded, escape impossible, but he would still kill her before he let himself be taken.

Because he had recognized her almost at once, and he had never liked her.

She and Hugh had been sitting in the Buick, waiting for Agent Blye to come back out of the driveway they'd seen her and the other agent going up. Hugh liked the big bands channel on the satellite radio, so they'd been listening to that, loud, and it was so hot out that they had the engine running so the air would keep blowing. If there was any noise from inside the house, they hadn't heard it.

But she was sure there must have been, because of what happened next.

The big black military-style truck had careened down the driveway, coming to a screeching halt when the driver saw that the exit was blocked. He had sat inside it for a full minute after that. The motion of the vehicle had caught her attention, so she was watching, wondering what it was all about. When the driver didn't get out, given the way he'd approached, she suspected he was considering whether he ought to try to ram his way through. Then he decided against it. He opened the door and climbed down, and Betsy felt her heart speed up. Then he reached back in and brought out a long black duffel bag, and that gun, and she grabbed Hugh's leg hard enough to leave marks.

Already, by that point, she feared that it was too late—that the man's path and hers were on some kind of collision course. She tried to look away, hoping he wouldn't notice them across the street. But it was clear that he had, and as he stalked directly toward them she realized who it was. Her grip on Hugh's thigh might have broken the skin at that point. He was aware of what was happening by then, and trying to start the car. But of course it was already running, and all he was doing was grinding the engine.

"That's Hal," she said.

"What?"

"Hal Shogren. The boy Agent Blye was asking us about."

"Doesn't look like a boy."

"Well, he's not anymore. Susan's not a girl, either."

"Susan's dead," Hugh reminded her.

She lost what was left of her composure then. "Do

you think I don't know that?" she cried.

Hugh started to say something in response, and at the same time tried to put the car in gear, having figured out that the engine was already engaged. But Shogren had reached them. Betsy finally thought to lock the doors, but too late. He yanked Hugh's door open and punched him in the face, without warning. Hugh cried out and fell against her. She caught his shoulders and tried to hold onto him, but Shogren got a grip on his shirt and hauled him from the car, sending him sprawling into the street. Hugh's glasses flew off and skidded across the pavement, and she could see then that the first blow had broken them. Hugh's face was cut and bleeding, and she started to scream, hoping to attract the attention of Agent Blye.

Or really, anyone.

But no one came. It was just her and Shogren, and he had a gun that looked wicked, like something forged in the fires of Hell, and there was blood all over his clothing and spattered on his face, and she knew it wasn't his blood. He shoved his bag into the back, sat down, pointed that gun at her, and growled, "Get behind the wheel."

"I won't," she said.

"Do it now, or I'll shoot your ass and take the car anyway."

She looked at Hugh, still sprawled in the street, pawing for his glasses. She knew if she didn't do what Shogren said, he would kill her and then, realizing that Hugh was a witness, kill him, too. He couldn't know how blind Hugh was without his glasses. Even with them, he never would have recognized Shogren if she hadn't named the man for him.

The only way to keep Hugh alive was to do what he

said. She scooted awkwardly over the center console and settled in the driver's seat. Then she thought of the pictures she had come so far to deliver to Agent Blye.

Those, she reasoned, were her only hope. Hugh would get the pictures to Agent Blye, and Shogren would take her to his family's old cabin, and Agent Blye and her colleagues would show up in the nick of time to save her life.

That was unlikely, even on TV. But she clung to it anyway, because she had to hold onto a glimmer of hope. Hugh had always called her his "incurable optimist." She embraced the tag; she hadn't wanted to be cured of optimism, after all. Optimists, she thought, considered optimism a positive trait.

So he directed her and she drove. When they neared a police roadblock, at the base of the hills on the Valley side, he told her to swerve down an alley instead. At the end of that alley, he told her to cut across the street, into the next alley. Three blocks later, the alley connected to a dirt road. She complained that the Buick wasn't made for dirt roads, but he said it was a good American car and could take anything thrown at it.

She wasn't so sure. But he was the man with the gun. So she tried to swallow her fear, which grew worse when she realized that he really was telling her to drive straight into where the fire blazed, and she put her foot on the gas and she drove.

40

Calvin Meadows had an office on the lot of Continental Pictures. The studio had once been one of Hollywood's biggest names, but the industry had changed and Continental hadn't always changed with it. Now the backlot had been sold off to real estate developers, and tall buildings loomed behind the remaining office buildings and sound stages. Having faced its near-death experience and survived, the business had finally adjusted to the new era of entertainment, and had become a major source of streaming programs for multiple online outlets.

Just as at the few big studio lots remaining, there was a gate with a uniformed guard. Callen and Sam waited in the line of cars while the guard chatted with a pretty blonde driving a red Tesla sedan. Eventually, she drove off with a three-fingered wave, and the guard got to work again. He checked their IDs and gave them directions to Meadows's office.

It was a pink building, which didn't narrow it down much, since almost all the buildings on the lot were pink. It was behind Sound Stage 14, which narrowed it down, as the sound stages were lined up along a single road, odd numbers on the left and evens on the right. The confusing part was that 14 was on the left.

It struck a chord of memory somewhere in Callen's brain. "I think I heard something about that once," he said as Sam swung the car around the huge building. "There was some kind of disaster on stage thirteen, maybe back in the forties or fifties. A fire or an explosion, something like that. One of the studio's biggest stars was killed, along with a few lesser luminaries. The powers that be decided it was because they'd had the temerity to paint the number thirteen on the end of a building, so they painted that out and made this one number fourteen."

"Might have made more sense to fire the pyrotechnics team," Sam said.

"Welcome to Hollywood."

Meadows's building had a sign on the front that said "Merrill & Sons Productions." Sam laughed when he saw it.

"What's funny?" Callen asked.

"Army Rangers like to trace their lineage to General Frank Merrill, who commanded the World War Two unit that became known as Merrill's Marauders. They were part of the Burma campaign. They fought their way through some of the toughest jungle on the planet, battling the Japanese every step of the way. They're legendary in military history. So the "Merrill" is Frank, and the sons are the rest of the Rangers."

"I've heard of them," Callen said. "There was a movie, right?"

"A classic. Merrill deserves to be remembered. So do his men. It's quite a tradition to live up to."

He eased the Challenger into one of the parking spaces in front of the building. Because this was

Hollywood, the red Tesla was already parked and plugged into a charging station.

Inside, a Japanese-American receptionist greeted them—proving, Callen figured, that old enemies could come together. The kid was probably in his twenties, and it was possible that he'd never heard of Merrill or his Marauders and had no idea what the company name meant. But since the company was owned by an ex-Ranger, Callen suspected that every staffer heard the story sooner or later.

Sam badged the kid, whose name, according to a nameplate on his desk, was Leo Nakamura. "Here to see Mr. Meadows," Sam said.

"You have an appointment?"

"Yeah. We told him we were coming over, and we'd see him when we got here."

"He's very busy," Nakamura said. "I can check with—"

A door opened on the far side of Nakamura's desk, and a tall African-American man smiled across the way at them. "It's okay, Leo. Come on in, Agents."

He was slender and handsome, with the kind of smile that impressed with its sincerity and made people want him to smile more. It wasn't until Meadows had introduced himself, shaken their hands, and they were all seated in comfortable leather chairs in a corner of his expansive office that Callen realized that both legs and his left hand were prosthetics. They moved almost like natural limbs, and didn't seem to inconvenience him in the least.

Meadows noticed him noticing. "DARPA is my favorite government agency, not counting the Rangers," he said. He raised his left arm, scratched his head with electronic fingers, then lowered it again. "It's not the same as my own, but it's close. I think it, and the arm does it."

"You get it in the sandbox?" Sam asked.

Meadows nodded. "IED. I was dismounted. Happened to so many of us. I was lucky enough to be wearing ballistic boxers, so my—anyway, that's enough about that. You didn't come here to talk about my junk."

"We came to talk about Hal Shogren," Callen said. "You served with him, right?"

Meadows sighed. "The Rangers is a great organization. 'Rangers Lead the Way' isn't just an empty motto. Most of those who serve in it are among the finest people anywhere. But you know what they say, there's a bad apple in every batch, or something like that."

"Shogren was a bad apple?"

"Nobody could tell, at first. He was just one of the guys. Distinguished service record. Tried out for the Rangers, made the cut, got through Ranger School with high marks. It wasn't until we were under fire that I saw anything wrong."

"What'd you see?" Sam asked.

"Just little things, at first. He'd maybe hang back a little when the rest of us were pushing ahead. You want to stay close to your battle buddy, to have his back and make sure he has yours. But Hal didn't always seem to do that. He acted like he expected everybody to have his back, but he didn't have anybody's."

He considered his next words carefully, the prosthetic hand rubbing his chin just as a biological one might have. "Then it got worse. In combat, people sometimes lose themselves, right? They lose the best parts of themselves, anyway, and it's hard to get that back. So they do things that they never would've imagined, never would have done back in the world.

Shogren was that way, too. He was a hell of a marksman, but I saw him take shots he didn't have to—shots that would kill slowly, instead of fast. I tried to tell myself he'd just missed the sweet spot, but I couldn't convince myself after a while. Then there were rumors of other things. Worse things. Torture, maybe rape. I don't know for sure, but that's what some people said."

"Were you there when he died?" Sam asked.

"No," Meadows replied. "I'd already been wounded. I was either in a hospital in Germany, or in Walter Reed. I wish I could be clearer, but a lot of that time is still a little fuzzy. I know he had left the Army by then, and gone to work for one of those contractors offering beaucoup bucks for Special Ops soldiers."

"Given what you'd suffered, a little fuzzy is probably an understatement," Callen said.

"What I heard is that he was riding in an MRAP. They had a makeshift Rhino out front—literally, a toaster on a long pole. It was on all the time, generating heat, to try to set off heat-triggered IEDs before the vehicle itself was in range. But this time, it didn't work. Everybody in the vehicle bought it. Shogren was reportedly one of them."

"Reportedly?" Sam repeated.

"Like I said, everything's a little vague. Somebody told me once that they'd seen him after that. That he wasn't in the MRAP at all. There had been rumors that he had money, that sometimes he paid other guys to take his place on missions. I didn't necessarily believe it. A lot of guys look alike when they've been in the shit for a few weeks. Everybody's dirty and unshaved and it's not hard to mistake one guy for another. Plus, I might have dreamed the whole thing. He got shipped home and buried, right, so I guess it must have been him."

"How long were you in the hospital?" Callen asked. Not that it had anything to do with Shogren, but he was curious about the man's remarkable recovery.

"Three years. And, you know, I still see a doctor and a shrink, but now I can afford ones in private practice."

"Looks like you've done pretty well," Sam noted.

"I came out here because a buddy from the Rangers recommended me to consult on a movie about the war. I did that, then took on some other consulting gigs. Eventually, I started to produce. Got a couple of features out, and now I have two TV shows." He gestured toward posters hanging on the rustic wooden walls. "*Bionics* is a physical challenge show for vets who have prosthetics—kind of meant to prove that we can do anything anybody else can do. And *Homeward Bound* is a drama about military families on the home front during what we used to call the Global War on Terror." He grinned, and once again Callen was struck by how infectious it was. "There's talk of an Emmy nomination for *Bionics*. Can you believe it? An old soldier like me, chewed up and spit out, bringing home one of those little statues?"

"Congratulations, man," Sam said. "I hope you win."

"You and my momma both," Meadows said.

"Let me ask you this," Sam continued. "If Shogren was alive, do you have any idea where he'd be? Where he'd go if he was in trouble? Who he might turn to?"

Meadows's smile faded. "No clue," he said. "Like I told you, I was out of it when he died. If he did. And he wasn't part of the unit anymore. So I don't know who his friends were, there at the end, if he had any. I remember being kind of glad, when I heard it, that he wasn't a Ranger anymore. That's petty, right? I'm a miserable excuse for a human being."

"Not at all," Sam said. "Unit integrity is key. Can't have that if you've got someone who's not pulling his weight. That puts everybody else at risk."

"Yeah, I guess so," Meadows said, his gaze downcast. Then he looked up again. "Hey, this doesn't have anything to do with what they're talking about on the news, does it? Something about an ex-Spec Ops soldier on the run, with a hostage?"

"Couldn't say," Callen said. "Would it make a difference if it did?"

"Only in how much sorrier I am that I can't be much help. If that's Shogren and he's still alive, all I can say is that I hope it's not for much longer."

"If that's him," Sam said, "you wouldn't be the only one who feels that way. Thanks for your help, Mr. Meadows."

"I'll walk you out," Meadows said. "Any excuse to show off my parts."

"Sounds good," Callen said. "And good luck with the Emmys. We'll be watching."

41

"A helicopter?" Deeks asked.

"What?" Kensi replied, looking at him in surprise. They were, after all, at a helipad and a helicopter waited on the pad, props spinning. Her hair was in a ponytail, but his wasn't, and he was starting to look like he sometimes did when he woke up, when it seemed like he'd styled his hair with an eggbeater. "You've been in choppers before."

"Ooh, chopper. That's a better word. Or maybe 'copter. Or what about whirlybird?"

"Call it whatever you want. Are you coming, or not?"

"If you're going, babe, I'm going. I'm just saying, flying in a whirlybird on a nice day is one thing. But flying over a mountain range that's basically entirely on fire is something else altogether. I thought they'd actually closed it to helicopter traffic, because of—and I'm quoting the TV weather infant here—'treacherous updrafts.'"

"They did," Kensi said. "But Hetty pulled some strings and got us cleared."

"So basically clearance to kill ourselves in a ball of flame that, in light of the incredibly more huge ball of flame formerly known as the Hollywood Hills, won't even be visible to anyone except possibly us. Until the point that our eyeballs melt."

"You can look at it that way, Deeks. Point is, we need to get going. We don't have all day."

"No, I suppose if we're hurtling toward our doom, we should do it while the light's good."

She'd had enough. She stalked toward the waiting aircraft. The pilot sat in it, watching, and when she started to climb in, he gave her a big grin and a thumbs up. "He coming, too?" he shouted.

"As far as I know," she replied, strapping herself into a rear seat. "But don't wait for him."

"You're the boss," he said. He opened up the throttle and started pulling up on the corrective. When Deeks saw the helicopter lifting off the pad, he ran toward it, waving his arms.

"Okay," she said. "Let him on."

"Roger that," the pilot said. He set the bird gently down, and held it there while Deeks clambered aboard.

"Welcome," she said. She had to shout to be heard.

"I thought you were going without me."

"I thought that's what you wanted."

"I told you, I go where you do."

"I thought that was hyperbole."

Deeks took her hand and squeezed it. "Kensilicious, it's one hundred percent true. Never leave me behind."

It was a touching moment, but badly timed. "Fasten your harness," she said. "We're going." She tapped the pilot's shoulder and jerked her thumb skyward. He grinned again, nodded once, and put the bird in flight.

"Why are we doing this, again?" Deeks asked as they raced toward the mountains.

"We're looking for a rock formation," she said. "Doing it from the air is a lot more efficient than on the ground. Particularly when the area's closed to vehicular traffic."

"I'm sure that's true," he said. "But it's also closed to helicopteral traffic, and that's not stopping you."

"It's the efficiency part," she said. "I don't know if we'll be able to find it, but we have a far better chance from up here. While we're at it, we should keep our eyes open for a gold-colored Buick LeSabre, and a red pickup truck, possibly pulling a trailer."

"The Buick belonging to the Peabodys," Deeks said. "And the pickup?"

"Being driven by Owen Granger, presumably."

"Oh. Then we should definitely watch for that one."

"We will." She pointed toward the pilot. "He already has the GPS coordinates for where the truck is. Or was, a little while ago. If he moves much, Ops will let us know."

"But no GPS for the Peabodys' Buick?"

"I think we're lucky it's not horse-drawn," Kensi said. "I'm not sure where the boundaries of 'Luddite' are, but I bet they're borderline."

She settled back and watched the pilot. He seemed to have absolute control over the aircraft. He held the cyclic steady, plunging forward as Los Angeles whipped by beneath them. Every now and then he adjusted his path slightly with the foot pedals. As they closed in on the hills, the air shifted from clear to brown-gray, and the stink of smoke filled the craft. "Sorry," the pilot called back. "Nothing I can do about the smell."

"We'll cope," Kensi replied.

Deeks was quiet, watching out his window at the city below, occasionally glancing forward at the thick clouds of smoke. He wasn't as neurotic as he came off sometimes, she knew. If he had been, she never could have fallen in love with him. It was in part a comedy shtick for him, and it had worked so he clung to it. And it was in part a persona he put on that helped him deal with stress.

The job they did was about as high-stress as they came, and everybody had to deal with it in their own way. She found that it fueled her, gave her energy that she had to burn off with action. For him, the sometimes goofy persona deflected it. When he let it fall, as he had now, he was calm even in the face of things that would terrify most people.

He'd been right, they were flying into a seriously dangerous situation. The updrafts made it hard enough to fly low over those hills at the best of times. During a massive wildfire was far from the best of times. The winds the fire generated could topple a helicopter right out of the sky, and the best pilot on Earth couldn't do a thing about it.

But Shogren was up there somewhere, with Betsy Peabody. Owen was there, too, and the fact that he'd been there so long without getting in touch implied all manner of things Kensi didn't want to think about.

The 'copter carved through the smoke like a hot Mixmaster through butter.

"Where to first?" the pilot called back.

"Head for those GPS coordinates you were given," Kensi told him. Owen was a survivor, and she was worried sick about poor Betsy Peabody. But because they had a good idea where Owen was, it made the most sense to take care of that first, then do the more difficult search.

"Roger that," the pilot said. He corrected course slightly, skimming over the luxurious homes of

Beverly Hills. The Beverly Hills Hotel passed beneath them, and then they were in the hills. The streets were weirdly empty. She understood—even here in the lower elevations, homes had been evacuated until the fire could be brought under control. She saw police cars prowling for looters, and staging areas for the firefighting crews. Then they were over the Franklin Canyon Reservoir, its water level far below the historical average. Despite that, until helicopter flight had been discontinued, choppers had been scooping water from the reservoir and dumping it on the flames.

Past the reservoir, the smoke was thicker, and she could only see glimpses of rugged hillsides, latticed with dirt roads. The aircraft lurched and bounced. Kensi didn't have problems with airsickness, usually, and she loved the fast rides at Magic Mountain, but this was getting to her. The pilot's back and shoulders were tense, the muscles in his neck standing out like steel cables. When he called "Getting close!" he didn't turn his head, as he'd done before, but held it rigid as he fought the controls.

"Any update on the GPS coordinates?" Kensi asked Eric over the earwig. He read off some numbers, which she reported to the pilot. He made another minor course correction. Approaching a ridgeline, he pulled up on the corrective to get some more altitude, but a powerful updraft caught the blades and heaved the helicopter higher. On the other side, it plummeted until the pilot got the descent under control.

"Sorry about that!" he called. "Now you know why they're not letting helis up here anymore."

"Did you call it a 'heli'?" Deeks asked.

"Yes, sir," the pilot said. "I usually use 'helicopter,' but sometimes I abbreviate it."

"Not chopper?"

"Choppers are motorcycles. Or teeth."

"Whirlybird?"

"Maybe pilots called them that fifty years ago. But I wasn't flying fifty years ago."

Deeks turned to Kensi. "Not choppers. Helis."

"I heard," Kensi said.

The aircraft started sinking again, slowing down. "Are we there?"

"Just about," the pilot said.

"Take it as low as you can. We're looking for a red pickup truck. Maybe towing a trailer."

The pilot nodded. All of his focus was on the controls, and Kensi was fine with that. The winds were batting them around, like a kitten lying on her back playing with a ball of yarn.

She watched out her window, and noted Deeks peering through his. Smoke hung in tendrils between the aircraft and the ground, and when it got low enough, the downwash caught the smoke and blew it into circular shapes that looked a little too much like targets for Kensi's liking.

The pilot spotted it first. "Red truck, dead ahead!" he shouted.

Kensi rose up in her seat as far as her harness would allow, and saw it through the front windshield, climbing a ridge on a primitive dirt road. It looked just as Hetty had described it, and it was indeed pulling a horse trailer. "That's got to be it! Let him know we're here, and try to get into a position where I can see the driver."

"Will do." He took the craft down lower and buzzed the top of the pickup, kicking up clouds of dust from the road. A little ways beyond it, he made a wide turn, approached the truck again, then hovered ahead of it.

Kensi and Deeks both looked out the windshield, and saw Owen Granger sitting at the wheel, an expression of deep annoyance on his face.

"That's him," Deeks said. "And we've pissed him off."

"There's no place to put down, so I hope you're not expecting to pick him up," the pilot said.

"No. I doubt he'd come, even if we tried. He's as stubborn as they come. But I need to get this to him." She held up a heavily padded cloth bag.

"Just toss it out the cabin door," the pilot said. "But make it quick, I can't hold her here much longer." Even as he spoke, he was gaining altitude, and furious winds were buffeting the aircraft.

Deeks was closer to the door. "Here," Kensi said. "Toss this down in front of the truck. Not so close that he'll run over it, though."

"What is it?"

The helicopter gave a sickening lurch. "Hurry!" the pilot shouted. He pulled up, and the aircraft rose still higher.

"Just do it!" Kensi said. "Before we get too high!"

Deeks took the bag, opened the cabin door, and gave the bag a gentle toss. They were maybe forty or fifty feet off the ground now, higher than Kensi had anticipated, and she hoped the padding in the bag was sufficient.

As Deeks closed the door, the helicopter lurched again, and started to turn. The pilot fought to control it. "We—we're gonna have to get out of here," he said. "These updrafts are gonna kill us!"

"Does that mean we can't do the rest of the search?" Kensi asked.

"Sorry. Later, after the fire's out, I'll fly you anywhere you want. But the safety of this aircraft is my responsibility, and the risk is too great."

Disappointment washed over Kensi. She was glad to have seen Owen, although the danger he was in was all too apparent. But she hated the idea of flying away without locating Betsy. She felt responsible for the woman's predicament; if it hadn't been for her suggestion, the Peabodys would have been nowhere near Shogren when he went on the run.

The helicopter was still climbing, but the winds were chasing it, lashing at it. The pilot pushed the cyclic and they started to pick up speed, heading back toward the city and out of the hills. "Okay," Kensi said, though she knew her permission made no difference. She had to let the pilot make the call. She'd have risked almost any danger to find Betsy Peabody and Hal Shogren, but she couldn't let him risk his livelihood and his life.

Deeks took her hand, seemingly reading her mood. "It's okay, babe. We'll come back on the ground. We'll find her, don't worry."

Nice words, she thought, *but empty ones*. Yes, they could come back in ground vehicles. It would still be a dangerous business, but they wouldn't be endangering anyone other than themselves.

But there were hundreds, if not thousands, of homes in those hills. Some were in high-end developments, others scattered in relative wilderness. And for the most part, they were empty, because of the evacuation orders.

Shogren and Betsy could be in any of them.

How did you find a needle in a haystack when you didn't even know which haystack to search in, and the whole farm was ablaze?

42

Granger stopped the truck and climbed down from the cab.

That had looked a lot like Blye and Deeks in the helicopter, but the downwash from the rotor threw up so much dirt it was hard to be sure. Then someone had thrown out an object, which had landed just off the road a dozen or so yards ahead of him. Since it hadn't exploded, he had to assume it wasn't a bomb. He walked along the right edge of the dirt road, scanning the fringe for whatever it was. Finally, he spotted a gray cloth bag with a knotted drawstring. It wasn't covered in road dust and ash, so it was most likely whatever had been thrown.

He picked it up, undid the knot.

Inside was a satellite phone. On the side was a sticky note, in Hetty's distinctive handwriting. All it said was, "You never call."

Granger smiled, for what might have been the first time in the last twenty-four hours or so.

He walked back to the truck. The sun was pounding down on the hilltop, the smoke only filtering it so much and doing nothing to mitigate the heat of the day. The truck's cab was the only shade available. He'd stopped running the air conditioner, to save fuel, so shade and water were his only friends.

He dialed Hetty's direct line, and she answered right away. "Owen. Good of you to get in touch."

"It's been a little difficult, Hetty. There aren't exactly a lot of payphones around here, and no cellphone signal at all."

"I know all about it," she said. "Are you all right?"

"Hot and filthy," Owen replied. "And hungry. But otherwise I'm okay."

"And the horses?"

"They're fine, too. I'm sure they're thirsty. Water's kind of at a premium, as you might imagine. I've found some empty houses with garden hoses, so we're doing okay, but we're being conservative."

"How safe are you?"

"Fine, for the moment, but I have to keep trying to outrun the fire. I'm above it, now, but it's hard to stay that way because fire climbs."

"I'm well aware. Can you get to Mulholland from where you are?"

"I'm not sure. I don't think I'm very far from it, but I'm traveling on dirt roads. It's been a while since I've seen blacktop, or any kind of road sign."

"According to Ms. Blye, you're about three miles south of it. Keep going north, and you'll get there. Mulholland is closed on both sides of you, because the fire has crossed it, but there's not much on the road's surface to burn, so you might be able to get through in either direction."

"That's what I'll shoot for then."

"And, Owen?"

"Yes, Henrietta?"

"I hate to ask—"

"But you will anyway."

"Well, yes. There have been a number of developments in the case that revolves around the murder of Navy SEAL Bobby Sanchez, the attempted murder of former SEAL Kelly Martin, and the shooting of LAPD officer Tony Scarlatti. I'll spare you the details, but the crucial point is this: the only remaining suspect is somewhere in those hills, and he has a hostage, an elderly woman who is tangentially related to the case. They escaped in her gold Buick LeSabre. Please keep an eye out, and if you see them or the car, let us know immediately. Don't be a hero, Owen. The man is Hal Shogren, a former Army Ranger and what's colloquially known as a really bad dude. I'm sure you're beyond exhausted. If you see them, just give us a location and we'll do the rest."

"I'll watch for them, Hetty. I can't promise more than that. I've been hauling these horses around for a long time; I don't want them to die of thirst now that I've rescued them from the fire."

"I'm not asking you to promise more than that. And, Owen?"

"Yes?"

"You're a good friend. I don't know what the owner of those horses ever did for you, if anything. But whoever it is owes you big-time."

"I'm working off a debt that can't ever be repaid, Hetty. This is just a small token."

"You've risked life and limb. I'd say the debt is settled, whatever it is."

"Thanks for the phone drop," Owen said.

"You're welcome. I can't get another helicopter in there until the fire's more under control, or I'd have you airlifted out."

"I can't leave the horses behind, anyway."

"I never thought for an instant that you would. Keep in touch, Owen."

"I will. Got to be moving again now, though. The fire's headed up the hill."

"Get out of there, then. Get to Mulholland. That's your best chance at this point. And, Owen? If you find yourself in a corner, let me know. I'll extract you, one way or another. Promise me."

Owen looked at the trailer, heard the horses shifting around inside. Could he leave them, if there was no other choice?

That was a hypothetical, though. He thought he knew the answer, but he couldn't say for sure unless he found himself in that position. Until then, he would do everything possible to avoid it.

"Gotta go, Henrietta. Thanks for the phone."

"Stay safe!" he heard her say as he lowered it from his ear and disconnected.

"I'm trying," he said to the empty cab. "I'm doing my best."

Betsy wasn't accustomed to taking orders. Sometimes Hugh tried, but long years of training had taught him to phrase them as suggestions or requests, and he always got better results that way.

But when Shogren issued a command, she did her best to obey instantly. Every time he barked something out, her heart leapt in her chest and her breath caught. She never knew which moment might be her last, which directive she might respond too slowly to. The higher into the hills they climbed, the shorter she expected her lifespan to be. Surely he didn't need her to drive anymore. There were no more roadblocks, no passing police cars. There was nobody. There were only flames and smoke and emptiness all around. Why keep her alive at all, at this point?

They'd found pavement and were making good time up the hill when he suddenly snapped, "Pull over! Off the road, under those trees!"

Startled, she almost lost control of the car altogether. She managed to brake, though, and crank the wheel to the right. She saw the trees he meant, a few feet from the blacktop. Cautiously, she left the road and drove across the dirt shoulder to them. "Stop here?" she asked. Her voice sounded foreign to her, quaking and timid, a stranger's voice.

"Yes, damn it!" he shot back. "Here! Shut off the engine!"

She came to a halt and turned the key. The shade was a blessing, but she was sure that wasn't why he'd told her to pull over. A minute later, she heard what he must have sensed long before. A helicopter, flying low over the hills.

Now she understood. If they'd been on the road— the only thing made by man that was moving for miles in any direction—they'd have been easy to spot. He couldn't have that, couldn't take a chance that the helicopter wasn't law enforcement of some kind. Smoke screened them from most aerial observation, but from the sound of it, the helicopter was traveling close enough to the ground to have seen them.

As it turned out, it never even came over the crest of the mountain. It was steady for a while, as if sitting still, then it moved away quickly in the opposite direction. Only long after its sound had faded to nothingness, at least to her ears, did he tell her to start the car again.

He got out of the backseat, stretched his legs, then got into the front passenger seat. He was still holding the gun. A couple of minutes after they were back on the road, he spoke in a calmer tone of voice. "You look awful familiar," he said. "Do I know you?"

Was it possible that he hadn't recognized her and Hugh? She'd been certain that he had, probably right from the start. The fury he'd shown in punching Hugh and hurling him to the street made her think he knew then who he was dealing with, and was expressing some long-held rage at them.

She didn't think he'd let her live, either way. But if he hadn't taken her because of who she was—if she meant no more to him than a hostage to get him past the authorities—then her chances might be ever-so-slightly improved. And she'd thrown her wallet out of the car with her purse, so as long as he didn't search the glove compartment and find the vehicle registration and insurance paperwork, there was nothing to give her away.

"I don't think so," she said. "I can't imagine how you would."

"I don't know. You seem familiar."

"I think I just have one of those faces."

That time, her voice had taken on an almost squeaky quality, she was so nervous. Could he tell she was lying? What would he do to her if he found out she'd known him all along? How much worse could he make things for her?

That was a question to which she didn't ever want to find out the answer.

She tried to console herself with the knowledge that at least Hugh was safe. If he'd still been with them, he would have tried to do something, and would have gotten himself killed. As it was, he'd been banged up but not seriously hurt.

That consolation only went so far, though. If he was indeed edging into dementia, as she was convinced, who would take care of him? Who would share his memories, store them for when they were lost to him? Who else knew his habits, his likes and dislikes? Steak medium well, no onions in the salad or the potatoes, coffee strong, with sugar. Who would laugh with him at corny old movies and contemporary rom-coms, when he was the oldest in the theater by at least a couple of decades? He would be lost without her.

Somehow, she had to make it out of this alive. She didn't know how—that seemed the most hopeless task she could set for herself. But so much depended on it. If making sure Shogren never knew who she was would help, she would become somebody else entirely.

But, but…

Hugh liked silly comedies, but her tastes ran more to cop dramas, the grittier the better. And she had seen enough of them to know one thing about hostage situations—if TV shows and movies could be believed—the key to getting through it was to make the hostage-taker see you as a human being, not as simply a means to an end.

She had to try to appeal to him as a person, but she had to do it without letting him know the person she really was.

Well, she thought, *here goes nothing*.

"Now that you mention it," she said, "I suppose we should get acquainted." She racked her brain for a name. "I'm Katherine Hep… umm, Hepworth."

"I don't need to know your name, lady," he said.

"It looks like we'll be spending some time together. I'd

rather you called me 'Katherine' than 'lady.' Or 'Kathy.'"

"I'll call you whatever the hell I want."

"That works, too, I guess. I don't see any reason to be antagonistic, that's all. I mean, we're more or less in this together now, aren't we?"

"There's no together here. There's me, and I'm the guy with the gun. And there's you, and all you have to do is drive and keep your yap shut. Think you can handle that?"

"Well, I'll certainly try."

"Good. Start now."

She shut her yap. Hard to tell if that had been at all productive. But he hadn't shot her, so that was something.

Anyway, talking made her marginally less nervous. She felt more confident at the wheel, now, more secure in the knowledge that he still wanted to keep her around, for the moment.

It wouldn't last, she knew. But it was a start.

43

Callen and Sam rode in one vehicle, Kensi and Deeks in another, and in still others were officers from the LAPD and the Los Angeles County Sheriff's Office. The ones the NCIS agents used were Forest Service vehicles, designed for the rugged landscape, and loaded with emergency provisions.

Hetty had told them about her conversation with Granger, and Sam was relieved to know that he was okay. For the moment, at least. Fire crews were doing the best they could, given the conditions. Hot, dry, and windy were ideal for spreading fires, not so good for fighting them. But on the ground they were cutting firebreaks, setting backfires, doing everything they could to contain the blaze. In the air, though conditions were too hazardous for helicopters, air tankers were still able to drop loads of retardant.

Watching the red gunk billow out of an airplane was an impressive sight; equally impressive was the chemical mix that included fertilizer, so the retardant would not only cool and slow the fire's advance, but help the landscape recover from the inferno.

"Do you like fire?" Callen asked.

"That's kind of out of left field," Sam said. "I guess in limited quantities, sure. Candles at the dinner table are romantic. So's a fire in the fireplace on a cold night. Or a good fire to get the coals lit in a barbecue grill."

"You're not a propane guy?"

"Propane's okay. Nice even burn. But nothing beats the taste of something cooked over charcoal or wood."

"Hot dogs on the grill," Callen said. He might have been salivating a little.

"Yeah," Sam agreed. "Tubes of mystery meat, but so good." He remembered what the original question had been. "But this much fire? No. Fire's scary stuff. It's like when nature gets angry, she might throw a hurricane or a tornado at you. But when she's really pissed, just enraged, then it's fire. The way it can just roll over everything in its path, incinerating whatever it touches. Fire gets its mitts on you, you might survive it, but you're never gonna be the same."

"That's how I feel too," Callen said. "Still, there's something fascinating about it. A primitive fascination, probably. The way it's never the same, from one instant to the next. If you're watching a flame, there's just no predicting what shape it'll have five seconds from now. I think if I could watch a wildfire from a safe vantage point—and know that it wasn't actually damaging the ecosystem it was tearing through—it'd be more interesting than any movie."

"Sometimes it's good for the ecosystem," Sam pointed out. "It's a natural force, after all. It thins out forests so trees can grow bigger, helps certain kinds of seeds germinate. In the moment, it's destructive, but in the long run it's healthy."

"Tell that to Bambi."

Sam chuckled. "Well, Bambi's kind of a special

case. Being a cartoon and all."

Before Callen could respond, Sam heard Eric's voice in his ear, and knew that Callen did, too. "Guys," Eric said. "I have some bad news."

"What is it?" Sam asked.

"I just scanned the video feed from the safehouse. It's been kind of crazy in here, so I know I should have been looking more often, and I'm sorry. Our guest has checked out."

"He's gone?" Sam said.

"I backtracked until I saw him leaving. Ninety-six minutes and fourteen seconds ago, give or take."

"Give or take," Callen echoed.

"But you're tracking him, right?" Sam asked.

"Yeah… no. I had him on a couple of traffic cams, but then lost him. Somehow he ditched that tracker you put on him, Sam."

"He's a pro," Sam said. "Probably knew it the minute I planted it."

"Let us know if you pick him up again, Eric," Callen said.

"I will. Sorry again for losing him."

"Like I said, he's a pro," Sam said. "If he didn't want to be kept, there was no keeping him."

When Eric was gone, Callen said, "Any idea where he'd go?"

Sam tilted his chin toward the vista ahead of them: a forest laden with smoke, flames faintly visible in the higher elevations. "I know just where he'd go."

"You think?"

"Sure. Dude's a warrior. Shogren killed his swim buddy, or is responsible for it one way or another. That calls for payback, and he doesn't want it to be second-hand."

"I guess you'd know."

"Yes," Sam said. "Yes, I definitely would."

He'd had enough of sitting around.

Maybe he would never serve in uniform again—though any of the services would probably try to find a place for an ex-SEAL, if he pushed it—but that didn't mean Kelly Martin was used up. After he did what he meant to do, he would have violated every oath he'd ever taken, and he wouldn't be able to bring himself to put on a uniform again.

But he had to do it. Loyalty demanded that he take action. The warrior's code allowed nothing less. And he no longer had to worry about being killed if he went home. He flushed the tiny tracker Hanna had planted on him, left the safehouse, and went to the nearest major road. There he was able to flag a cab. At his place, he loaded a pack with weapons, ammunition, binoculars, and the gear he'd need for a couple of nights in the woods. He had a car stashed in the garage, so even though he'd left his primary ride in Texas, he had wheels.

He knew he was taking a risk. The fire was far from contained, for one thing. If the NCIS agents spotted him, they just might shoot him to save themselves the trouble of detaining him again. And if he found Shogren, then of course Shogren would try to kill him.

And his chances of finding Shogren were slim to none. The TV news had said he was believed to be holed up in the hills somewhere, with a hostage. They described the gold LeSabre, and showed a picture of the hostage, an old woman whose name was meaningless to Martin. There had to be thousands of homes in those hills, most them empty, and still more wilderness where a skilled Ranger could easily lie low for days or weeks.

None of that mattered. He would find Shogren or die trying. If the authorities found the Ranger first, they would try to take him alive. Maybe they'd succeed, though that seemed unlikely. In that event, he would watch the trial bitterly, knowing that Shogren would probably die in prison and not by his hands.

If *he* found Shogren first, the outcome would be different.

Maybe this was really what he'd trained for, worked for, fought for his whole life. The opportunity to avenge his best friend's torture and murder. He had loved Bobby like a brother. Strike that—Martin had a brother, and they didn't get along very well. He loved Bobby more. In the end, Bobby had given him up, but that wasn't his fault. The guys who'd tortured him were also Spec Ops, also trained in resisting torture, and therefore skilled at administering it. They had caused Bobby unimaginable agony, then they'd killed him.

And Shogren was the ringleader.

Shogren had to pay.

He had to die, and Martin had to kill him. It was as simple as that, really. Life, in its purest essence, was the process of dying. You started dying the moment you were born, and when you were finished, however long or short a time you'd had, you'd succeeded in doing the only thing every living being really *had* to do.

Martin was determined to push Shogren to succeed right away.

When he got to the hills, he found one roadblock after another, and a robust law enforcement presence. He'd been up in those hills before, raced down the length of Mulholland Drive, which he believed was one of L.A.'s most magnificent wonders. Looking at them from this angle, though, he felt weighted down by the impossibility of the task he had set himself. They were so big. There were so many places to hide. He was one man.

He had only one slim advantage: Shogren was on the run, hiding out from everyone and everything he had ever known. Martin knew exactly how that felt. He knew what he would do.

He took to the smaller roads, and found an unstaffed roadblock. It was a simple enough matter to move the barricades, drive through, then replace them.

He was inside the perimeter.

Time for a little search and destroy.

44

Deeks was driving, for a change.

Kensi preferred to drive, but Kensi was an odd combination of control freak and chaos witch. She thrived on what would appear, to an ordinary human being, to be an absolute lack of organization. To her, though, it all made sense. Her legendary messes were like complex spells that bestowed magical powers on anyone who could understand them. And woe be unto anyone who dared disturb them!

By the same token, she liked to drive because it bothered her not to have her hands on the wheel, not to choose the vehicle's speed and direction. It had probably driven her nuts to be a passenger in the helicopter earlier, reduced to giving the pilot verbal instructions rather than just taking the stick and flying it herself.

When they traveled in her car, she insisted on driving. But this old thing wasn't hers. It was a Forest Service 4x4 that had 214,000 miles on it. Judging from its performance, most of those had been hard miles, maybe climbing uphill over boulders and trees. It reminded Deeks of some mules he'd heard about, who didn't want to get going but then once in motion, didn't want to stop.

And it was a kick to drive on roads closed to all other vehicles. He swerved back and forth, from his lane into what would ordinarily be oncoming traffic, then straddled the center line, weaving this way and that.

"What are you doing?" Kensi asked.

"I'm enjoying freedom."

"Freedom? That's what freedom means to you? The ability to drive like a toddler with one of those fake steering wheels that straps onto the back of the front seat?"

"I don't think they make those anymore, Kens. I haven't seen them for a long time, anyway."

"Sure they do," Kensi said. "They're just a lot fancier than when I was a kid. They have electronics now, and—"

"Wait, you had one of those?"

She met his gaze, just for an instant. "Watch the road," she said.

"For what? We're the only vehicle on it."

"Bears, then. Or deer, whatever."

"Bears. I'm watching for bears, now."

"Anyway, yes, I had one. It didn't do anything, though. Well, it turned. And the horn beeped, for a while. Until one day it was cracked. I guess it only beeped when it was airtight."

"So you think you just beeped it so many times that it cracked?" Deeks asked. "Or do you think maybe your dad took a razor blade to it, because you were driving him nuts?"

"I'm sure he didn't…whoa. I never thought of that. Do you really think that? A man would take a razor blade to his beloved child's favorite toy?"

"Stranger things have happened."

"I don't believe it. I can't."

"Denial is a river—"

Kensi cut him off. "Don't say that. It's the stupidest thing there is."

"Oh, you think? There are a lot of contenders for that title."

"You probably know all of them. You probably comb the internet looking for the stupidest things someone could possibly say, just so you can say them. But not now. Not while I'm having a parental identity crisis."

"Parental identity? You know who your dad was."

"I know *who* he was, but if he slashed my car horn, I don't know *what* he was. Some kind of a monster? Maybe he had multiple personalities."

"I'm just kidding, Kensi. I'm sure you just wore it out. You probably punched it too hard. You always did have a good left jab."

"Maybe," she said.

"I'm positive."

"How could you possibly know?"

"Because I know you. And you're wonderful. Therefore, your father was too good a man to do something like that to his loving daughter."

Nell's voice sounded in their ears before Kensi could respond. Deeks hoped that whatever it was would distract Kensi from the whole business about the horn, because he had dug himself in so deep he couldn't even see the sky anymore. "Calling all cars," Nell said. "Calling all cars. Sorry, I always wanted to say that."

"What's up, Nell?" Kensi asked.

"I might have something for you. You said the Peabodys lost track of the Shogrens, years ago, and the Shogrens pretty much disappeared from the radar.

Well, it took a while, but I managed to track them down. They moved to a town called Geneva, Alabama, near the Florida Panhandle. I'm reading between the lines a little here, but it looks like they went because Woody Shogren's father was ill. I can't find any real estate transactions, so either they rented from a private party, or they lived in the father's home. Anyway, he died, and not long after that, Woody and Dinah divorced. She married a cosmetic surgeon she met in Florida, who—get this—had a practice in the Valley. They came back to L.A., and after a year or so, bought a home off Coldwater Canyon."

"Small world," Kensi said.

"No joke. I guess she really likes it there," Nell continued. "Anyway, they lived there in wedded bliss for about two years, when he divorced her and married one of his patients, who he had turned into a kind of living Barbie doll."

"Yuck," Deeks said. "That's really putting the plastic in 'plastic surgery.'"

"What happened to Dinah then?" Kensi asked.

"She traded up. She's currently married to a Wall Street investment banker, and living in the Hamptons, in a house that's been featured in *Architectural Digest* twice."

"Nice work if you can get it," Deeks said.

"Exactly. Point is, the house in the hills is empty. It's been for sale since they split up, but you know what real estate's been like. Hal Shogren was already in the Army when all this happened, so neither of the stepfathers adopted him, and he never changed his name. But chances are good that he visited his mom when she was back out here as Dinah Spellman. Now she's Dinah Douglas, or Dinah Shogren Spellman Douglas, or whatever."

"So where is this empty house?" Kensi asked.

"I said 'Calling all cars,' but I was really just calling you, because you're the closest to where he saw it."

"Okay," Deeks said. "Where do we go?"

"It's complicated," Nell said. "Get to Mulholland, and I'll direct you from there."

"Roger Dodger," Deeks said. "Over and out."

"Like I was saying," Kensi said. "The stupidest things."

"Turn here," Shogren said.

Betsy eyed the road. "Where? There aren't any—"

"There!" He pointed, throwing his arm right across her field of view. She batted it away.

"Use your words," she said.

"Just make the turn."

"That's not much of a road. More of a path."

"It's wide enough."

"Do you know where you're going?"

"Do you always ask questions? Just do it."

She slowed, flipped down the left turn signal—not that anyone was around to see it—and swung onto the narrow track. He was right, it was wide enough for one car. Not for two, but there were some turnouts where somebody could pull off and let another vehicle pass.

She wouldn't need to use those, not today.

She felt like she'd been driving all day, pulling off the road whenever aircraft flew overhead, taking side roads any time Shogren thought there might be Forest Service personnel or firefighters out. She had breathed in so much smoke she thought her lungs must be at least dark gray. Sometimes they'd gone right by flames, so close she could hear the roar and feel the heat. She was more than ready to get out of the car.

After about a half mile, the road met a perpendicular one that was still dirt, but considerably wider and more frequently used. "Which way?" she asked.

He studied for a moment. "Right."

She turned right. "I hope you know where we're going."

"You don't have to worry about that," he said.

"Mister, you threw my husband out of our car, pointed a gun at me, and kidnapped me. I think I have a right to worry about anything and everything."

"The only thing you have to worry about is doing what you're told," he said.

"Why? Why do you even still need me? There's nobody up here. The fire's still raging, and wherever you're taking us is probably going to burn down while we're there. So what good do I do you now?"

She was taking a chance, she knew. If he decided she was right, he might just kill her now. But if his natural opposition to everything she said held true, he would defend his decision not to have killed her yet, and in so doing, be arguing in favor of keeping her alive. Once he had taken that position, she hoped, he would have a harder time reversing course.

"God, you talk a lot."

"I talk when I'm nervous. Forgive me for being a little on edge."

"There's a driveway up there, see? On the right? Turn in there."

"Is this your—" Betsy caught herself just in time. She'd been about to say "your parents' cabin," but that would have given her away. Instead, she shifted gears. "—your place?"

"It doesn't matter to you what it is, or whose place." He spoke the next words slowly, as if she were a first-grader. "All. You. Have. To. Do. Is. Drive."

"I'm driving! I'm just curious. And like I said, nervous."

"We're there," he said. "Turn!"

"I'm turning."

Two stone columns flanked the driveway. A stone gargoyle sat at the top of each one. The one on the right seemed to be laughing, and the other was scowling fiercely. Beyond them, the driveway arced around to come to a stop in front of a beautiful contemporary house, mostly glass, it seemed, and white where it wasn't. It swept along the curve of the hillside, graceful as a bird in flight. Most of it was elevated off the ground, adding to the birdlike aspect; at ground level there was just a door, with a full-length window beside it.

"Okay," he said.

"Okay, this is where we're going?"

"Am I speaking English? Yes, this is where we're going."

"Can I get out of the car? Because I really have to pee."

"Like I need to know that. There are bathrooms inside."

"Does the water work?"

"How the hell would I know?"

"If this is—"

"What?"

"Never mind," Betsy said. "Are we going in?"

"Yes," Shogren said. A pile of logs, at least a cord and maybe more, were stacked against a low wall across the driveway from the house, underneath a slanted roof. He picked one up, carried it across the drive, and hurled it through the big front window, shattering the glass. "Yes, we're going in."

45

"This would be so much faster from the air," Callen said.

"Yeah, but you heard what that helicopter flight was like," Sam replied. "No way to fly low enough over these hills to really search until the fire's out. Or at least considerably smaller. We're getting satellite imagery all the time, wherever the smoke is thin enough. If he's up here, we'll find him."

"Even with all the bodies looking, it could take weeks to check out every corner of these hills. If he's here, he's not going to stay long. He had an escape route ready before any of this started. They all did, we know that. He just needs to hole up until it's time to go. Then he'll be out of the country, probably to someplace with no extradition to the United States."

"He thought he was conducting a simple transaction," Sam reminded him. He was driving the light-green Forest Service pickup on a pavement covered with so much white-gray ash it looked like a dirty snowfall. "If it had gone according to plan, he could have chilled in a fine hotel for a couple of days, until departure time. He wasn't expecting to be on the run, with every cop in the county looking for him. He had to change plans in a hurry. So he's gone to ground, probably someplace he's familiar with. He'd want to know the ways in and out, know the neighborhood so he could spot anything that looked out of place."

"I get it, in theory," Callen said. "I'm just not sure the theory is right. What if he came up here, then changed his mind and went to the beach? Or back to someplace like the Sea Vue, where nobody asks questions?"

"He still has the hostage," Sam said.

"Unless he's killed her and dumped the body."

"Granted, that's a possibility. But even if he did that, if he came back into the city, we'd have picked up the car."

"Unless he stole another one."

"There are always going to be other potential scenarios, G. We can't check out all of them. Best we can do is go with what seems to make the most sense, given the facts we know. We know Betsy Peabody was still driving the car when it turned up this way, out of the Valley. We know the car hasn't shown up on camera again since then. So we proceed on the assumption that they're still here in the hills, until we know something definitive that contradicts those facts."

"Yeah," Callen said sullenly. He agreed with everything Sam was saying. At least, on the surface. But he couldn't shake the feeling that Shogren was too smart to do what made the most sense for him. He would change it up, somehow. The trick was figuring out how.

Probably, Callen figured, what was upsetting him was not the futility of searching the whole of the Hollywood Hills—at least, those parts not currently ablaze, which narrowed it down quite a bit—but his own failure to nab Shogren at Belyakov's rented house. He'd genuinely believed that Belyakov hadn't told any of his men that he was undercover. He thought he'd convincingly played the part of a Russian tough guy. Granted, it had all had to happen quickly, because they hadn't known when the deal was going down. And as it turned out, they'd pulled the switch just in time; twelve hours later and it would've been done.

His guess was that Belyakov had let something slip to Yegor when they'd been drinking together by the pool the night before. Yegor was no fool, and with his background, no doubt a suspicious sort to begin with. Belyakov might have said something he hadn't considered dangerous, and Yegor had put it together with his naturally distrustful outlook. Callen didn't know what he could have done differently, to ensure a better outcome, and that still bothered him.

He hadn't intended for all those men to wind up dead. That had always been a possibility, even if he hadn't been involved, because of the nature of the transaction. But if his presence had not made it almost inevitable, it had certainly upped the odds.

And then Shogren had escaped, with millions of dollars and a hostage—whose daughter, not incidentally, Callen had just shot to death on an L.A. street. It was no wonder, he decided, that he felt so jaundiced about the whole affair. It was the kind of thing that the acronym SNAFU had been coined to describe.

Finding Betsy Peabody alive and reuniting her with her husband would help improve his outlook. Arresting Shogren and ensuring that he faced justice for his many crimes would, too. But even those results couldn't bring the dead back to life, or heal Deeks's friend Tony Scarlatti.

Callen wasn't predisposed toward depression, although sometimes he wondered if there was a darkness at his center that was responsible for his seeming inability to form lasting romantic relationships, his preference for solitude over company. Sam Hanna was the best partner he'd ever had—maybe the best friend, too—but still, there were plenty of times they parted ways at the end of the day that he was glad to be seeing Sam's back. Certainly Callen's early life had not been something out of a storybook, unless perhaps one written by Charles Dickens or filmed by Tim Burton. That kind of upbringing doubtless had long-term psychological ramifications, and Callen was still dealing with those. Always would be, he guessed.

Fortunately, a call from Eric Beale interrupted his thoughts before they could veer any further toward the morose. They were using Earwigs, because the cell service had not been restored yet. They had satellite phones for backup, but for the moment, the Earwigs would do.

"Guys," Eric said, "I have a possible lead."

"What is it?" Callen asked, anxious to hear some good news.

"You've seen the Peabody pictures, right? The cabin with the unique rock outcropping behind it?"

"Sure," Sam said. "We have 'em on our phones."

"Right. Well, I consulted with a UCLA geologist who's been studying the Hollywood Hills for decades. He narrowed those pictures down to one of two locations. He can't be certain which it is, he said, because so much of what you can see in the photographs is determined by the lighting, the time of day, the weather, and so on. But both sites are relatively close together, and not that far from where you are now."

"Is there a cabin?" Callen asked.

"I've been looking at satellite imagery," Eric replied. "One has a small, rustic house that could be described as a cabin. The other has a much bigger house, but it's also newer—built sometime within the last decade, anyway, and probably more recently than that. I've been trying to find historical imagery of that precise location, to see what was there before the house, but so far, no luck."

"How do we find these sites?" Sam asked. "We'll try the one with a cabin first."

"Okay," Eric said. "First, you need to make a U-turn…"

They followed Eric's directions to the cabin site. Pavement ran most of the way, but the last quarter mile was on a stretch of unpaved road that appeared to have been maintained by a chiropractor desperate for new patients. The cabin was nestled in a shallow bowl, shaded by live oaks, with a rock wall behind it that could have been the one in the photographs. They parked the truck out of sight of the cabin, and hiked in far enough to get a glimpse.

"What do you think?" Sam asked. "That look like the place?"

"Might be," Callen said. "It's not exactly right, from this angle. But those were snapshots, taken more than a dozen years ago, and they were trying to capture people and activities, not show off the location."

"I don't see any Buicks."

"Could be behind the house," Callen said. "I don't

think we can tell anything useful from here."

"Yeah. You ready?"

"I've been ready. I want to get this guy."

"I feel you," Sam said. "So do I."

"Not like I do."

"I feel that, too. Check your emotions at the door, G, and let's go."

Rather than approaching from the road, they circled around on foot, keeping the cabin out of view to their left, so they could come at it from the least likely direction. Their path took them through thick underbrush; more than once, thorns snagged Sam's pants. It would have been nice if the federal government could spring for an apparel allowance, considering how many of their assignments ended with what had been perfectly good clothing turned into rags.

Callen was a little on the grumpy side, and Sam understood. Their work sometimes required killing. Typically, the dead were bad guys, involved in the commission of crimes or terrorist acts, and their deaths were in the interest of public safety. Callen felt a special obligation to that—like all of them, he hated seeing innocents threatened, but G took it more personally than most. To do their job, they needed to be able to compartmentalize. Taking a human life was always hard, but they couldn't let it cripple them.

Every agent had his or her own way to cope with it. Sam tried to sort his knotted feelings about each killing into individual threads: pain, sorrow, fear, rage, loss, blame, and anything else particular to the event in question. Once he had identified those, he could close them into a mental box and set it aside. Later—when the case was closed, when he was alone or walking on the beach with Michelle, both of them lost in their own thoughts—he could open the box and address each one separately. Most such incidents were kill-or-be-killed, or they involved the certain death of another person or people, if that action wasn't taken. That gave him a place to start, a way to rationalize the necessity of the act. From that point, the rest could be considered, one by one. The hurt he felt, the knowledge that every person he killed was somebody's son or daughter, was special to someone, was more than the sum of his or her crimes, would never go away. Ultimately, though, the knowledge that by taking one life he had saved others was what pulled him through, enabled him to go on.

Callen might have felt responsible for the deaths in the Brentwood house, and for whatever became of Betsy Peabody. But he wasn't. Hal Shogren was responsible for Betsy's fate, and was in large part responsible for all the other deaths. The participants in the shootout shared that blame with him. All Callen had been trying to do was to save the lives of people he had never met, never would meet, but who would have been endangered by yet another major blow to American-Iraqi relations.

Theories about why people became terrorists were easy to come by, but it was usually a combination of factors that included poverty, hopelessness, a sense of isolation, and the perception that others disrespected one's beliefs or culture. The theft of an important Iraqi artifact might not have been enough, by itself, to make anyone join a terrorist organization. But it could have been the last straw for some.

From the far northeastern corner, Sam still couldn't be sure if the rock face was the same one in the photos. Even if it was, erosion could have changed its profile in the intervening years. Rockslides and earthquakes could make significant alterations in what amounted to the blink of an eye, and wind and weather sculpted stone slowly but surely.

Parked in back was a dark-blue pickup truck that looked like its best days had been in the 1970s, and a Dodge so rusted that its original color was impossible to discern, sitting up on crumbling cinderblocks. No gold Buick, but as Callen had said, Shogren could have switched vehicles. Sam read the license plate to Eric, who reported back that the truck was registered to one Louis Bilsen, whose residence was indeed this property. "That complicates things a little," Sam said. "Any idea if Bilsen evacuated?"

"He should have," Eric said. "That area hasn't been opened for return yet. But there are no records for people who did, unless they're staying in one of the official shelters or checked into local hotels."

The flames hadn't reached this protected alcove, and were currently burning thousands of feet higher, so it was probably likely to survive. Not a bad place to hide out for a few days, if one needed to.

He and Callen moved forward, keeping to the cover of trees and brush for as long as possible. Finally, there was nothing but open space for a span of about twenty-five feet. The house itself had a lower tier of native stone, then logs above that, painted brown but raw and weathered. The roof was shingled, and overhung the walls by a couple of feet on all sides. In the back was a small porch, made of logs painted to match the house, with a couple of Adirondack chairs on it. A coating of leaves and ash made it look as if nobody had been here in a long time.

Which, of course, was what Shogren would want

anyone to think, if he was waiting inside with a gun.

The eastern side of the house had no windows, so they would move in there, then make ingress through the door off the porch and the front door at the same time. They'd been partners for so long that they could easily communicate without words; a gesture here, a nod, a twitch of the eyes was all it took in a case like this.

Callen went first, darting across the open patch while Sam covered him. When he was safely against the wall, Sam sprinted to his side. Sam pointed, Callen nodded, and they went in their separate directions. Sam's took him to the front corner. He peeked around, saw nothing out of line, then took a longer look.

From here, there were two windows, each about five feet from the ground, before the front door. On the far side of the door was a bigger window, almost floor to ceiling, then another pair of windows like the first. Above the door was a dormer window; he couldn't tell if it was real or maybe just decorating a crawlspace/ storage space above the ceiling.

When he saw Callen take off toward the back door, Sam crouched and hustled to the front, passing below the two windows. He flattened against the wall beside the front door, counting down and listening for Callen's footsteps on the back stairs. He didn't hear a thing, so when his countdown got to zero, he went for it.

"Federal agents!" he shouted as he kicked in the front door. At the same moment, Callen went in through the back, issuing the same warning.

A shotgun boomed, and Sam hit the deck.

46

Kelly Martin unfolded a map of the Hollywood Hills and studied the roads marked on it. He liked paper maps; they gave him a better sense of space and proportion than a little map on a screen, and there was a certain tactile satisfaction to be had from opening them up, tracing the lines and shapes marked on them, noting the colors, gauging the distances. When he'd spent a few minutes with it, he took a topographic map from the same waterproof pouch and examined it. In his head, he superimposed the elevation lines on the topo map over the road map, and converted it to a three-dimensional image more accurate and more securely embedded in his mind than anything he could get from an electronic device.

He used digital maps when he had to, but then he found himself having to refer to them more often. They just didn't stick like his own internal 3D picture did. He had developed the technique out of necessity. The American military had the best GPS technology in existence; a soldier, sailor, airman, or Marine could strap a device to his arm that showed where he was, what his position was in relation to the rest of his unit, mounted or dismounted, and instantly communicate that information back to the command post running the show, a mile away or around the world.

But technology failed. Batteries died, an unexpected impact could break a screen, and sometimes there was no evident cause for a malfunction. Paper and his eyes and his brain gave him a sense of confidence that no device could match.

Having done that, he turned his attention to the actual landscape ahead of him. He had parked off Benedict Canyon Road, a little less than a third of the way up the hill. Fire still raged above; if he drove much higher, he would be in the thick of it. As it was, he could taste smoke; his tongue felt like he'd been licking ashtrays.

His gut told him that Shogren wouldn't have gone to ground in the middle of the fire. He couldn't know when it might reach his hideout and drive him out, possibly right into the arms of firefighters or the law. That's what had led to one of notorious outlaw John Dillinger's various arrests, after all; some of his gang were staying in a hotel in Tucson, Arizona, when the hotel caught fire. The gang members tipped firefighters to rescue heavy trunks from their room—trunks loaded down with guns and cash. One of the firefighters identified a gang member from a magazine picture, and the men were arrested, along with Dillinger and his girlfriend. Whether Shogren knew the story, Martin couldn't say, but instinct would tell him to avoid hideouts likely to catch fire while he was in them.

All the news reports he'd seen said that Shogren and his hostage had entered the hills from the Valley side. That, Martin was convinced, was intentional. Shogren had obviously been careful about avoiding cameras on the way there, so the fact that he'd allowed his unwilling driver to be photographed there meant he'd wanted it that way.

Martin's conclusion was that Shogren's destination was on the far side of the hills. He wanted people to waste time searching on the Valley side, but it made more sense to be on the L.A. side, closer to LAX, I-10, and Mexico. If he wanted to get out of the state or the country in a hurry, he wouldn't want to be stuck in the Valley.

So he entered from the Valley side, intending to go over the top and wind up not too far from the city, on the south side. The next thing to consider was what road he would take. There were only a handful that went all the way across: Laurel Canyon, Coldwater Canyon, Benedict Canyon. Combining a few others with some travel along Mulholland offered more options, but Martin thought Shogren would want the quickest up and down he could find. The Buick had been photographed near Coldwater, so that was where Shogren wanted people to think he was going. But it was an easy shot to Benedict from there, too. Martin thought that was likelier. Shogren wanted to throw the authorities off his trail, not leave breadcrumbs for them to follow.

Having made that determination, he cut over to Benedict Canyon via some back roads—roundabout, but with no traffic—and started working his way up. He ignored the side roads in the relatively densely populated lower elevations. The fire hadn't burned down this far, and the residents might be allowed to return home at any moment. Shogren would want to be higher than that—close enough to the fire to ensure his solitude for at least a couple of days, but not so high that he'd be burned out. That left a relatively narrow band to search.

Above the developed areas, Martin slowed down. He drove up the middle of the street, scanning both sides of the road. Fine ash covered it like virgin snow, so tracks would be easy to spot. Even if new ash fall had covered them, the side roads beyond this point were mostly unpaved, so might show signs of recent passage.

He realized that all his conclusions were guesswork. He also knew that law enforcement personnel, including the NCIS teams, were searching these hills, and had the advantages of technology and numbers. But he was in Shogren's head. He understood the man, knew what he was going through and how he'd be thinking. Shogren was focused on survival. The city was too hot for him at the moment; all potential escape routes cut off. In another day or two, something else would take his place at the top of the news, and he could slip away.

Martin meant to find him before that happened. He was certain that he was already close.

Heading west on Mulholland Drive, Granger made good time. There were incredible views from up here—views that people paid millions of dollars to wake up to every morning—but all it cost for anyone else to experience them was a tank of gas and a couple of free hours. He was starting to think he'd make it to the San Diego Freeway, and safety. But then he rounded the bend between Benedict Canyon and Beverly Glen, and was quickly disabused of that notion.

Firefighters had blockaded the road. It wasn't hard to see why—flames roared across it with the force of hurricane-driven rain. Even the firefighters were standing well back from the inferno; no tools at their disposal could tame that beast.

Granger pulled up to the roadblock and rolled down the window. "How's it going?" he asked.

"You're not supposed to be up here," a firefighter said. She was a stocky woman with straight, dark hair and smoldering eyes. Native American, Granger guessed, maybe from one of the coastal area tribes. "These roads are all closed."

Granger showed the woman his badge. "NCIS," he said. "We're tracking a fugitive."

"Oh, I heard about that." She glanced at the trailer he pulled. "On horseback?"

He smiled. "Whatever it takes."

"Well, if he's in the middle of that, he's already cooked," she said.

"How long till I could get through here, do you think?"

"You got a tent? This is gonna burn for a while."

"I'll backtrack," Granger said.

"Good idea."

"Thanks for what you're doing. You folks do good work."

"Thank you," the firefighter said. "I hope you find him!"

"So do we all," Granger said.

He was getting pretty good at backing up the trailer. It helped that the road was wide open behind him. He managed a three-point turn in about six points, and drove off toward the east.

47

"Drop it!" Callen screamed. "Drop the gun! Now! Get on the floor!"

He had his HK416 pointed at the man with the shotgun. The man was slow to lower the weapon, and Callen thought for a few horrible moments that he would have to shoot him to prevent him from shooting Sam.

Before that moment came, the man seemed to notice him, there, shouting at him. He saw the machine gun. His eyes widened and his mouth fell open, his jaw quaking. He bent over and, with trembling hands, laid the Remington pump-action on the floor.

It wasn't Hal Shogren, unless Shogren had disguised himself by adding twenty years and sixty pounds, lopping off about eleven inches, and growing a patchy gray beard. This man was wearing camo, from his boots to his shirt. The shotgun was camo, too.

Sam picked himself up from the floor. "Louis Bilsen, I presume?"

The man jutted his chin out defiantly, a pose made slightly less convincing by the tremor in his voice. "Yep."

"Did you not hear us announce ourselves as federal agents?"

"I did," Bilsen said. "You ever heard of the Bill of Rights? I got a right to defend my home. Even against federal agents. Maybe *especially* against 'em. "

"Yes," Sam said. "Yes sir, you do."

"We're searching for a very dangerous fugitive," Callen said. "He has a hostage. If we just knocked on the door, he'd probably kill her."

"Well, he ain't here," Bilsen said.

"You shouldn't be, either. You're inside the evacuation zone."

"Hell, the fire ain't comin' down this far. It's all burnin' higher up. How can I protect my property if I ain't here?"

"Point taken, sir," Sam said. "We're sorry to have disturbed you."

The man's adrenalin rush was already fading. "Hell, probably good for my ticker to get a good fright once in a while. Jump-starts the circulation system."

"We'll get out of your hair, Mr. Bilsen." Sam handed him a business card. "If you see any strangers around here, please get in touch. And don't approach—the man we're looking for has no compunctions about killing, and he's good at it."

"Will do," Bilsen said.

Sam and Callen headed out the front door. "You okay?" Callen asked.

"Barely," Sam said. "If I hadn't been so close, some of that shot would've hit me, for sure. I was just near enough that he missed me altogether."

They were still in the yard when Bilsen called after them. "Hey, who's gonna pay for my door!"

"NCIS will," Sam replied. "Just send us the bill. Address is on the card."

"I'll do that," Bilsen said. "And I'll get one hell of a good door, I can tell you that."

"You do that, sir. Sorry again for the trouble."

"Hetty's going to love that," Callen said.

"That's why she makes the big bucks, isn't it?"

"Yeah." Callen nodded. "Yeah, I guess it must be."

"It's really pretty here," Kensi said.

"It'd be a little nicer without the fires of hell raging around us," Deeks replied.

"A fire of this magnitude only happens here every couple hundred years, Deeks."

"I know. I'm just saying, the smoke and ash kind of counter the natural beauty a tiny bit."

"You can look at it that way. Or you can look at it as part of nature, and we're lucky enough to be here on an incredibly rare occasion."

"We'll be lucky if we don't spontaneously combust."

"There!" Kensi said, pointing. "That's the Spellman place!"

Deeks braked the SUV. They were on a road, looking downhill at the house. "I believe you're correct."

"Of course I'm correct. Would you ever doubt me?"

"I might. Once in a while." He noted her look and quickly amended his statement. "A great while."

"We should check it out," she said, choosing to ignore him. Sometimes that was the best approach. Often, actually. "Anybody would have to look out the windows and uphill to see us here."

"Yeah," Deeks agreed. "Awkward angle for them. Of course, it means we can't see in the windows very well, either."

"True."

He pulled to the far side of the road and killed the engine. They each had binoculars, so they took those and their weapons and crossed the street. At the hillside's edge, they trained their glasses on what windows they could see. The house was clearly new, and just as clearly had cost plenty of money.

"So that's how plastic surgeons live," Deeks said. "Not a bad gig."

"If you want to spend your life cutting into people," Kensi countered. "Most of whom are just doing it out of vanity."

"Not my idea of a good time. But it looks like the pay rocks."

"You see anybody? Or are you too busy dripping with envy?"

"I'm only dripping with sweat. But no, I don't. Do you?"

She scanned all the visible windows again before she answered. "Not a soul."

"No vehicles in sight, either," Deeks pointed out. "And the ash is pretty thick down there. Looks like it hasn't been disturbed since the fire started."

"I'm thinking they're not here," Kensi said.

"Not unless they levitated into the house."

"From where? There's not a car or truck in sight." She looked beyond the house. The roof of another was visible a short distance farther down the hill. Beyond that, it looked like most of a mile before there were any more manmade structures. All was still.

"We should get closer," Deeks said.

"That's fine. We can get closer, but no one's home."

"You're pretty sure of yourself, Kens."

"That's right, I am. That's because I'm pretty sure. Very sure, in fact."

"Still, we have to see."

"I *said* we can check. I just know I'm right. You

should stop doubting me."

The road curved around as it dropped in elevation. They walked along the edge, stopping every couple of minutes to scope out the house again. There was still no suggestion of life in or around it.

They stopped at the end of a short driveway leading from the road to a three-car garage attached to the house. From there, they scanned the windows once more.

"Nothing," Kensi said. "Like I said."

"Maybe he's hiding inside. In a closet. Or a panic room. A house that big must have a panic room, right?"

"When was the last time you went to a movie, 2002?"

"Okay, dated reference, I admit. But still—"

Nell's voice in Kensi's ear blocked out anything Deeks might have said. "Kensi, Deeks. Wherever you are, get back up the hill, quick."

"We're at the Spellman house," Deeks said. "We were just going to approach and see if anyone's inside."

"Nobody's inside," Kensi said.

"I don't know about that, but I'm sure Shogren and Betsy Peabody aren't inside."

Kensi shot Deeks a satisfied grin. He might have seen it as a smirk. She didn't care. "What do you have?" she asked.

"Satellite imagery has picked up a gold sedan, parked in front of a house on the other side of the hills, off Benedict Canyon. From above, it matches the profile of a Buick LeSabre. The resolution is such that we can see clear tracks through the ash. The car's only been there for a couple of hours, and it's in an area that's still under an evac order."

"We're on our way," Deeks said. "It'll take us a little while."

"Callen and Sam aren't far away. They'll be there way before you."

"They should wait for us," Kensi said.

"I'll pass that on," Nell said. "But with a hostage in the house, if they have a clean shot, they'll probably take it."

Kensi met Deeks's gaze, and nodded once. They took off running up the hill, back to the borrowed SUV. "We're en route," Kensi said. "We'll be there as soon as we can."

Ash made the road slippery, but they reached the vehicle in a few minutes, and soon were racing back up the hill, once more heading toward the flames.

This time, they had a good reason to hurry.

48

Shogren had assured Betsy that the fire wasn't going to come down the hill to where they were. She wasn't sure she believed a word he said. He had been a soldier, and presumably knew about such things. But she'd known him before his Army career, and she didn't trust him for an instant.

She was already sick of being his prisoner. She wanted to know how Hugh was. She wanted to hold his hand. She would feel safe when she was back in his arms. Never mind that she was the one who kept their household safe; who made sure the doors were locked, who followed their bank accounts to ensure that they hadn't been breached. As Hugh's memory went, she was worried that he'd become vulnerable to telephone or email scams, so she tried to be the first to grab the phone when it rang, and she checked his email account regularly.

But when he held her, she felt as she had when they were younger, just married. She felt secure, loved, cared for. He had told her time and again that he would never let anything bad happen to her. They'd both known that was a promise that couldn't be kept.

It didn't matter. It was the promise that counted, the effort to protect each other from life's tribulations.

She missed him so.

She'd found some food in the freezer, and other ingredients in the pantry. The power was on, so she prepared an early dinner for them. She was still determined to make him see her as a human, not a hostage, and if cooking would help with that, she was glad to do it. It was another reason for him to keep her alive.

The house had a landline. He'd checked it, determined that the phone service was still down, but then broke every handset he could find, anyway.

The house was even more luxurious than it had looked from the outside. The décor was very contemporary, with modern art pieces that she didn't understand the appeal of accenting low-slung, expensive furniture. The kitchen was state-of-the-art, with stainless steel appliances that looked like they'd come straight out of a four-star restaurant. By the time dinner was finished, although it was simple—a couple of steaks she'd thawed in the microwave, some frozen French fries, fresh green beans with some light spices— she thought it smelled like one of the best meals she'd ever prepared.

Of course, part of that might have been that she hadn't had a bite to eat since breakfast, and it had been a busy, eventful day. To say the least.

When dinner was ready, she found him in a den, watching a TV that seemed almost as big as some movie theater screens she'd seen. He had the local news on, and both their faces were in a split-screen shot, bigger than life.

"I look terrible," she said.

Shogren turned around. "You look fine, Mrs. Peabody."

With a start, she realized that her name had been plastered across the screen, underneath that gigantic face.

"No," she began. "That's… a mistake. I'm Kath—" She couldn't even remember what name she had told him. Her heart was pounding in her chest like a drum solo from Woodstock, and she couldn't catch her breath. The room seemed to swim, and she was afraid she would faint.

"I knew I recognized you," Shogren said. "I just couldn't place you. I guess it's been a long time, hasn't it?"

"Dinner's ready," she said. "In the—" She flailed her hand toward the doorway, groping for the word. "Kitchen. In the kitchen."

"I don't know that I'm very hungry," he said. "More, I don't know, curious. Did you really think I wouldn't figure out who you are?"

"I didn't—I didn't know. Like you said, it's been years. I've changed. You've changed a lot."

"You recognized me, though? Didn't you? Otherwise, you wouldn't have lied about who you were."

"I—" She had been about to tell him she'd been warned, that NCIS had told her that he was involved in Susan's death. But she didn't want him to know that. Definitely didn't want him to know that she had tried to help them find him. This place wasn't any cabin in the woods, so she figured her photos hadn't been helpful after all. "I did eventually," she lied. "Not at first."

"You know Susan's dead?"

"I—I heard that. The police. They said there weren't any clues."

Shogren grinned. It was awful. "Thanks for confirming," he said. "I was only guessing, because she disappeared. No contact, no messages. Just gone. We had a protocol. If she was able to, she'd have been in touch, so I knew she was either arrested or dead."

"She's dead because of you, isn't she? I always knew you'd hurt her in some way."

He barked a laugh. "I saved her. I freed her. You wanted to make her another you. Another boring white American who never knew the first thing about the world, living in a bubble. If you had your way, she'd go to school, get a job, go to church on Sundays. She'd spend her life thinking she was safe, maybe birdwatching and belonging to a book group, giving money to charity a couple times a year."

"That doesn't sound so bad," Betsy said. She backed up until she felt the door jamb behind her, and leaned against it, unable to trust her knees. Her legs were shaking. She tucked her hands into her pockets so he couldn't see them quake.

"It's hell," Shogren said. "It's a lie. You're not safe. Nobody's safe. The world is a vicious, spiteful, dangerous place. It's filled with hate and fear and death, and the only way to not be a victim is to be the baddest dog on the block. Of course Han shot first—if he didn't shoot first, he never would have made it to the new movie."

"I don't know what you're talking about."

"I'm not surprised. It's the first time you've had to see the real world."

"This isn't the real world, Hal. We're inside somebody's house; I don't think you even know whose. We're hiding out from the law because—I don't know why, but you have blood on you, and a gun, and a bag that you won't let out of your sight. There's a massive fire burning all around us, and you've taken me prisoner. Does any of that sound remotely real to you?"

"It's all real, *Betsy*. That's your name, right? Betsy. And Hugh—he was the old man I hit this morning. I would have hit him harder if I'd known. I just thought he was some useless old coot. This is real life. Life on the edge. Life and death. That's what it's about, Betsy. That's where things get real, on the edge."

"I… I don't understand that. No, I don't accept it. I never thought you were any good, Hal, but I didn't think you were insane. Now I'm starting to wonder."

"The blind always think those who can see are crazy," Shogren said. "It's the way of the world."

"Anyway, dinner's in the kitchen if you want it."

She spun away from the doorway and hurried down the hall before he could say anything more. She shouldn't have insulted him. She should have played dumb, acted like she was on his side. Who knew what he'd do to her now? He couldn't let her live, not knowing she could identify him, say where he'd been.

She had to get away from him, somehow.

Back in the kitchen, she looked out the glass wall that faced onto the front yard. The sun was almost down. Night came early in the canyons. Maybe under cover of darkness, she could escape.

But of course, he was a soldier. He was used to hunting and killing. He probably enjoyed it.

Still, she had to try. It was the only chance she had.

She took a step toward the door, but he was already coming down the hall.

She was too late.

49

The tracks in the ash were a giveaway. Martin was surprised that Shogren hadn't come up with some way to disguise them. It would have been hard, he supposed, in a regular passenger car. Ordinarily, he'd have counted on other traffic to obscure his tracks, or in the case of something like a heavy snowfall, for the snow to quickly fill them in. But the fire was mostly at higher elevations, and the ash tended to float on the wind, which blew uphill. Tracks farther down remained evident for a while.

But he wasn't certain until he saw the lights on.

It wasn't the only house with lights on, of course. People had evacuated quickly. They'd rounded up children and pets, grabbed the things that they considered irreplaceable, piled into cars and headed down the hill. Checking the light switches was the furthest thing from their minds.

It was, however, the only house with lights on and people moving around inside.

He couldn't help feeling pleased with himself. His read on Shogren had been correct. It had still taken a while to spot the tracks, and longer to follow them to the right house. But he'd done it. He didn't see any law enforcement around, either.

Perfect.

Dusk was settling in fast. That was perfect, too. He could see in, but it would be hard for anyone inside to see him. He moved closer, careful but not slowly. He wasn't worried about the neighbors spotting him; there weren't any.

It was him and Shogren.

It was payback time.

"Bobby," he said aloud. "This is for you, bud."

"Left turn!" Eric called. "Left turn, now!"

"I'm turning!" Sam said. "If you could give me a little more warning next time, it'd help. Maybe a tenth of a second or so."

"I'm sorry," Eric replied. "There's a minute lag in the signal. By the time I see where you are, you're a little ahead of there."

"So you're saying your technology is inadequate," Sam said.

"No, I'm saying—right! Turn right!"

"I think I see it," Sam said.

"You should be able to by now."

"I'm stopping."

"What? Why?"

"Because there's an armed man, a former Army Ranger, in that house, with an innocent hostage who, believe me, has already been through more than enough grief in the last couple of days. I don't want him to kill her, and I don't want him to see us coming. So we're going on foot from here."

"Okay," Eric said. "Yes. Those are all good reasons. Just, you know, hurry."

"Of course we'll hurry, Eric. We're not here sightseeing."

"Sorry," Eric said. "I know, you're on the scene. It's your call. I'm stuck back here. Just trying to help."

"It's a big help, Eric," Callen said. "You found the place, and told us where it was. But we'll take it from here."

"It's all yours," Eric said. The feed went silent.

"Lot of windows," Sam said, getting out of the truck.

Callen climbed down on his side, grabbed his weapons, and closed the door silently. They'd already turned off the dome light. "Good for us, bad for him."

"Unless he's watching with night-vision goggles."

"If he's using thermal imaging, he's probably going blind," Callen pointed out. "Everything's hot around here."

"Image enhancement's more common, though," Sam argued. "And not as sensitive to heat."

"He probably doesn't have any night-vision gear."

"Probably not. Why would he?"

"Exactly."

"You see him yet?"

"Not yet."

"Neither do I. It'd suck if this was the wrong house, wouldn't it?"

"A lot," Callen said. "A whole lot."

Sam grabbed Callen's arm, stopping him in his tracks. "You see him?" Callen asked.

"I don't see Shogren." Sam pointed to a vague shape in the near-darkness, ahead of the house. "But who's that?"

50

A pan on the stove was sizzling. Betsy spun around; she'd been so nervous she had walked away and left the burner on under the steaks. Pan-frying was so easy, and she didn't mind cleaning up the sprayed grease. She hadn't wanted to do anything requiring a lot of thought or creativity, not for Hal Shogren's dinner.

The fact that the steaks would be burned disappointed her for a moment. *Don't be stupid*, she told herself. *He's not going to let you live long enough to worry about it.*

Then another thought struck her.

He was coming down the hall toward her. "Bet-syyy," he said, stretching it out in a sing-song voice. She thought he had gone completely insane. Or he always had been. "What's for dinner, Bet-syyy? Smells delish. I hope you enjoy it, because it's your last meal. But don't worry, little Susie's going to be waiting for you on the other side of that glowing white tunnel. Isn't that how they say it works?"

By the time he finished taunting her, he was in the kitchen. It was the biggest kitchen she'd ever cooked in by a wide measure, so he was still more than fifteen feet away.

Not far enough. He hadn't brought the big gun with him, but he had a pistol. How long would it take a bullet to reach her? A fraction of a second. A single beat of a hummingbird's wing.

"Keep away from me," she said. She edged toward the stove.

"I think that's wrong, though. I've seen a lot of people die. More than you'd probably believe. And not one of them—not a single one—looked like he was traveling down a glowing tunnel of light. Not one of them looked happy to be going. No, I think it's a pretty horrific trip. I guess you'll find out, though. Soon. Too bad you won't be able to come back and tell me. I'd kind of like to know before it's my time."

The knife block. It was on the counter, closer to her than the stove was. She'd only used one of the knives from it, but it was good and sharp.

Could she reach it in time?

"Don't even think about it, Betsy," Shogren said. He gestured with the gun, holding it casually. He didn't even have his finger on the trigger. She was so insignificant to him, so pathetic a threat, that he didn't even feel the need to have the gun ready to use. "By the time you could free a knife from the block, you'd be dead. You'd never reach me with it, and if you did, you wouldn't know how to use it. In your picture-perfect phony world, people don't have to kill other people. Don't fool yourself into thinking that you could."

"But you—you can kill an old woman without a second thought, is that it? Is that what the real world is to you? One where life is that cheap? I never did anything to hurt you."

"You tried to poison Susan against me. She told me the things you used to tell her. How I was worthless. Nothing but trouble. How she shouldn't let me drag her into the muck with me."

"And they were all true, weren't they? Look what happened to her. Look what's happened to you."

"Look what's going to happen to you, Betsy. Whoever lives here will come home, maybe tomorrow, maybe the next day, and find an old lady's corpse. That'll be a surprise, won't it? Think that's the kind of thing that'd trouble their sleep for a while?"

"God, you're... you're a sick, sick man. I never knew how sick."

"Guess you found out just in time." He raised the pistol, and slipped his finger over the trigger.

And the world exploded.

The huge window shattered, glass crashing like frozen rain.

Shogren fired, but his shot went into the ceiling.

Betsy snatched the pan off the stove, still spitting hot grease, ran toward him, and threw it, steaks and all, into his face. He screamed and screamed.

And she ran out into the night.

51

"Ma'am! Mrs. Peabody!"

Her name had been all over the radio on the drive up, along with Shogren's. Martin raced toward her as she bolted from the house. She veered away from him, as if he was Shogren, still chasing her. But Shogren was inside, trying to claw hot grease out of his eyes. Martin had seen the whole thing. It was priceless.

"Mrs. Peabody!" he shouted as he ran. "It's okay. Nobody's going to hurt you!"

"Martin!"

A voice from behind him, loud and commanding. He almost stopped, but he didn't. Another couple of paces and he'd have her. He didn't want her running off into the darkness. She could get hurt out there.

"Martin, stand down!"

He recognized it now. Sam Hanna. He kept going. The old woman was faster than she looked; fear had given her wings. But he had longer legs, and stronger ones. Lungs to match. He lunged, caught her. They both went down, but he twisted in midair so she came down on top of him, the fall cushioned. Last thing he wanted was to break her hip or something.

"It's okay, Mrs. Peabody. You're safe now. You're safe. We're the cavalry."

"Martin!" Hanna and Callen had caught up to him. "Martin, what the hell are you doing?"

"Hostage rescue op," he said. He helped Mrs. Peabody to her feet. "Here she is, safe and sound. Ma'am, these men are with NCIS. That's the Naval—"

"I *know* what it is. Is Agent Blye with you?" she asked.

"She'll be here soon," Callen said.

"I only had one shot," Martin said. "I wasn't sure how thick the glass was, so I didn't know how much it'd deflect my round. Instead of trying for him, I just fired a burst at the top of the window, to shatter it. She took it from there. I knew she would."

Hanna looked toward the house. "Well, he's gone."

"She threw hot grease right in his face," Martin said. "He's not far."

"You'd better hope not," Hanna said. "Come on, G. Martin, we have a truck back there. Take her to it, and stay there. That's an order, sailor."

"Sir, yes sir!" Martin shot back. He put an arm around Mrs. Peabody's waist, helping support her. "Come on, ma'am. They'll be back in a few minutes."

He glanced over his shoulder. Hanna and Callen were silhouetted against the bright light spilling out of the broken window.

They were pissed, and they probably had good reason. But he had to admit, he kind of liked those guys.

52

"If he was still in the Navy, I'd have him court-martialed," Sam said. "Maybe I'd see if they'd be willing to bring back keelhauling."

"He might have saved her life," Callen said.

"We were right here. We could have done that."

"He was closer."

"Okay, G. You're right. He did the right thing, and I'm glad he did. But if he let Shogren get away…"

"Like he said, she threw a hot frying pan right in his face. Wherever he is, he's hurting."

"Doesn't mean he's not dangerous. A cornered animal—"

"I know."

They'd reached the house. "He could be anywhere," Sam said. "He's got his guns, and his money, and he's desperate."

"One room at a time," Callen said.

"There's a lot of rooms in that house."

"Maybe we'll get lucky and he'll be in the first one we check."

Betsy Peabody had left the front door open when she'd raced out. Even if she hadn't, the big window next to it had been smashed. Some glazier was going to make a lot of money redoing the glass here, Sam thought.

They went through the door. It led directly to a staircase, with floating steps leading up half a flight. The kitchen was on that first main level. Whatever had been cooking in Betsy's frying pan, it smelled delicious.

They cleared the kitchen first. Glass everywhere, and lying in it were two steaks. Answered that question.

Beyond the kitchen was a dark hall. In the distance Sam could hear a television. He and Callen took it slowly, cautiously. They spun into the first room, a den, where the TV was. Empty. They followed the hall to the next opening. It was a large bedroom, with its own bath, and a door to the outside, up the slope from the front door. They cleared the room and the bathroom, then checked outside. "Footprints in the ash," Callen said. "Fresh. He went out here."

"Yeah," Sam agreed. "So he's out there, somewhere. In the dark. Maybe watching us right now. Did I mention keelhauling?"

"You did," Callen said.

"Just making sure." Sam activated his Earwig, "Eric? Can you see anything from the sky? Shogren's on the run."

"Not a thing, Sam," Eric said. "I can try to get a UAV up there with thermal imaging capability."

"Not enough time," Sam said.

"On the bright side, you're about to get reinforcements."

"Don't send them here," Sam said. "Have them go north of our location by a hundred yards or so. Maybe two hundred, depending on how long it takes. They can work their way down toward us."

"Copy that," Eric said.

"Let's find this guy, G. I want to end this."

"You and me both," Callen said. "It's been a long couple of days."

53

"You're about parallel with the house," Nell said. "Keep going. Say, two hundred and twenty yards."

"You have a tape measure, babe?" Deeks asked.

"Estimate," Kensi said. "Never mind, I'll estimate. Just stop when I tell you to."

"Usually you tell me to keep going."

"Deeks!" Nell said. "Still listening."

"Sorry, Nell."

"Stop!"

Deeks braked the SUV. It fishtailed on the ash-slick road, but came to a stop.

"That's good," Nell said. "Now go west. To your left. On foot, cross country. Your fugitive is out there somewhere, probably between you and Callen and Sam. You'll work downslope toward them. Remember, he's—"

"We know," Deeks said. "Armed and dangerous."

"Hey! Finishing other people's sentences is my thing."

"Deeks wants to step in on everybody's thing," Kensi said.

"Maybe we could stop insulting Deeks long enough

to find the bad guy," Deeks said. "What do you think?"

Kensi sighed. "Can we start again after we've caught him?"

"Sure. Not like I could stop you."

"That's right. Okay, Nell. We're going in."

"Good luck," Nell said. "I'm here if you need me."

"Good to know," Deeks said. "Over and out."

"Over and out," Nell echoed. "Be safe."

54

Callen and Sam walked into the trees. They were exposed for a couple of minutes, limned against the lights from the house, but nobody shot at them. Was Shogren blinded? Hunkered down somewhere, unable to see well enough to shoot them?

Or was he just waiting for them to get closer, so he'd be less likely to miss?

Callen heard a vehicle go past on the road, then stop up ahead. Kensi and Deeks, he guessed. If Sam's plan worked, they'd trap Shogren between them.

But he was a Ranger, and he had a head start, so they couldn't take anything for granted. The fact that he hadn't already taken a shot was a little disturbing. Maybe he was running. He could be a half mile away already, gaining more distance with every passing minute. He and Sam were walking, trying to see through the dark, listening for any stray sound.

If they lost him, Callen was going to be furious. He was used to long, difficult assignments, but he didn't relish the idea of spending a night out in this wilderness. Higher up, he could see the glow of the fire. That would keep Shogren from going too far, he figured—the guy wasn't likely to run right into the flames. But he could cover a lot of ground to the east or west, if he hadn't been too badly injured.

"Listen!" Sam whispered.

Callen stopped, listened. It came again. Up ahead and to the right, the unmistakable sound of a foot coming down on brush or twigs. But was it Shogren, or Kensi and Deeks?

"I think it's him," Sam said quietly. "That way."

He took a step to his right. Callen followed. His foot was still in the air when he saw a muzzle burst up ahead, heard the blast, and rounds whipped through the air around them. He slammed his arm into Sam's back and drove them both to the ground.

From higher up the hill, more guns sounded, and bright flashes of light cut the dark, then faded, leaving only ghostly echoes burned on Callen's retinas. He and Sam opened fire, too, but didn't want to aim too high for fear of hitting their teammates.

Shogren ran off to the west, away from Kensi and Deeks. Callen could hear him tearing through the brush, and fired a burst toward where he thought the man was. Still on the run, Shogren fired again, keeping Callen and Sam pinned down.

"He knows where we all are now," Sam said. "So he's heading the other way."

"We're not losing him," Callen said. "Let's go."

"I'm with you," Sam said. They took off after their quarry. Above, they heard Kensi and Deeks doing the same. Still, Shogren had a head start, and one could travel more quietly than two—or four.

They'd been running for about five minutes. Callen couldn't hear Shogren anymore, and his heart sank. If he was gone…

Then he heard a different kind of sound crashing through the trees and brush. Louder—much too loud to be just Shogren. And accompanying it, something unexpected.

"Was that a horse?" Sam asked.

"I was just about to ask you."

Ahead, Shogren fired wildly at something Callen couldn't see. He emptied his clip, crying out in terror at the same time. Sam took careful aim and fired a quick three-round burst. Shogren went down.

"You got him!" a familiar voice called from the darkness.

"Owen?" Callen asked.

"In the flesh," Granger said. "The somewhat odoriferous and dehydrated flesh, but the flesh, just the same."

He clicked on a flashlight and trained the beam on Shogren, who was just getting to his knees.

"I thought you shot him," Callen said.

"I didn't want to kill him," Sam said. "I want him to rot in prison."

"Works for me."

Shogren heaved himself to his feet, and took a couple of staggering steps. Owen shifted the big, dark horse's position, blocking his path. They continued that way: Shogren trying to lunge past, Granger and the horse cutting him off, until Sam and Callen reached him, followed closely by Kensi and Deeks. Sam grabbed the ex-Ranger's wounded arm and wrenched it behind his back, slapped a bracelet on the wrist, then brought the other arm around and did the same. "Harold Shogren," he said, "you're under arrest for murder, attempted murder, bank robbery, and so many other things it'll take the entire ride to central booking to enumerate them all. You have the right to remain silent, which I strongly advise you take advantage of. If you choose to ignore my advice…"

Epilogue

"You really are special," Sam said. "Hetty doesn't let just anyone into this place. It means you're practically family."

"I appreciate it," Kelly Martin said. "Especially considering how much trouble I caused all of you."

"That you did, Mr. Martin." Hetty's voice preceded her into the bullpen. She appeared at the top of the stairs, and continued speaking as she descended. Eric Beale, Nell Jones, and Owen Granger stood by the railing upstairs, watching. "It's a pleasure to meet you in person, despite the fact that you ran my people ragged."

She stopped at the bottom, and extended a hand. Martin took it.

"It's good to meet you, too. I thought you'd be... " He let the sentence trail off.

"Taller, I know. So did Robert Redford, but he was able to adjust."

The expression on her face didn't vary for an instant. Even Callen wasn't sure if she was joking.

But he wouldn't have put money on it.

"I still haven't finished tabulating the expenses generated on your behalf," Hetty said. But I will let you know when I have a total."

"I'm sure you will, Ms. Lange."

"Don't forget the old man's doors," Callen reminded her.

"I've had a long discussion with Mr. Bilsen," Hetty said. "A very long discussion, in fact. He has some quite... let's say, colorful ideas about the Constitution, and the role of the federal government therein. And I will be including my time in my final accounting."

She reached the bottom step and stopped, hands down at her sides. "My hourly rate is considerably more than you want to think about."

"You can send me the bill," Martin said. "I don't know how I'll pay it, but—"

"There will be no bill," Hetty said. "I want you to know what this has cost the taxpayers, but you're not expected to cover it. I understand you were instrumental in rescuing Mrs. Peabody. Mr. Peabody was delighted to have her back. They'll have a difficult time of it for a while. Possibly for the rest of their lives. To lose a daughter the way they did, then endure such a traumatic experience immediately thereafter... it's not easily brushed away."

"I'm sure not," Martin said.

Hetty broke into a smile that was, for her, effusive. "Nobody's blaming you, Mr. Martin. You were a victim of those criminals, as much as anyone else was. I can't say that I approve of all your actions, but I can't argue with the results."

"I was just trying to do what I thought was best."

"All anybody *can* do," Sam said. "That's how we get through the days."

"I understand you're recently retired," Hetty said.

"That's right."

"I've taken the liberty of having a conversation with the commander of the Naval Special Warfare Command at Coronado, Mr. Martin. He would be delighted to welcome you back at your parting rank, if you'd like. Failing that, he said the base could use a new training officer. It would be a promotion."

"I was going to keelhaul him," Sam said.

"You don't have my generous spirit," Hetty said.

"I don't have your pull with Navy brass, that's for sure."

"Very few do." She turned back to Martin, who had a kind of stunned smile pasted on his face. "Take a few days to think about it," she said. "There's no rush, and no pressure. If you'd rather not re-up, that's fine. I just wanted you to know that the option is there, should you choose to exercise it."

"I don't know what to say."

"'Thank you' would suffice."

"Thank you, Ms. Lange. Thank you all."

"Oh," Deeks said. "She gets an individual thank you, and the rest of us have to share tiny thank-you shards? Collectively we only merit the equivalent of one personal thanks?"

"Thank you, Deeks," Martin said.

"No, it's okay. It's just good to know where we stand."

"Ignore him," Sam said.

"We do," Callen added.

Kensi took Deeks's hand and squeezed. "Deeks," she said, "you're an idiot." She leaned closer, and stage-whispered the next four words. "And I love you."

"Sorry?" Deeks asked. "What was that? Couldn't quite hear you, Kensileena. A little louder, please?"

"Later," she said, flashing him a grin. "At home,

we'll work on our non-verbal communication."

"That's my favorite kind," Deeks said.

Hetty's voice cut through the laughter. "Mr. Deeks," she said. "Ms. Blye. The entire bullpen does not need to be subjected to the sordid details of your personal lives."

Kensi's smile faded. "Sorry—" she began.

But Hetty's grew at the same time. "Go home, you two. And stay there tomorrow. We'll try to keep the national security crises to a minimum for twenty-four hours, while you get whatever is in your systems out of them."

She started up the stairs, then stopped and turned to face the bullpen again. "And I know I don't say this often enough. In fact, you might never hear it again, so listen closely, everyone. Thank you all for your service. Your coworkers appreciate it, your nation appreciates it. And *I* appreciate it."

She paused for a beat, then added, "And as we all know, *that* is what's most important."

Acknowledgments

Great thanks to the folks at Titan Books, my good friends at CBS TV, Howard Morhaim and his fantastic team, and of course to Shane Brennan and the entire cast and crew of *NCIS: Los Angeles* for bringing us one of the most consistently entertaining shows on television. Additional thanks to Jason Zibart, Steve Mertz, Chuck Sellner, Lisa and the Tech Pubs gang, Vicki and Dia, and especially to Marcy, for pulling me through.

About the Author

Jeff Mariotte is the award-winning author of more than fifty novels, including thrillers *Empty Rooms* and *The Devil's Bait*, supernatural thrillers *Season of the Wolf*, *Missing White Girl*, *River Runs Red*, and *Cold Black Hearts*, horror epic *The Slab*, the *Dark Vengeance* teen horror quartet, and many others. With partner (and wife) Marsheila Rockwell, he wrote the science fiction/horror/thriller *7 SYKOS*, and numerous shorter works. He also writes comic books, including the long-running horror/Western comic book series *Desperadoes* and graphic novels *Zombie Cop* and *Fade to Black*. He has worked in virtually every aspect of the book business, and is currently the editor-in-chief of Visionary Comics and division chief of Visionary Books.